The Director
and
the Daemon

The Director
and
the Daemon

Pitaya Chin

PUNCHER & WATTMANN

First published in 2024
Published by Puncher and Wattmann
PO Box 279
Waratah NSW 2298

https://www.puncherandwattmann.com
web@puncherandwattmann.com

ISBN   9781923099166

Edited by Ed Wright
Cover design by Miranda Douglas
Typesetting by Morgan Arnett
Printed by Lightning Source International

 A catalogue record for this work is available from the National Library of Australia

Australian Government

Creative Australia

This project has been assisted by the Australian Government through Creative Australia, its principal arts investment and advisory body.

*For Abdallah
and for the best birds.*

Freedom is worth everything that you can give.

– Sekou Odinga

Chapter 1

Kit has the most beautiful hands in the world. Always alive, always in gesture.

"Should I bring it in a little closer this time?" asks the camera guy.

Kit's eyes skate over mine, shaded with an implicit question. I know they are worried with the camera so close they will be tempted to aim for sheer bigness, emoting as a substitute for authenticity. I know the fact they can ask this question is a sign that they know how to guard against this. It is this capacity for both spontaneity and self-knowledge that makes them the most brilliant performer I have ever known.

"Cut!" yells the assistant.

"Great work! That was perfect," says a producer. It wasn't, though. I don't know why he bothered saying it. Perhaps he wanted to assert his existence in a world that so often fails to recognise this.

I have played out this scenario so many times. All eyes on my hands, my hands adjusting the camera, the eye of the camera resting on the scene written by my hand, which we now usher into life. And then, without warning, perception and feeling swim away – a flicker in my vision – and I turn to find myself de-realised, disoriented. I try to summon my intent when I was first writing this scene, what I was trying to achieve by arranging these non-existent people into action and reaction, cause and effect. It seemed so vital at the time, so urgent and expressive of some broader truth. Now it seems alien to me and I to it.

At times like these, I am reminded of certain moments I have been riding a train towards a place I didn't want to be at, looking out the window at the passing buildings and the lives that they contained. Feeling in my very bones that no such life nor location could hold any real interest or desire for me. Yet equally unable to imagine some alternative way of life which might have been desirable or interesting. These experiences are not common, but they have begun to occur more frequently. They began shortly after the episode when, for no reason I could discern, I left work to find the tyres of the SUV that I was renting had been slashed.

"Um, not my call, but maybe we could move on from this at some point," says the camera guy. Weary glances exchanged across the fake room. Everyone else besides me is so competent, so good at what they do. It is moments like these which induce me to pause and consider if my entire life has been the preamble to a nasty joke.

At such times it has been as if desire itself has gone dark for me, the shutters drawn permanently on my interfacing with the world. And so it was three years ago that in walked Kit, standing shyly and elegantly in the audition room. Lowering their eyes as they declared, in a burst of sincere, childlike cliche, that they wanted to work for me, that it was their lifelong dream to work for me. It was then possibility crept back, that there might be some value to the process of being after all.

While I am lost in this mix of ennui and nostalgia, Kit goes off to one side. Expression utterly blank, like the cut face of marble. I wish I could understand even a small portion of what goes through Kit's mind at these moments. That even some little part of their interior world could become legible to me. At other times I wish wildly and to no-one that I, like Kit, could learn to speak using the vocabulary of the body. As opposed to being trapped always within myself, head in a ridiculous jar.

"Didn't used to get this windy," says the camera guy. The sound of air whistling overhead. A fake room, a soundstage with three walls. The whole set, the lighting rig starts to shake; and this, too, seems to telegraph my failures professional and personal.

"One more take," I say, with what is left of my authority.

Kit looks up. Head cocked to one side, the intelligent young fox. And in that moment we are synced. I don't know what it is, this jolt of shared confidence that passes between us.

Kit steps into the light. And suddenly the air, the physical environment changes. Impossible, but there it is. Words spool from Kit's mouth: still just the words I wrote, but suddenly they are the right ones, the perfect sentences which slip into the scene like a knife into a body.

"Cut!" yells the assistant. And we break for lunch.

There are brownies and fruit juice. There are sandwiches and fruit platters with cheese and ham and melon slices. Kit eats like a racehorse, folding wraps into their mouth as shoals of people move past. On the surface they are nervous, but underneath there is no fear. This strange mix of humility and mastery. Because Kit knows their own talent.

Where do they go, these performers, when their eyes turn in on a landscape only they can see? Strange, Kit is so open with their feelings yet preserves this basic privacy. They want my approval, I can tell. But something is always withheld, true passion always kept back in reserve. I want to see what it is. Because there is nothing of Kit which is not precious to me. Colleague, shapeshifter, muse.

What is love? The cheapest, oldest question. An affect state? A behaviour? I wouldn't know. For me, the most compelling thing is someone else who is absorbed in their intensities, their own private magic. There's nothing else so beautiful in all the world.

Chapter 2

"Hi," I say.

"Hi," says the rich guy.

"Sit down," says the assistant. A smile – parched and efficient like her gestures – abbreviated. "Can I offer you a glass of water?"

I sit.

"I heard about your parents," says the rich guy. "Very sorry, such sad news."

"Very sorry," says the assistant.

I say nothing.

"We've been looking at your streaming figures," says the assistant.

"They've been going up," says the rich guy.

"They've been going up quite a bit," says the assistant.

"Oh," I say. "Good."

"But not enough," says the rich guy. "Not nearly enough to reach a level that would justify us extending the run for another season."

"Very unfortunate," says the assistant.

"Oh no," I say.

"Nevertheless," says the rich guy. "We've been very happy with what you've been doing. There have been some positive reviews. Some great critical buzz. As a result, we are looking for alternative funding channels."

"We have certainly been looking," says the assistant.

"We are a prestige network," says the rich guy. "Quality, not quantity. We don't just appeal to mass consumption, the lowest common denominator. Someone with your gravitas... by the way, do I hear on the grapevine that you're in line for a Lifetime Achievement Award? Oops, that was meant to be embargoed, don't spread it around. What an honour, eh? Same year that your memoir is being released... what was it called again, *My Life*?"

I say, "It's called '*My Life So Far*'. Actually, we were going to launch it at the Gala..."

"Can't wait to read it," says the rich guy. "Love to know how the magic really happens."

I say nothing.

"Nonetheless," says the rich guy, "while we aim for quality, TV for those who think, we still need to be bringing in network growth in the form of subscriptions."

"Growth is the word."

"Like being a shark."

"It's exactly like that."

"Can't stop swimming."

"Can't stop swimming," agrees the assistant. "If you stop swimming, you die."

I say, "Does that mean our show is getting cancelled?"

"Oh, no."

"No, no, no, no."

"You slow right down," says the rich guy. "Don't jump the gun."

"There's still a chance."

"A good chance."

"An excellent chance."

"Sponsorship," says the rich guy. "From Nilsson Services."

"A truly new opportunity," says the assistant. "A new source of investment in the arts."

"Oh," I say. "But aren't Nilsson Services the company that…"

"They have offered," says the rich guy, "to cover thirty percent of our production costs over the next eighteen months."

"Thirty percent," agrees the assistant. "And no product placement."

"All they want," says the rich guy, "is a simple, discreet, end-of-episode acknowledgement of their contribution. And to use *Red Jade Ravine* in their promotional materials."

I say, "But aren't Nilsson Services…"

"It's a very generous offer," says the assistant. "Unprecedented, even."

"How much longer does Kit's contract go?" asks the rich guy. "I think it's three more months."

"I think it's less than that," says the assistant.

I don't say anything.

"What do you think Kit will want to do after this is over?" asks the rich guy. "Bright young thing, unlike us, ha ha ha."

"Can't imagine he'll want to stick around."

"He's not the type to stick around anywhere, from what I've heard."

"I've heard some things… an artistic temperament, to put it mildly."

"That last show he was doing, in New York."

"*They*, not he," I say.

"*They*, of course," says the assistant.

"Is there even a point to the show without Kit?" asks the rich guy.

"I don't think so," says the assistant.

I don't say anything.

"Anyway, this is great news!" says the rich guy. "Because with funding from Nilsson, we can just about make up the shortfall."

"We just need your commitment."

"Some assurance you're on board with this."

"Just a formality, really."

I don't say anything.

"Think it over," says the rich guy, pressing my hand across the table. "An offer like this, it's once in a lifetime stuff. Quite an honour, even. We can't wait to hear what you decide."

To Sanction All Revolts, All Desperate Actions

We are not pragmatists, since nothing about this is sensible.
We are not dreamers, since the catastrophe is real, not
speculative. Our historic mission is to sanction all revolts,
all desperate actions. How do you live in the aftermath of
the catastrophe that has already occurred?

Chapter 3

I follow the climate imperialist home after a conference. It's easy to do because after all, he's just a man. It's just some steps to follow. It's hard to do for the same reason.

I message Tamina and J. "He's getting an Uber," I say. "Follow my location beacon."

I follow from the hotel and I know that it's him because of the photos Tamina sent over. I can tell from his jaw and how his ears are shaped. They don't show their faces so much, these days, but you can tell from just that.

"It's him," Tamina confirms.

Kabir waits for me in the borrowed car on the corner. He looks large, nervous, nondescript. We follow the fossil guy through the CBD where office workers go for bento boxes, things like that, then left and right between the sandstone, across the bridge and out through suburbs with the greenness of parks and the purple fall of jacaranda. It's that time of year.

"J on their way," Tamina messages.

Once we get closer to his address, we slow down and turn off so as not to be too obvious. We park a couple streets along and I get out while Stickie waits, feeling cold because I'm underdressed, I do this on purpose 'cos it keeps me awake. I used to wrench myself into focus but I have since found that allowing a buzz of surface thought actually helps to preserve a greater level of alertness underneath. The scene around me is beautiful, there is just so much colour. Drooping trees with purple blooms crushed underneath. It's familiar 'cos I scoped it out last week and saw that the imperialist lives in an incredibly ugly house. Stacked levels, like a Rubik's cube. It's a recent renovation, you can't see it yet on Google maps. I took some pictures 'cos you never know when they will come in handy.

"Turn left," messages Tamina.

It's such a comfort to see J's familiar silhouette. Tall, hands in pockets, head slightly bowed, mask, sunglasses, grey hoodie and those trackpants from Kmart, paid for in cash. Him on one side of the street, me on the other. It's so different when you're with someone else, you feel like you can do anything. Like you are bigger than the limits of yourself.

"OK, he's gone indoors," messages Tamina. "Probably getting changed before his workout. Wait at the park. I'll let you know."

The square of grass with its swings and shady seats. Cherry trees heavy with blossoms, the smell of eucalypts – the beauty of cliché, but it's still beautiful. Over the peeping fence you can see a hint of the blue ocean, green laws which spill out to the water.

Boredom, boredom, boredom, violence.

"He's close," messages Tamina. "Be ready."

Here he is wearing trackpants, T-shirt, sneakers. Workout gear, he's the kind of wealthy man who pays attention to his diet. He probably knows how to punch things, but only in the gym. He comes into the park and his eyes kind of slide over me, this is a gift that I have, to just slide blackly into someone's vision. "Excuse me," he says, hardly even bothering to look me in the eye. And it is then then that I hit him, a one-two punch, jab and a cross; and then a left right hook so that his head whips around at an ugly angle; forcing the breath from his chest. I strike him with full force and momentum, third time connecting on the flattened plane of the right side of his skull. As he goes down I hit him with my elbow, the full pivot so the blow comes with my body's weight; I feel his nose cave in so that the blood is lurid, strands of the brightest scarlet in the fading light. Oh, there is so much colour in this evening. And now J is here, that human force of the possible, kicking him again and again in the ribs while I am holding him down; noises are coming from his orifices and it's disgusting but beautiful. And the contempt goes through me in a shudder, and each blow feels harder than the last, contempt moves through my body like arousal; then a light flicks on. J and I look at each other and scram. J's legs are so long but I keep at it, I keep up and I am at his side, and then we're in the car with Kabir driving off, ecstatic with release.

I look back once and see two figures. A baby in a stroller, abandoned by the roadside, its small fists moving in and out towards its eyes as it starts, uncontrollably, to cry. Also a blonde woman, clothes askew as she runs towards the prone figure in the playground. Hair unkempt, mouth stretched out as she goes off with fear like a car alarm.

"Yes," I message Tamina.

"Nice work," she messages back.

Chapter 4

In January the temperature in Penrith passes fifty degrees. Thankfully this doesn't occur on a day of high humidity. Heat at this level is technically survivable if there isn't too much moisture in the air. And this is, after all, a wealthy country: people have their air-conditioning, their insulated houses; they have baths and pools. So far, so good.

But the heat lasts one hour, two hours, three. A transmission line sags in the heat, touches some trees and bursts into flames, causing the electricity to be cut from two thousand homes. The air con goes out; and with pipes heating up, the water warms up too. The temperature climbs: fifty-one, fifty-two. People want to escape, they get in their cars and start to drive to where the electricity still works. Some of these cars are battery-powered electric. Because of the heat, five of these batteries experience thermal runaway, causing the entire vehicle to burst into flames. In three of these incidents, all of the passengers get out in time. In the other two, they don't.

The heat lasts three hours, four hours, five. Two of the flaming cars, driverless now, continue rolling down the street. One of them rolls onto a grassy verge framed by drooping eucalypts. Soon the whole cul-de-sac is on fire; smoke blankets the horizon across the suburb. People stagger from their homes, terrified and bleary with the temperature. More try to flee, taking their cars. And now there are fears for the stability of the power system: an influx of people into neighbouring suburbs may cause further strain and larger blackouts. To avoid this contagion, police issue a stay-at-home order. A helicopter is deployed to circle overhead, barking out orders through a loudspeaker. But it's too hot to care.

A line is drawn around Penrith LGA and four additional suburbs. Emergency orders are issued and signed, and the police set up blockades to stop people from leaving. They wait inside their huge, air-conditioned eggs, black four-wheel drives. Some residents resent this. One, a Lebanese man in his mid-thirties, emerges from his car. He gesticulates angrily at the police and is shot at point blank range with a rubber bullet; when his brother protests, he is pulled from the car and tasered. Later there are reports the man has been hospitalised with internal bleeding.

The heat reaches a maximum of fifty-four degrees; then with nightfall, subsides to a more survivable forty-five.

Over the coming weeks, several dozen corpses are discovered in homes, dead of dehydration or heat exhaustion. Ten more are discovered on the street, probably homeless; most of the housed fatalities suffered from at least one pre-existing issue with their health. This does not include two people killed from being run off the road at the checkpoints, or the eight who perished in the fires.

Labor Senator Katherine K. Kelly asks why the army was not called in earlier to enforce the blockade.

A few weeks later, when conditions are more bearable, Kit and I catch the ferry to go and visit the home of Deirdre Yuen, who is hosting one of her bi-monthly 'Creatives In Colour' dinners. These are events where artists from Culturally and Linguistically Diverse backgrounds, and a few well-chosen allies, meet to share experiences and swap tips on navigating a white, settler-colonial artistic environment. Deirdre is an important contact in the industry – I would use the word 'friend', but the word and the currency of feeling have become so debased over time, I am no longer convinced it is appropriate. Deirdre was a filmmaker once, though this side of her career has all but ceased since her first feature, *Mooncake Mirage*, won third prize in the inaugural (and as it would turn out, final) iteration of the *Intersections* film competition. These days she describes herself as an 'imaginative enabler': someone who soothes, flatters, uplifts and occasionally bankrolls other people's creative endeavours. I see her as a sort of eternal older sister, possessed of an unshakeable yet somewhat indiscriminate belief in the power of the arts.

Some teenagers gather round us, giggling, asking for selfies with Kit. For a moment I hover, uncertain, waiting to see if they also want a picture or an autograph with the director of *Red Jade Ravine* – until it becomes clear that they are followers, not of our show, but of Kit's TikTok. I don't have TikTok – the quick editing and mix of text and speech confuses me – I'm unfamiliar with the contents of Kit's channel, except that it features attractive foods such as snowskin mooncakes, or a bear made out of rice reclining in a bowl of curry. Kit poses obligingly, arranging themself on the ferry's prow with one hand in their pocket and the other on their vape. They look disengaged, artful although, I notice, they continue interacting with the teens for some time, until everyone is satisfied with their shots. I hover round them for a while then go and huddle inside, avoiding the spray and smell of salt. The harbour is grey and beautiful, sky grey and dim like a folded screen.

"Helloooo! *Helloooooooo.*" Deirdre, wearing a smock from Gorman paired with bright coral lipstick and white tights, kisses me on either cheek. "It's so good to catch up. Congratulations on your memoir! I can't wait to read it – what was the title, '*My Life Story*'? Sorry, '*Story Of My Life*'? And you must be Kip – sorry, Kit. My bad. Come inside, come inside."

"Hello," says Deirdre's husband Andrew. As a human being he is mostly unnecessary. He and I have an easy, low-stakes relationship. On the rare occasions circumstances force us to converse, it is mostly on the topics of urban planning, documentary film and occasionally sports. Deirdre's house is large and so, so white. If you've seen the movie *Parasite,* you can probably imagine the decor. There is what feels like an infinite quantity of floorspace. Other surfaces extend without obvious bound: white tiles; white kitchen countertop; a huge white platform dedicated entirely to the TV. There is an enormous living space which is normally adorned with children's toys and a sumptuous yet minimalist rug. For the purpose of the evening's festivities, these have been replaced by an extendable white dining set around which are seated Dhanya Patel, who works for the Centre for Copyright, Michelle Widjaja, who performs at slams and writes lyric poetry, and Ali Marshall, an emerging literary critic for the *Weekly Review*, and their respective plus ones.

"Oh no," says Deirdre. "Kit, I'm so sorry, I forgot to set a place for you... do you mind if I put you at my daughter's table? I hope you don't think you've been left out? You're too special to sit with us... young and beautiful, ha ha ha."

"That's fine," says Kit, and shrugs. It occurs to me they may be slightly stoned.

The talk turns to the state of the arts in this country. It is agreed that funding for the arts, as well as the cultural and institutional processes surrounding them, are generally inadequate, gatekeeping and systematically discriminatory.

"It's horrible. Horrible!" Michelle waves her hands and shakes her head at the same time, earrings swinging energetically. "Poets are the worst, I tell you. The way they tear each other down, instead of supporting each other. The other day, I was getting ready to go on stage. I was so nervous... you know me, as an artist, I'm always up in my feelings. And then this other performer – and I don't think you'll be surprised to hear he was a white man – comes up to me and says, 'Oh, are you doing another piece on your identity? Nice work if you can get it.' As if *he* doesn't have an identity. Sometimes I wonder when I'll be left alone to find peace in this world. Because we are all going to die, you know? All I am trying to do here is to speak my truth, to exist in this sad, lonely, challenging, yet incredibly beautiful world."

"Awful," says Deirdre, shaking her head. "I admire that so much about you, Michelle. That you are willing to share so much of yourself. Artists are the most vulnerable people in our society."

"It's the most extractive experience," agrees Dhanya. "White men acting like they are entitled to exploit our identities, our lives. I see it all the time in my work in copyright law. Just the other week we had to issue a 'cease and desist' notice to these people, they call themselves a radical book swap or is it book stop? Either way, they were circulating pdfs, clippings from essays, passages from books. Such a level of entitlement in this kind of behaviour. That you can just get access to someone else's labour, without paying – it's just stealing from the mouths of artists, writers, activists!

Especially marginalised and First Nations creators."

Ali nods earnestly. "It's the whitest thing in the world, isn't it. I'm so sorry you have to deal with that. Living in this white body, I will never know what it is to move through the world as a woman of colour. But as an ally, though I know I will never really *understand*, I can still stand… as artists, I think it's important for us to dignify our work as labour. Time in rehearsal, preparation, so much more than the time we are paid for, isn't that right, Kit?" Speaking in an unnaturally high voice, as if talking to a child.

Kit blinks exaggeratedly. "I dunno… I mostly just rock up."

"But you do it so well! Gen Z is really something. You just woke up like this, did you? Ha ha ha." Kit does not smile in response. The scene is awkward: Ali graceless, trying to be charming; Kit remaining gracelessly uncharmed. And yet more graceful than all of us, cocooned in their elegant slouch, long fingers toying with their vape.

Michelle comes to the rescue: "These dips are amazing, Deirdre, you've outdone yourself."

"All thanks to Ottolenghi. That man never misses."

Kit looks vaguely at the wall and shoves a fistful of pita chips in their mouth.

"I love vegetarian food," Dhanya says. "My family have been vegetarians for hundreds of years, it's our ancestral tradition. So don't lecture *me*, white vegan Karens. Although these days, I do cook some meat. Mike," looking at her husband "can't really do without it, tee hee. I started off by learning to eat chicken, but not on the bone – ugh, it's awful! And I still can't bring myself to eat beef."

"It's so much better for the environment," says Ali. "We white Australians have so much to learn from other cultures. The first step is to talk less and listen more."

"Speaking of the environment," Deirdre says. "Something really quite shocking happened recently. You remember Tim, Andrew's brother-in-law. Really helped us out in setting up the sponsorship arrangements for the Young Poet's Prize last year. Such a kind, soft-spoken man. Well, it was quite terrifying… he was just coming home from work when he was accosted by the members of some gang. He was severely beaten up… his wife and his one-year-old even saw some of it happen! So traumatic for them. But the strange thing is, he wasn't even robbed. Apparently, the police think there may have been a political motivation."

"Oh, how awful for your friend!" says Ali, covering her mouth. "Have they caught the perpetrators?"

"No! Oh, I know, it's shocking to me, too! But Andrew says there's been a few of these attacks occurring. It's opportunistic, almost random. There doesn't seem to be much rhyme or reason, other than targeting people who are linked to fossil fuels. It's hard to track because these people are criminals, not protestors – they hide their identities, they cover their faces. The police are at a loss. Andrew says they just don't have the powers to deal with things like this."

"That is horrible," says Michelle. "What is wrong with people. As an artist, it's the job of my heart to really *go there*, you know? The darkest places of the human psyche. But I can't think what kind of darkness you would have to have inside. Of course, I want climate action, but violence is never the answer. Maybe as an artist, I just have too much empathy. Deirdre, I so hope your friend will be OK. I heard a podcast about these vigilante groups – they call themselves, what is it, 'anti-industrialists'?"

"Anti-imperialists," corrects Dhanya. "The idea is, they are our self-appointed defenders from climate collapse. Truly disturbing stuff. No matter your beliefs, everyone deserves to be safe at work, don't they? Tim went back to work too early, well before he was fully recovered. They couldn't find enough senior staff to replace him. Then he ended up quitting his job anyway, because of PTSD. And now it looks like they will cancel the entire project he was working on, an ore refinery – well, what is going to happen to his family? To all the families who were relying on that business? I just find this terrifying – don't you think so, Andrew?"

Andrew clears his throat. "Awful," he agrees. "And expensive, too. Really eating into the budget for new projects. It's getting to the point where people won't take on the job without private security. Not to mention the insurance! You know, if I could talk face to face with one of these goons, what I would say to them is: if you have a problem with what we're doing, take it up in parliament. Go and hold a rally, protest all you want – *peacefully*. Hell, I might even join you. But no violence – we still live in a democracy, you know."

"Absolutely!" says Ali. "As an artist, the thing that really gets me going is the epistemic violence. Elevating their own voices above all others. I listened to this amazing podcast by my friend, she is so passionate. Does the most brilliant work with this group called the Green Revolt – they do NVDA, it stands for Non-Violent Direct Action. Just like Dr Martin Luther King. They held a beautiful event, a picnic outside parliament. Adults, kids, the elderly – there was music, speeches – a completely family friendly event. There was one beautiful moment, I saw it on Facebook – a police officer was crying. He stopped to give the protestors a hi-five, one of the little children – well, I teared up. To make real change, you have to bring everyone on side. Doctors, lawyers, politicians, artists, poets, cops. We're all in this together!"

Deirdre's cleaner, an old woman with a severely hunched posture, comes into the room. She is dragging a vacuum which makes a disconcerting sound as it scrapes against the tiles.

"Oh, excuse me," says Deirdre. "Please don't stop the party on my account." We look politely at the walls, the light fittings and the floor while they converse in Mandarin. At last Deirdre throws up her hands and waves the woman from the room. "I am so sorry," she says. "It's such a battle to get her to follow my instructions. In my own home! I don't know how many times I can explain, *hard* plastics go in this bin, *soft* plastics go in the other… Don't you think?" she adds, rounding on her husband.

Andrew jerks back into full consciousness, as if he is a laptop that has been left idling and gone into power saving mode, and someone has just accidently swiped the mousepad. "Yeah… definitely," he says.

Michelle and Dhanya's respective partners adopt expressions of pre-emptive innocence. Their faces convey an ambient sense of 'I didn't do anything'.

"I couldn't have said it better myself, Ali," says Dhanya, covering the lull in the conversation. "As a woman of colour, I condemn these violent actions. People claiming to speak on my behalf. After all, my family is from Basavanagudi, Bangalore. We know what it means to suffer under racialism, colonialism – Hinduphobia is growing every day. It reminds me of the time they brought the, what do they call it, 'black bloc', to a conference at my uni. Men in black wearing balaclavas, masks, their faces hidden, rampaging through the campus. It's just more toxic masculinity, really. The one thing we don't need is more white men centring themselves."

Kit says, "How do you know they are white men if they're hiding their faces?"

There is a silence, which Kit fills by picking at a falafel that has fallen onto the table, sticking their fingers in their mouth.

"Time for dessert!" says Deirdre.

"But it's not just white men who can't help centring themselves," Michelle goes on, while Deirdre spoons portions of Ottolenghi's halva pudding on our plates. "Men of colour, Asian men, can be horrible as well. Just these last few days, if you look at what's been happening to Mandy, with these trolls on the internet."

"Oh my *God*. Mandy is a *goddess*."

"Lyrical, intellectual, embodied, intense."

"She has truly gut-renovated the TV serial form."

"Mandy is an incredible artist and person," says Michelle. "I wish I had half of her talent and strength. But even she isn't safe from the online MRAsians – you know, Men's Rights Activists. Patriarchy, but make it POC. Really terrible guys – I mean, welcome to intersectionality, hel-*lo*! It makes me sick to see such hate directed at an Asian woman. All for sharing her truth, her vulnerability with the world."

"Abso-*lutely*," Deirdre says. "I'm so proud of her for standing up to them. Speaking her own personal truth about who she, personally, feels attracted to. It's time someone said it – Asian women aren't the property of Asian men! What these misogynist trolls refuse to acknowledge is that when we look at them, we remember the oppression we had to witness our mothers, our grandmothers, our aunties going through. Ain't nobody got time for that!"

Michelle's husband, a tall white man in a cable-knit jumper, Deirdre's husband, a thin white man in a good-quality zip-up hoodie, Ali's boyfriend, a smiling white youngish man, and Dhanya's husband, a broad-shouldered, well-manicured white man in a blue suit, all nod in unison.

"Hetero-patriarchy, sexism. It's a problem the world over, isn't it?" Ali says. "Of course, in my white body, I can't speak for myself to this lived experience. But that's the meaning of intersectionality, isn't it? The patriarchy oppresses us all. As women, of course – but also men, girls, boys, every colour of the gender rainbow."

"Yes!" Deirdre exclaims. "The gender spectrum – I find this space *very* exhilarating. Young people doing their little experiments – playing games with their pronouns – well, not *games*, but you know what I mean."

Everyone turns to look surreptitiously at Kit, who takes a moment to realise what is going on. "Uhhh… OK," they say, drawing patterns in the halva on their plate with the back of a spoon.

"Let's have some chai," says Dhanya. "Yes, that's right, chai. Not 'chai tea'. That's like saying 'tea tea' in our language."

"I'll go and get you some soy milk," I mumble to Kit, leaving the table.

It is a relief to be alone, silence and space standing in contrast to the claustrophobic social continuousness of the dinner table. For once I am comforted by the size of Deirdre's home. On the side of the stainless-steel fridge there is a framed poem-fragment:

My Mother's Dumplings by Mandy Lo

As a child I watched
My mother's
Hands
Prepare dumplings

For our family.
From her wrists
Hung green bangles
Of moss-jade.
Now I too
Prepare dumplings
For my family…

I read it slowly, finding it hard to keep my focus in a kitchen of such splendour. To soothe my nerves, I take a moment to observe the range of appliances on display. There is an air-fryer, a dehydrator, a food processor, an electric garlic press. A convection cooktop with an industrial-strength extraction hood and eight different hotplates of varying sizes. A Thermomix, a pink KitchenAid (I detected some envy in Kit's expression on observing this) and a rice cooker of great technical advancement, featuring various heating, re-heating and pressure-cooking functions. There are two fridges, both stainless steel: one of them ceiling height and one a chest freezer. There is however, as far as I observe, no electric toaster, only a pair of red ceramic vintage toasting irons. After consideration, I am able to deduce that you are supposed to heat them manually over the stove, before applying them to the cut surface of sliced bread.

When I get back Deirdre turns to me and says, "Speaking of serials – how are things going with your show? Have you been renewed for a second season? I've been hearing on the grapevine, the funding environment has been growing even tighter than it was."

I steal a glance at Kit, who unbeknownst to me seems to have migrated to the couch and fallen asleep in a dramatic fashion. "Yes, we did get renewed, but with conditions. The network isn't willing to pay for it all. But there has been an offer of additional sponsorship from Nilsson Services. I do feel somewhat conflicted about accepting that funding stream, though. There has been this call for divestment related to, what is it, the migrant camps?"

"*Ohhhhh.* Nilsson do the security, right? For the detention centres."

Deirdre' face is stricken. "I heard about – it's quite terrible, isn't it? That poor boy who died. I wrote an email to Katherine K. Kelly, did you know we're in her seat? She brought a motion before the Senate, we're so lucky to be in her electorate. One of the few moments in recent years I've felt truly proud of a politician, as an Australian."

"Yes, of course," I fiddle with my fork. "I've been wondering, actually… perhaps I should turn it down."

The response is instantaneous.

"No."

"What are you talking about?"

"Don't sell yourself short!"

"These are difficult issues," Ali says. "In my white, middle-class body, I can't know how it feels to seek asylum in Australia. But please remember, you are a migrant too. Your work is also part of breaking down these walls and boundaries."

"Don't give in to whichever voice chooses to scream the loudest," Dhanya says. "Some of those holier-than-thou protestors need to remember that we are all living here on stolen land. If you can't own your privilege as a non-Indigenous Australian, all your boycotts, your rallying, your protests, mean nothing. *Nothing*. You are just as complicit as any cop. Oh, here's an idea! Maybe you can use the show to make, you know, a statement! Say something about how strongly you disagree with what Nilsson is doing."

I say, "But if they're still sponsoring our show…"

"What else have people been up to these last few weeks?" asks Michelle. "Does anyone else here watch *Parliamentary Pantry*? Oh my God, that lamb *curry* Julie Knight made."

Parliamentary Pantry is an exceedingly tedious reality TV show dignified with a thin veneer of political relevance. It follows the adventures of a well-known journalist, a white lady who goes from house to politician's house cooking meals with them. During their working lives, these politicians do things like melting glaciers and putting children into gulags. However, the journalist looks past these petty grievances when they sit down one-on-

one and share dinners like beef bourguignon or the afore-mentioned lamb curry. Thus we, the audience, learn that those who wield power and use it to wreak misery on others also, on occasion, successfully cook and metabolise food. That is all that it takes to engender empathy for the powerful. The soft bigotry of low moral expectation.

"Of course, I don't believe exactly the same things as Julie Knight," Dhanya says. "But at least now I have some empathy for where she's coming from, as a person… my goodness, look at the time. It's been wonderful, Deirdre. Superlative hostessing, as always."

The rest of us take this as our cue to start moving. I am the last out the door, owing to the need to shake Kit into consciousness on the couch.

As she hugs me goodbye, Deirdre winks surreptitiously and says: "I can tell you're still uncomfortable about, you know, that thing with Nilsson. Here's a little suggestion – if you want to do something for the refugees, why don't you try calling your MP? If you want to make a real difference. I love how passionate you are about these issues, I find it so inspiring."

"Thanks Deirdre. That sounds like a good idea." I hesitate on the threshold, unsure of how to broach the topic. "It may sound a little odd, but can I ask you a personal question? What is happening with your toaster?" I gesture at the red handheld ceramic plates, now framed in a little mis-en-scene of open-plan living room, aircon, air purifier with HEPA filter, electric dehumidifier, heater, smart bulb set, household alarm system, Roomba and wall-length TV. "How come you don't have a normal one? For making breakfast."

"*Ohhhh.*" Deirdre glows pink with embodied satisfaction, like Kirby from the Super Mario-verse. "It saves electricity."

While we are waiting for an Uber, I say to Kit: "Thank you for being so patient tonight. And sorry Deirdre is the way she is."

Kit takes a moment to respond. "She's not a bad person," they say, sucking reflectively on their vape, which has an aroma of weed and artificial strawberries. "I reckon there'd be times when, like, she would be cognisant of human pain. Like, if it were spread over her shoes."

Chapter 5

"Good afternoon. You've reached the office of the Honourable Jo Hartcher, your local member."

"Hi there. Hello. Look, I'm just calling as a concerned, um, a concerned Australian citizen. To discuss your, um, our government's policy on the detention camps."

"One moment, please."

(Hold music playing.)

"Hello? Hellooo? Is anyone still…"

"Good afternoon. Thank you for calling the office of the Honourable Jo Hartcher, your local member for Tannehill. We've been experiencing a higher than usual volume of calls lately. Thank you for your patience."

(Hold music playing.)

"Hello? Hellooo…"

"Hi, thank you for calling the office of the Honourable Jo Hartcher, how can… "

"Hello? Hellooo? Is this an actual person?"

"Yes, it is. How can I help you?"

"Oh – hi – hi! Sorry, I thought I was stuck on the pre-recorded message. Um, I'm just calling to…"

"Just a minute, I'll be back with you shortly."

(Hold music plays.)

"Hello? Hellooo?"

"Hi, you've called the office of…"

"Yes, I know who I called! Look, I want to protest, I mean, register my strongest disagreement…"

"Oh, is this about the mandatory detention?"

"Yes, it is."

"Give me your postcode, please."

"What?"

"I said please give me your postcode."

"Right. It's 2002. As I was saying, the camps…"

"The Member for Tannehill values your input very much. Thank you for calling today. Goodbye."

"Hey, wait! I … "

(Call disconnects.)

*

"Hi, thank you for calling the office of the Michael Drury, your shadow minister for…"

"Hello, is this an actual person?"

"Yes, it is. Is this about the detention centres?"

"Well, yes, I … "

"Thanks for calling. What's your postcode?"

"2033. I … "

"Thanks, we take your input very seriously. Michael is committed to securing the integrity of our nation's borders."

"OK, but…"

"Thanks for calling, have a good afternoon."

(Call disconnects.)

Headline 1

MINISTER HARTCHER: 'WE WILL DO **WHATEVER IT TAKES** TO SECURE OUR BORDERS AGAINST UNAUTHORISED ARRIVALS BY BOAT.'

Headline 2

SHADOW MINISTER DRURY: 'UNLIKE THE GOVERNMENT, WE ALSO HAVE A PLAN TO STOP UNAUTHORISED ARRIVALS BY PLANE.'

On revolutionary defeatism

Climate change is not 'like' colonisation, it is not 'related to' colonisation; climate change is colonisation. It is a literal occupation of atmospheric space, secured by violence and raining violence in the most literal sense on the world's poor and coloured peoples. It is the flow of death from the core to the periphery, and of resources from the periphery to the core. Whether these flows are explicitly in the name of empire or some notion of green industry, whatever neo-empire you call it. This is war and we are the aggressors. The phone call is coming from inside the house.

Chapter 6

The vibe on the street where the NGO guy lives is different from the jacaranda avenue. Terrace houses, lots of native plants. Young professional
couples with no children, or just one, small ones; bowls of water left out
for soft cats and for jubilant dogs. There are signs which say FRACK FREE
ZONE and RECONCILIATION NOW.

Following the NGO man home is easier than the fossil fuel dude because
he catches public transport, as a man of the people. It's also easy to find
pictures of his face, which he posts constantly on social media. He has a
lot of that – Twitter, Instagram, LinkedIn, Facebook. As many forums as
possible, where people congratulate him for putting solar panels on his
roof. Stickie by my side again. The comfort of the human and familiar.

"Yes, you're at the right place," messages J.

The street is narrow, with cars on both sides though there is no-one driving at the moment. There's a small basketball court where some teenagers
are playing beneath the light. The sound of the ball striking the asphalt feels
unnaturally loud. Stickie walks ahead, carrying a round yellow bucket, a
mop and a handheld vacuum cleaner whose snout protrudes from a back-
pack slung over one shoulder.

"Going in," I message J.

Stickie enters first, through a metal gate with peeling paint at the vined
entrance, a latch that falls open at the slightest touch. I move to the side
of the house, a small wound-up hose, brown bricks and a magnolia tree I
saw when I came by to scope the place out. At the time it was flowering;
now it is bare of leaves with one lingering blossom. I hear them talking
on the doorstop – Stickie's feminine half-whisper, the fresh-off-the-boat
accent, though she's been in the country for eight years. Hamming it up
a bit. And then, deeper, an Australian man's voice, a tone of weary entitlement, faux-polite.

"I am here for the cleaning – yes? For your house? So you let me in now?"

"No, you don't understand. I didn't schedule you to come today, you were supposed to come tomorrow. Not *to-day*. *To-mor-row*. I – "

Various indistinct noises. Stickie is arguing, sounding increasingly plaintive; at last the man agrees to let her in. There is the sound of a bag being unzipped, and then I hear the door close; muffled, abrasive hum of the vacuum cleaner. The awaited ping from Stickie's phone. I walk back and find the door unlocked. The squeak as I open it can't be heard over the vacuum.

Inside the house the front hall is dark and narrow, then spreading out into a golden-panelled living room. Warm pool of yellow light in the blue evening. The interior is homely but slightly askew, with odd absences where some physical object appears to be missing. There are ochre-coloured couches and several shelves of magazines – *The Monthly*, *Meanjin* and *The New Yorker* – but also gaps in the shape of a single book, so that the remaining texts lean sideways. A round imprint on the wooden mantlepiece where a vase would go, but no vase and no flowers.

Just alongside the vacuum noise, not so much over or under as adjacent to it, you can make out a thread of music. Good quality speakers. The NGO man is cooking something or other in the kitchen:

"*…don't think twice now, it's alright…*"

Vacuum still in Stickie's hands. Her eyes a reflection of mine. Vortex of anticipated violence.

The NGO man comes back out of the kitchen. He looks so banal, so aggressively harmless.

Kitchen knife in his hand, his gaze catching me full in the face. 'What…?' he begins. Stickie slams him with the vacuum from behind so the knife clatters to the ground. The NGO guy moans, more in surprise than anything else. 'Fuck!' The machine is still going, they're wrestling, rolling over the brown-gold panelled floor, her arms pinning him from behind. Then I'm onto him as well, he is surprisingly easy to hold down, a skinny piece of work, we're bending him over the table, he's trying to rear up and we are slamming him, again and again; Stickie pinning his arms while I bash his head again and again on the surface like a parody of one of those toy drinking birds.

"Please," he moans, dribbling. "We are on the same side."

The vacuum is still going. Stickie turns it to max with her foot, so that the noise intensifies. Through the walls, which are thin, we hear movement in the house next door. I glance back at his shelf, which has a certificate of thanks from the Renewable Jobs Alliance as well as one from the Tiddaroo Foundation. A row of framed photos, also with gaps – the pictures that remain depict professional accomplishment, not intimacy. Three white men, all with a very divorced look to them, wearing suits. The picture has been taken from a terrible angle, in worse light – everyone's face looks beefy, red and distorted. On the dining table are some unopened letters, prob-ably bills, and there's junk on the chairs – this is a man who lives alone. I take as many letters as I can, just in case it turns out useful.

"Please," he moans. There is red foam on his mouth. "I support green energy." Then, unexpectedly, he bucks; Stickie has to push her elbows into his back to hold him down. A glass of water falls. The crash and the expansion of volume feel more violent than anything which went before.

Next door a dog begins to bark. "Time to get out," Stickie says. I hit him one more time on the head, with definitive force, to knock him out. We scram.

Once we are back on the street time feels different, it seems to move very fast. The dog is still barking. A voice calls: "Are you alright?" Both of us stiffen, but someone else answers: one of the teenagers has tripped and fallen on the court. Kids are playing basketball still, their game unin-terrupted.

Stickie and I walk quickly in the dark; then, out of sight, we start to run. Out of the gaze of the pooled streetlamps we pull on different jump-ers, then keep running past the houses and through a construction site, only slowing down when we reach the main road and its lights. Almost at the station now. The world seems bigger and smaller, like we are in a distortion field. I can't tell if I am entering or leaving the zone of reality.

"Oh no," says Stickie. "I stepped in dog poo, look at that."

J messages, letting us know we should meet him on the corner. There's a car parked underneath the light; J's friend Brian is there, flicking a spent cigarette out the front window. Stickie and I hop in the back and we drive without speaking to the station. Thank goodness J handles things. I don't know what Brian knows and I don't ask.

Once we are on the train, it feels like a different world. Like we are deep sea fish pulled out of water. We sit in different carriages and Stickie gets off first. I watch her crossing the concourse, bag slung over her shoulders. Mop and bucket were abandoned at the NGO guy's house – although she has brought the vacuum cleaner. Seems like a risk, given how fast we had to go. But, well, a good vacuum can be hard to find. Seeing her from behind, I feel a surge of love. I feel so happy and affectionate, warmed all over by the sense of a job well done. I can almost forget that we slammed a man's head into unconsciousness, listened to him beg through his own spit and froth. I forget about the wave of oncoming death which makes these actions both necessary and desirable.

And, honestly, kind of fun. There is something in the way you can strike into a human face using your fist, a perfect fit. In these seconds you realise it is possible to live for such moments, when the dream is the reality, and reality is re-shaped around the moment of desire as it is instantiated in real life.

Chapter 7

"How, in one sentence, would you describe the story you're telling here?"

"Well, where do I begin? This is a story about contrasts, the tension where two different worlds collide. East meets West, pop culture meets high art. If you could get a cross between *McLeod's Daughters*, and, uh, *In The Mood For Love*..."

Alden Park is a representative from AP Entertainment (initials unrelated). This is a mid-sized entertainment agency in South Korea, which from our perspective means that he has access to more money than God. At the behest of the network, I am taking him on tour round our set, for reasons not yet disclosed but likely related to some potential cross-platforming agreement. Though I believe he grew up in the US – whether as migrant or adoptee, I am unsure – his Korean is as fluent as mine is diaspora-halting. Very skinny, dressed all in black and with a well-tended face which looks almost comically youthful – he could be anywhere between eighteen and thirty – he has an oddly androgynous, physically disconnected quality, as well as a way of articulating words veiled by a scrim of irony. It is as though he, personally, is merely the conduit for expressing an interest not entirely his own.

"Oh, I adore Korean cinema," interrupts the Actress. Young, ascendant, not completely untalented, she and Kit are leafing through the pages of tomorrow's script. "So much better than the boring, cookie-cutter, Hollywood stuff. I was at the Korean film festival, and some of the guys there... *rawr*. The hair, the skincare – Australian men could learn a thing or two." She looks meaningfully at Kit, making sure they have grasped the racially transitive nature of the compliment.

"Cool story, bro," says Kit.

"It was incredible! Although, did you hear? On the opening night, some people came to yell about bad funding, or something like that. To do with climate change. And then – well, you wouldn't believe it, but they actually threw a can of soup. Like, that's crazy, right? What is that supposed to mean? Obviously, *I* support protest, but – ”

Kit looks up, a corner of their attention snagged. “So, when you say they threw soup – did they, like *pour* it out? Or was it the whole solid can? Because…”

“Hello Kit,” says Park.

“Hey,” says Kit. Half distracted, still ruminating on the logistics of the soup-throw. “Nice to meet – *oh*.”

There is an elongated pause, during which each appears to size the other up, but without hostility. I say, more brusquely than I'd intended: “Can you two just get on with the table read?”

As we leave, I see from the corner of my eye the Actress touch Kit lightly on the chest. “Goodness, this jumper is so pretty on you. Wish that I looked as good in this colour. Lavender just does not suit me, but on *your* complexion, rawr.” A door is closed behind Kit's eyes. Still, I notice they continue to smile, even moving in closer so the Actress can rub against their jumper with her fist.

“It's a fascinating industry, isn't it?” Park says as we move on. He has a way of speaking that is simultaneously intimate and distant, as if the words are addressed both towards me and to some unseen studio audience. “There's the ostensible product, which is the show we are creating. And then there's something outside of that, overlapping but not quite co-extensive. I often say, a movie star is different from an actor. This comes across in our agency's core business, which is training idols. These days, very few singers compose their own music or lyrics – of course our market wants beautiful people, but it isn't only that. Often the composer of the song is not the best, most affecting performer of their own material. There is something absent from their delivery, a kind of sparkle round the words. Kit has that quality.” Abruptly, Park stops talking and smiles – a sleek, Apple-watch version of a smile.

We are out of the shade now. The sun golden and unpleasant, the ground hard and dry beneath our feet. I say, “Well, you know, I don't like to think of it in those terms. Markets and outputs – it's not a manufacturing process. More the expression of a personal inspiration."

"Of course." Park makes a gesture that could be a nod or a half bow. "Can you remind me, how did this series come to be?"

"Well, the inspiration was historical. We wanted to do something speaking to the national story, Indigenous Australia – decolonisation is big right now. You may have heard the phrase 'another world is possible' – we thought we could take some of the themes a bit further by using a science fictional approach… 'another world is possible'… there was also a tax break." We pause before a group of raucous and hormonal Aboriginal teenagers, aged between about eleven and seventeen. Alden says, "What are these children doing here?"

"Those are extras. We're shooting a crowd scene today, it's pretty exciting."

"I see. And what role do they play in the story?"

"Well, they're living on an asteroid. And Kit's character, who is the protagonist, is one of the agents from the company. Which is mining, um, these precious stones, using child labour. But then, Kit's character falls in love with one of the natives. Did you ever watch *Avatar*? Or was that before your time?"

"I haven't watched it." Alden smiles politely. "Don't worry, I've seen memes."

The teenagers are running round in circles, with some boys finding reasons to grab girls around the waist. Shrieking and squirming ensues. A harried set-assistant, a white woman with a ponytail, calls ineffectually: "Settle down now, settle down." I notice one of the kids is wearing a T-shirt which looks like it is has been painted by hand: the word BLKPWR in red, yellow and black. There is a picture of a panther, teeth bared, mid-pounce.

Park and I enter the make-up trailer. We find ourselves intruding on a heated dispute between the make-up artist and one of the producers, who was part of the cinematic New Wave in the 1970s. His hair is white and his face is pink. "No, no, no," he is saying. "Not good enough – these children look too soft. They look like a fashion advertisement. We need to see pain inscribed on their faces."

"Oh, I hear you, I do." The makeup artist's cadence is soothing. "But don't you think that we need to be capturing both sides of this story? The beauty *and* the brutality of colonial struggle. There, that looks perfect, don't you think?" She turns to the girl of about fifteen sitting on a high seat, using a long brush to apply a final flourish to her cheeks.

"Aw yeah, I look fucken sick!" The girl pulls out her phone. I see a glint of colour – purple, orange, pink – as she uploads to her Insta story, before running full tilt towards the door. The makeup artist gives the producer a look of demure triumph, which he receives with the worst possible grace.

Park and I leave the trailer – his mood is now contemplative, inward. I ask, "How old are you, Alden?"

"Oh, can't you guess? Twenty-six next January."

"Goodness, you're hardly older than Kit." Park grins, uncharacteristically roguish. "And how long since you migrated back to Seoul?"

"It's been seven years now. I migrated shortly after high school. I didn't plan to stay so long initially. But one thing led to another, and there was never the right moment to go back. It's exhilarating to work in a growing industry – you feel that things are really happening. The production of an international culture, the confluence of global currents." Park's smile seems lightly tinged with mockery. "If I may ask you a personal question, do you and Kit live together?"

"I keep a room for them in my apartment."

"How interesting. We like to keep our performers close, as well." I notice for the first time that, just visible beneath his linen collar, Park is wearing a small gold crucifix. "Kit must be grateful to have a supportive mentor. Young actors struggle so much." It's lightly comical to hear Park describe Kit as being young. We have returned to the group of Black teenagers, who are now being herded into the back of a shipping box mounted on a truck. "What is going on here?"

"Ah, well, they're being human trafficked. Taken off world to be used as forced labour to mine minerals. Wait, no, it's spices, or is it water? Anyway, they're going to get it from the asteroid belt."

"Right, and you say this is historical?"

"It's meant to be a parable for the Stolen Generations."

The assistant director shouts out a command and the box starts to rock. The kids begin to scream, rent their hair and pound their fists against the walls. They do this with great volume and enthusiasm.

"Beautiful, beautiful," says Park, somewhat at random. I am unsure as to what he is referring – the acting, the scene in its entirety, the teenagers themselves. The assistant shouts again and the truck ceases rocking. She sees us and glowers.

"This is a big opportunity for these young people," she says. "Some of them have had very difficult lives. I hope that they make something of themselves."

My phone vibrates with Kit's tone and I excuse myself.

"Is everything OK?" says Park when I get back.

"Ah, it's just Kit letting me know that they have gone home early. Apparently they're not feeling very well."

"Oh, how sweet. It's nice for you know where they are going. Some of these young performers become hard to control, once they have grown a bit famous."

"I didn't mean to say I monitor Kit's movements all the time." All of a sudden I am weary, with an urge to the confessional. "I was so tired before I knew Kit. Tired to my very bones. Kit was like a wrench prying open my life."

"They have that effect on people, don't they?" Another Apple-watch smile. "I remember, it was like that when we were together in the US."

"Wait." I straighten up. "You and Kit know each other? You've met before?"

"Our paths have crossed."

I am about to ask more, but the rocking of the shipping container recommences. At the climax of the scene, one of the children takes it on himself to improvise a fake heart-attack. The others get in on this with gusto, wailing for help and pointing at the body. "Well, that was the best take so far, I think. Let's call it a day."

It has begun to spot with rain. Assistants come running carrying tarps for the equipment. As Park and I head towards shelter, he says – casually? Faux casually? – "I'd like to chat with Kit at some point, if that's alright with you."

"Well, I don't own Kit. They don't need my permission to talk to other people." Taken aback by the brusqueness in my own voice. For a moment I fly out of my body, seeing myself through Park's eyes: a large-ish fish circling a small-ish cultural pond. Career no longer in ascent, if not precisely in decline. "You still haven't told me how you know each other."

"Of course! We met in the US." Park breaks off his step to look me in the eye. His gaze is professional and oddly marked with sincerity. "Let me be straight – I have no wish to undermine your work. I'm not an artist myself, but I am honest with regards to the nature of my output. What I produce is, as you say, a product. Mass entertainment. Whereas you are creating original, insightful cultural work. A means for the nation to see itself – hey, excuse me!" Park beckons at one of the teens, now chewing gum. "May I ask you, please: how do you feel about this story? The experience you have had today, as an Aboriginal person?"

The girl looks at him dubiously, then laughs in his face. "I literally don't care," she says. "I'm on TV." And runs full tilt in the opposite direction, across the open field where clouds are banking overhead.

Chapter 8

I'm hanging out on the front porch, enjoying a bit of a vape when DojaCat!!!, my friend who doesn't live here and yet kind of does, comes wandering past. She has persistent suicidal ideation, an amphetamines problem when she can get hold of them, and an alcohol problem when she can get hold of that. Which is all the time. Today she is wearing a binder, combat boots and a boiler suit. Her hair, which used to fall down to her waist, is now cropped close.

"Oh, hey," she says. "Did I tell you that I think I might actually be a boy?"

"Oh," I say. To be honest, I already knew DojaCat!!! was in the process of transitioning, I just couldn't remember which direction it was in. The other day I overheard her say she was about to start a course of a drug which sounded like 'ee', but it was noisy where we were. It could just as easily have been T(estosterone) or E(strogen). "Am I using the right pronouns?"

DojaCat!!! shrugs. "Eh, I don't care. Some people use pronouns accurately, but I use them with wonderful expression. Gender is a shitpost, anyway."

I was born in Sydney, but it could just as easily have been either Kuala Lumpur (where my dad is from) or Kochi, Kerala (the hometown of my mother). My parents met during business school in Australia; they came here to study but were always planning to go back to their respective homes where they had 'friends in every corner', as my mother used to say. But after the wet bulb event where a few friends of hers dropped dead – caught in the heat while they were touring slums as part of some resume-building, NGO-complex bullshit, upper-caste kids doing that gross, poor-watching thing, not that they deserved it – it kind of dawned on them that it was better to stay here. To die in a wet bulb event is terrible; all of your organs shut down progressively. I know this because my mother re-explains it to me every time it gets a bit humid. It is her way of punishing me for being alive.

I grew up in the south-eastern suburbs of Sydney; my own home was comfy and middle-class, though the area we lived in probably not. They used to put security guards on my bus, to stop people chucking bricks at the windows. The bus shelter was perpetually smashed; I don't know why they kept rebuilding it using the same materials. Recently I went swimming in the pool near my parents' old place and, would you believe it, I didn't see a single band-aid in the water. That is how I know gentrification is real.

Racially speaking I am Brown, although I sometimes say borderline-Brown given how I am able to, not 'pass' exactly, but significantly change how I am perceived depending on how I choose to present in any given moment. My mother used to make a big deal of my fair complexion. She used to buy me Fair 'n' Lovely, which I refused not from incipient political consciousness but because I had heard that it was made from lard. Though I am not yet a vegan, I draw the line at smearing pig fat on my face.

For these and other reasons I am a disappointment to my parents. It all comes down to my failure to achieve. Career-wise, I do shifts in a shop that sells educational puzzles for children. This is fine, I guess. I also did sex work for while, which was also fine. Well, it wasn't more gross than other stuff I've done for money.

My parents went to English language schools; they are proud of this. When I was growing up my dad said 'lah' for emphasis, but when I said 'lah' they would both shout; they told me I should die. I was young and didn't understand why, but I internalised the message. These days I don't say 'lah'; I am physically unable to. You would have to literally kill me to make the sound come out.

How I got to this point: honestly, it is hard to tell from this distance. There was the death-wave in Kerala, obviously, but that was tertiary trauma, at most, not my direct experience. These days everyone is two degrees of separation from disaster. One of my memories from the first round of megafires: how the sun looked like blood and my mum, a Christian who is big into Revelations, lost her shit and started hoarding Panadol and sparkling water. My cousin had an asthma attack and, according to my mum's second-hand reportage from the family Whatsapp, almost perished – although I don't know how much of that was real and how much was her morbid relish of proximity to death. It makes her feel significant, though she is not. I still had to go to school, even though everything was dying. This was my first lesson in how catastrophe and normalcy can co-exist.

Actually, when I say I remember, I'm sort of lying. I know this stuff happened, I know it exists in my memory somewhere, but talking about it now feels like rote – I can't call up a sense-image of these things. I think maybe it is like that when you experience something which is just really big, and you do not have a schema to fit it into. No-one tells you the emotions you should use to populate your mind, so you just don't. I don't believe we are just born into feelings, we have to learn our way into them. When no-one teaches you what's what, there is this flatness around your emotional response.

I guess it was because I wanted to learn a different way of thinking that I started to lurk around Bombadil's anarchist reading spot, a library slash zine palace. Bombadil is white and owns property as a result of never actually having come out to his parents. He uses it as a reading room where he puts on this monthly social event, it's called 'Radical Zines for Radical Teens (In Rad Scenes)'. To be honest most of the people in attendance are at least in their late thirties. In an odd way, they seem like they are all the same person – just something in the way they dress, how they move. Telling jokes they understand and I don't. I just wanted to join, like a small child in the middle of the bus listening in on conversations from the back seat where the cool kids are.

I remember wandering in there, kind of shy, seeing Bombadil and J for the first time. Bombadil was holding court, talking about philosophy or something; J was silently stacking the chairs. Later, I saw them lurking in the courtyard, talking in a way which seemed to indicate historical physical intimacy, but also a relationship whose nature exceeds mere touch. Like a long conversation that continues even through the ostensible silence. I thought it would be nice to have a friendship like that. Bombadil himself is kind of ageless and has always been around.

"Well, how are you, how is the LARP going?" he says each time he sees me. "Nice little Live Action Role Play of the revolution, your little game of ultraviolence."

On Thursdays there is free food (mostly stew, lentils and carrots). There are pamphlets and a store of A4 posters which are free to collect, mostly made by this older dude called Robbie. If you put up enough posters, he and others may congratulate you for 'doing the work'; they may also favourably or unfavourably compare individuals, organisations and whole suburbs on the basis of who 'does the work' and who does not. Here are some examples of the posters: a millionaire who looks like the Monopoly guy being chased out of town by guys with pitchforks. A crowd of workers rising up in a factory; you know that they are workers because they are wearing Soviet worker caps. There are stickers with slogans like 'Good Night Far Right' and a fist punching an exploding swastika. You are supposed to put these over other stickers which say 'AFF', which stands for, 'Australian Families First,' kind of a right-wing group who show up every now and then, say some shit about minorities, and then *siegheil* their way off. This is known as 'fighting fascists in the streets'.

There is also a button on Robbie's Instagram page which you can click to donate to his crowdfunder, supporting the production of such media as well as his personal living costs. This is our channel of agitprop, our political education programme, reaching out to the masses. I donate fairly often: not because the art moves me, but because I feel guilty that it doesn't. To be honest, I don't really get much out of it at all; it doesn't seem to show anything that I really recognise from my own life. I do not say this out loud, since I don't want other people to know I am not radical enough. Once day, when I have learned to be more radical, I am sure that I will learn to properly enjoy this art.

Then there is the written stuff – pamphlets and the aforementioned zines which are of variable quality. Lots of quotes and collage and sometimes even poetry, which by and large I do not touch. I mean, you never know where that stuff has been. But the first time I dropped in I came across this one photocopied pamphlet, pages bound with a lovely red cord. This came loose while I was browsing, so I ended up tying it around my wrist. Which then meant I had to take the pamphlet home. There was this one fragment that stuck with me – I don't recall the full context, but these were the words:

But first the state sets the scene for such violence, you see. We will retaliate with violence against his violence. It's true that we'll be hurt by his violence but we're determined not to let him wipe out the people. We will tear his legs off, we'll tear his head off and we'll take the example from George Jackson. In the name of love and in the name of freedom, with love as our guide, we'll slit every throat of anyone who threatens the people and our children...

So we will be very practical, we will go on and live very realistically. We know that all of us will die someday, there will be pain and much suffering in order for us to develop. But we know that there are two kinds of death, the reactionary death and the revolutionary death. One death is significant and the other is not... Even those who support the oppressor now will not support them in the future, because we're determined to change their minds. We'll change their minds, or else in the people's name we'll have to wipe them out thoroughly, wholly, absolutely and completely. ALL POWER TO THE PEOPLE.

This was framed by two epigrams:

WE WILL GET FREE REGARDLESS

and

IF YOU TAKE THE SKY FROM US, WE'LL SLIT YOUR THROATS

I can't tell you exactly what I was feeling, at that moment. Only that I was dismembered, just absolutely owned by the intensity of vision I was privy to. Even now I don't know what it was 'about', in a deep sense – why it touched me so much. I just know that it burned right though to the structure and the superstructure and the pillars of my little mind.

Not to put too fine a point on it, I bawled. It was all too much, I went home and filled a bath and sat in it for hours while I cried out my little eyes. Then I got out of the bath and read the piece again.

Chapter 9

At the zine palace I find Tamina and Robbie chatting. He is white and forty-something, as is she. "I'm sick of this shallow, performative, call-out culture," he is saying. "All these radlibs throwing round terms they heard on social media. Instead of getting out there on the streets, doing the work. It's like Badiou says, you know – they cling to their identities, afraid of the unknown." Robbie has recently commenced a Ph.D., he talks about Badiou a lot. "Oh, and I think you heard about the issue with Kabir. No biggie, just that he made Krissa feel... uncomfortable."

Tamina nods her agreement. "That's exactly right, Robbie. I'll get cancelled if I say it, but it's true. Where were these kids when we were at the Tuggerah detention centre breakout in 2005. You and I have spent decades trying to build up a radical scene in this place. Oh and don't worry, I'll make sure Kabir doesn't come along to the next meeting." She breaks off, seeing me. "Hi there, dear. Lovely to see you. Can you do me a favour? Pop up to the pharmacy and get me one pack of ibuprofen, a bottle of melatonin and some Hydralite – the tablets, not the liquid – purple flavour, not the green. Also Blackmores probiotics, if they have any? Thank you so much."

We have a joke, Tamina and I, that I am her gopher. She is kind of a mentor, I don't know exactly where she's from or what she does for a living – security, you see. I know everything about her and yet nothing at all. Before I go to fetch the meds I transfer her the files, pictures I took of the climate imperialist's house. This makes me happy, like a dog dropping a stick into her lap. These are pics for her to use, not all the others. Some people find the restrictions annoying, but I actually enjoy having these private intensities, a secret bond. Sharing things other people aren't supposed to see.

The first time I went on an SUV-run was with Tamina. It was the day we met. I saw her for the first time at the bus stop, tall and amused, all masked up and with her blonde hair tucked under a beanie. I thought she was warm, brisk and very admirable, as she briefed me on what we were about to accomplish. "There are six cars parked on this street, more the next one along. With a bit of luck we can get them all. You two team up –" gesturing towards this tall Black guy and a young yellow dyke, I later learned were J and Stickie. "And you and me, since it's your first time, we can go out together." J nodded silently. Stickie smiled so wide that I could see it in her eyes, even though she was wearing a surgical mask. She had this bright, awkward energy about her, which I warmed to right away.

The thing that is intrinsically hilarious about messing with an SUV is, they are so huge and simultaneously so pointless and helpless in a city environment. Disabling them is very simple, I encourage you all to have a go. There are so many ways. You can put gravel in the tailpipe. You can insert something long and sharp into the tyres, so that they gradually deflate, or you can just slash them if that's the mood you're in. You might need to use a drill bit for larger vehicles. Do your due diligence, obviously – check and dress for the cameras and study the map before you go, just in case you need to get away. Arrange for someone else to keep a lookout, if you can. It all depends on the availability of your friends and your capacities at any given moment.

"Nice work," said Tamina. She watched me push the screwdriver into my first tyre. Ineffectually at first, then with greater confidence. "Feels good, doesn't it?" And it did, the resistance and the give. "Alright, let's check in with the others. Always keep an eye on each other, OK? Look out for your pals."

When Tamina and I arrived at the next cross street, Stickie and J weren't there yet, so I had a minor freakout. Then J messaged, saying they'd spotted a cop car so they would meet us somewhere else, two streets along. And they did. It was fine, they were both there. This was the first time I experienced anticipated loss and then reprieve from loss.

"We got five cars," said Stickie happily. "It's silly, no-one needs to own a Lexus."

By the end of that little expedition, we had disabled nine 4WDs, one

Lexus, one Mercedes, two BMWs and one Honda Accord. This last vehicle was not as fancy as the rest but we could not go past the Australian flag.

"Tacky as hell," said Tamina, shaking her head.

Once we were done with the deflations, we turned our minds to the dissemination of propaganda. "I have a few posters left," Tamina said. "On the off chance, does anyone have some wheatpaste?"

"I do," said Stickie.

"You're a marvel," said Tamina. "I love the way you just carry wheatpaste on you all the time."

I held the posters flat while Stickie used a brush to spread. J and Tamina kept lookout. "J is really good at choosing spots," Tamina told me later. "He has this amazing spatial awareness, like a whole sixth sense." While Stickie brushed, I looked at the design. There was the outline of a circle and, in the middle, a black flag. Half of the space inside the circle was red and half of it was green, with a slash down the middle. There were words round the top and the bottom, but I hadn't worn my contact lenses.

"What does that say?" I asked.

Tamina gave me this cagey look. "Diversity of tactics, diversity of targets," she said.

"Oh, I get it," I said. Though at the time I really didn't.

And that was how I first came to join the battle against climate imperialism. One of those moments whose full romance and embedded loss can only be known in retrospect.

Chapter 10

Nobody hears from my housemate, DojaCat!!! for seventy-two hours. On the first day no-one notices because, what is time. On the second day a few of us start worrying, but privately. On the third day a general alert goes out and we start exchanging notes.

"She was on Twitter last week," I say, remembering.

"The last text I got from her was this," says Leafie, a white dyke who by the way is Stickie's girlfriend. Showing a jpeg of Squidward lying face down on the ocean floor: the caption reads, 'The Vibe Continues To Deteriorate'.

"I don't get it," says Stickie. Blunt and anxious. "This is too much internet for me. Is it a coded suicide note?"

"I very much hope not!" says my pal The Rat. "Imagine ruining memes for us like that."

The first place we go looking is the memorial park where we sometimes train for self-defence. This is where DojaCat!!! was found, semi-conscious, the last time she OD'd on whatever it was that she OD'd on. On that occasion it was J who found her. He wasn't even searching, just went there to train because he likes exercise so much.

Today by coincidence he is there as well, hitting pads with Kabir and Kabir's white girlfriend, who by the way has dreadlocks. She also has a dog named Kaya – this is short for Kartikaya, aka, the Hindu god of war. Kabir's girlfriend is not a Hindu and Kaya frequently shits inside the house. All of them express polite, unhelpful concern with respect to DojaCat!!!'s wellbeing and whereabouts.

"Have you tried asking any Mob?" the girlfriend asks. "I heard, you know, they have telepathic powers. They might be able to sense where she is without looking. I heard that when they're in a group of their own people, they all get up to go at the same time. They don't need to say anything. They can read each other's minds."

Kabir looks embarrassed on her behalf, but he doesn't say anything. The man is kind of a magnet for the white chicks – well, you know how they can be when there are men from the Orient. 'Dick curved like a scimitar,' as Edward Said said, probably. Not that it doesn't go both ways – where white girls are, Kabir will be. The only cost is his dignity, lmao. Infinite sex in exchange for a lifetime's racial degradation.

Without speaking J makes it politely yet firmly known that he wishes for us to move on, and we keep going.

"Not to be a doomer, but what if DojaCat!!! has slashed her wrists?" Leafie wonders. "Like the last time she tried… no, I think it was actually the time before that."

"No, last time it was pills," The Rat corrects. "In any case, we should find her before she bleeds out or whatever. Once there's brain death, it's irreversible. Hey, why don't we go check out Brian's house?"

Brian lives down the road. He is an Indonesian punk who lives with his brother and cousin amidst scenes of generalised squalor. DojaCat!!! likes to hang there for this reason, she feels better when she feels someone's life is going to hell faster than her own. When we show up, there are chords reverberating from the back.

"What's up?" Brian asks, emerging with a guitar. "Ah, Doja's run off again? Have you got a car – you could go and take a look for her down the creek? Maybe she's gone and drowned herself? Bro, you know what, you can borrow the van off my cousin when he gets back home."

"Thank you," says Leafie. "Brian, can I please have some tea? We can use my homemade mix from the dandelions. I'm feeling anxious, it will help to soothe my nerves."

Leafie has a point, we do require tea. Unfortunately this requires traversing the floor of the filth-kitchen to procure cups. These are buried beneath a huge pile of mouldering crockery, a kind of improvised Jenga-tower currently balancing in the sink. As he washes them, after a fashion, Brian holds forth on the condition of things. "You know what gets me about the fucking Left? Everyone is so fucking self-righteous. Politics this, politics that – everything just has to be turned into a big ideological issue, you

46

know? Even just doing the fucking dishes."

"Yeah," says The Rat, *sotto voce*. "But doing the dishes *is* political."

The boiling water for the tea sterilises the cups; I consider this good, from a microbial perspective. I get anxious and go to the living room to decompress via a TikTok from that actor, Kit Phuong, the one who is cuter than God. To be honest, I don't really watch their show, which sort of tries to be deep, but I do like Phuong's cooking TikToks – even though when I tried to make the cute bear made from rice reclining in a curry onsen, it just looked like it was comatose in a pool of slop.

Brian produces bottle of Amyl, which is more relaxing than the tea. To pass time, we begin to discuss worst case scenarios.

"Maybe she has been murdered," Stickie speculates. "Maybe right now she is lying face down dead in a ditch."

"Maybe she's actually a Fed," says Kabir. He and J have just shown up. "Maybe even as we speak, she's giving names to the cops. Inshallah she is alive," he adds, inconsistently crossing himself. Kabir says 'inshallah' a lot, though he was raised Coptic Christian. It started off as a bit 'ha, ha, all Arabs look the same' but has since grown into a load-bearing pillar of his personality.

"Hey, J," I say, wanting to change the subject, though it also feels like a good time to bring it up. "I think that it's cool to start looking into, you know, the non-profit angle… what do you think about doing more actions specifically focused on green extractivism? You know, the West annexing resources for their batteries and stuff."

J's expression is closed. "Mm, be careful who you say this around."

"Why, who would I not want to talk about it with?"

And J just looks at me.

The Rat says, as if speaking through a fog: "The ambient dread of caring for the ambiently suicidal."

As a kind of talisman, I touch the red cord from the pamphlet, which I still wear around my wrist.

At last, well after night has fallen, Brian's cousin gets home. Brian explains the situation and we all pile into the car, carrying one handheld flashlight and our respective phones, which we plan to use as torches. It is raining; a dull, soggy, continuous rain that seeps into our hopes and consciousness. We search for twenty minutes, getting wetter and wetter, until Leafie cries out in sudden pain. Turns out she has fallen and twisted her ankle.

"This is fucken ridiculous," says Kabir. "Let's go back."

Me and The Rat have to help to carry Leafie, hobbling and shaken. When we get back we find DojaCat!!! in the living room, sitting next to the heater. She has cranked it up to the max and is wearing just a T-shirt.

"Oh, hey," she says. "What's happening with you guys? Sorry I went quiet, I just met this dude on Tinder, he invited me to see him at his new place out of town. It was only, like, our second date. He was kind of weird but also really hot. He put a blindfold on me and stuck a sharpie up my ass. I bled, but not too badly. There were spots all over the sheets."

Stickie launches into an account: the meme, the fear of suicidality. Traipsing round the memorial park, darkness and Amyl, searching by the river and Leafie's sprained ankle.

"Wow," says DojaCat!!! in honest admiration. "It's amazing how you guys did all that. It sounds like something I would do, but somehow even dumber."

Chapter 11

Speaking strictly for myself, everyone I know is just a little bit fucked. Physically, mentally, there is something wrong with all of us, as if someone had cooked a meal and chosen to substitute ingredients which were subtly yet significantly wrong for that particular cuisine. If you're just looking at one person on their own, you can't quite tell. When there are two, you start to wonder. Once there are three or more of us assembled in one place, you can definitely tell something is amiss.

Right now Kabir and DojaCat!!! are not coming to Bombadil's zine nights because of something to do with Brian. It goes like this: a while back, the two of them were having an argument outside of the IGA. Nothing serious, it was going to get sorted. But Brian was there and took it on himself to pass comment.

"Woof, woof," he said. Like, dog noises. It was supposed to be a joke – look at the leftists fighting, ha ha ha. I mean, Brian is OK, he is young and a hothead but totally not a bad guy. But Kabir and Tamina are not having a bar of him.

"Brian is fine," Leafie tried to explain. "He is annoying but he's also fine. Sometimes people are annoying and bad and sometimes they are just annoying."

Leafie is a real sweetheart, a nice white dyke. I feel a little bit warmer each time I remember she exists. We've known each other for years, but before she and Stickie got together – it was on her vouch that Stickie joined the crew – I never really met up with her on purpose. She would just sort of appear in my life without warning. Every time I would see her she was all geared up, full makeup, and the outfits – e-girl meets goth maiden, studs and black and black. Even at the supermarket getting organic chickpea flour or something, she'd be dressed like she was on her way to a cyberpunk uprising. Now that we live together, I get to see her home wardrobe which consists of black band T-shirts and black trackies. I trust in her good judgement and her good heart.

Although, I wouldn't discount Tamina's opinion, either. She's seen it all, to a degree that even I don't know the full extent of. I would trust her with my life and think she feels that way too, although it's hard to tell just what 'trust' would entail for her, whether it is a habit that she's learned to make dormant or just totally eliminated. She's very open in describing events, like how her dad died of asthma in the last round of fires, or how she needs dialysis every few months. But she doesn't talk about her feelings. She's lived through every iteration of the so-called Left and still nobody is pettier on the internet. I know that she will always be there for me, though. She's taught me so much.

"You have to sweat the small stuff," she explained to me once. "When you do this kind of work, relationships are all you've got. Pick your people carefully. Only work with the people you can work with."

That said, the 'woof, woof!' incident occurred five years ago.

J had a blowup with Kabir and rage-quit the entire group but then came back a few weeks later.

Recently we all survived the great Lead Poisoning Saga. It went like this: Leafie, bless her heart, took it into her head that we should eat more vegetables. She really got stuck into it, working on our garden for three months. It was so wholesome, DojaCat!!! and the others would just pull vegetables from the ground and eat them without washing off the dirt. Punks, you know. Basic hygiene is too bourgeois for them. Well, it would have been fine, except that our house is in an old industrial precinct. We didn't even know until Stickie lost sensation in her fingers, and that was how we learned we were all slowly being poisoned by lead. We had to go for treatment, but they say some of the damage is irreversible. That's why we're so stupid, ha ha ha. Well, that and many other reasons.

"Has anyone else had a moment to do a close read of those new laws they've been debating?" Robbie asks. "*The following shall be punishable by a minimum of twelve years' imprisonment: acts of violence, intimidation, or any other acts causing persons to have genuinely held fear as a result of their participation in projects with relevance for national infrastructure and security.* A 'genuinely' held fear? That makes it sound like it doesn't even need to be substantiated."

"Interesting," says J, voice almost silent. Everything he says feels like it should be in parentheses, like <Death> from the Terry Pratchett books. "Whose support in the Senate does this bill need to get passed?"

"Looks like it's Katherine K. Kelly," says Scott H. "She is left-leaning, isn't she? MPs for Climate Action. Hopefully she can put a stop to this scary stuff." Scott works for a non-profit, making this radio broadcast, he kind of talks like he is talking to a child. He has good skin and is always smiling even when he is delivering bad news. He and Robbie and Tamina run together, they go right back to the Tuggerah breakout of 2005. Frankly, there are a lot of whites around this stuff, which makes me sort of uncomfortable – they all talk the same way and hang out the same way and kind of know all these things that I don't know, and I feel silly when I see how much they know compared to me. I am embarrassed to say this – it shows I have been brainwashed by identity politics, which is a personal deficiency I'm trying to fix. DojaCat!!! is white but I don't care because I love her so much.

There is also this group of diaspora kids hanging round, they keep on changing their name. Last I heard they were called 'Dragon Philosopher Z', which I found pretty hilarious. They seem kind of cool, although I know them mostly from a distance. There is quite a bit of infighting, callouts on *Medium* and stuff – Tamina says they are clout-chasers, also tankies and radlibs, which is why I haven't really gotten that involved. But when I see them together in a posse, looking so cool together, like they are the keepers of the most impossibly romantic shitpost of a secret, I find that I must tread carefully lest I be pulled into a vortex.

"I'm the fucking subaltern, you're not the subaltern."

"You're not the subaltern. You're a Brahmin, for Chrissake. The worst oppression you ever faced was hearing someone say 'chai tea'."

I spend much time on the internet, and oh my God, you would not believe what has been going on in the Asian-baked-goods-meme-based community. Here is the origin story: once we all memed in harmony on a page called **understated** asian baking, sharing such wonders as naan prepared in an Instant Pot or macarons shaped like Sanrio characters. Over time, this supportive environment grew into a forum where people could vent about their personal struggles: 'I hate my strict Asian parents', stuff like that. You can probably tell that things were taking a liberal turn. The group composition grew progressively more East Asian and relatedly, more model minority-inflected, causing tensions which eventually exploded in a pyrotechnic (400-plus comments!!) fight about whether it was acceptable to post a cake which said, 'YELLOW PERIL SUPPORTS BLACK POWER'. Questions were raised as to whether this offensively appropriated Black history (representation politics critique), or co-signed non-non-violent approaches (the classic liberal appraisal). This then evolved into some soul-searching regarding the relative status of yellow (East), Brown (South) and other Brown (Central) Asian participants within the group, to which the panicked mods responded by banning all non-baking-related content. Sadly, it was too late; too much blood had been spilled for our unity to be preserved, causing a faction to splinter off into a new page, Asian Bakery Obsessions. Both groups have since degenerated roughly equally towards liberalism, but for some reason South Asians have primarily congregated in the latter, where there are now complaints it has been taken over by Indians. Life is so hard. Sometimes I just want to look at boba memes.

Anti-colonial, anti-border, anti-imperialist, well, it's important, but you do get tired of it, you know? Being against literally everything that structures our lives in this stupid colony. By definition anybody who is willing to do this shit will be 'a lot', it just comes with the territory. Hurt people hurt people – well in that case, we are a human centipede of trauma. Everybody can hold a grudge and no-one, not one single person, possesses any kind of chill.

"You know what I hate about the Left?" says Kabir. "This obsession with identity, it's consuming us, it's driving us apart. Idpol this, idpol that – like, you know what part of the *discourse* made me want to glass someone? Whether it's OK to raise your fist if you're not Black. Have these people never heard of history? The other day I heard someone hanging shit on Sophie Scholl, for fucksake. Because she was a white woman – as if she could help that! Inshallah one day these woke cunts will all choke on their own vomit."

"Well, everything is about position in the end," J says in his considered way. "So, all politics is identity politics. But also, nothing is only about that, because individuals are not tendencies. If they were, no kind of solidarity would be possible." J isn't confrontational but he has a kind of gravitas, I can't tell if it's because of his knowledge or just because he speaks relatively slowly. His dad is Malagasy and his mum is Korean; they met when his dad's relatives were displaced from their land by his mum's family business, mining rare metals for green cars. I've never found a moment that was right to ask him how he feels about it.

Tamina and Bombadil don't get on, I don't know the full context.

"Do you know what I think?" says Tamina. "Everybody needs to get over this fetish for moral purity. Cancel this, cancel that – thank God *I'm* not an anarchist. I'm not an academic Leftist either. Their stupid reading groups, seminar nerds, clout-farming communists – I have no more respect for these stupid cunts." Tamina is my heroine but, God help us, she does have a lot of thoughts.

There was somebody else who used to run with us, Bridget, but not anymore. Tamina and her had some falling out, I never heard the whole story. There are things you are not supposed to ask. When someone is dead to Tamina, they're dead. You just have to roll with these periodic excisions if you want to keep with it.

And honestly, that is not really particular to this set of relations. Man hands on misery to man – comrades passing on misery to comrades. Might as well be living in a walk-in freezer, packed with wall-to-wall beef. I tell you, sometimes it feels like we are all playing pass the parcel with each other's bullshit. Riding round in circles, we think we're going somewhere but it's really just a rotating carousel of each other's trauma. But in the end it's OK – take Tamina for instance, I don't know much about her but I know that she'll always be there for me. She's taught me everything I know.

I tell this to Bombadil, who laughs. "Yeah, yeah, I get ya. To you Tamina is a puzzle that can only ever lead to the right answer." He looks at me shrewdly for a moment, and then sighs, "Oh, you're young, aren't you. You're very young."

Living where I am right now works for me, I guess. I enjoy living with Stickie and I enjoy living with Leaf. I also like being around DojaCat!!! but sometimes it is too much, there is this unhinged need like an open wound. I guess a loss foreseen is not the same as a loss averted.

I've been here for three years, which is pretty good for this kind of arrangement. Why then do I still feel like I'm just passing through? Shoes in the hallway so temporary. Of course there are lots of things I could blame: capitalism, precarity, etcetera, etcetera. Don't get me wrong, these are all real things. But I know in my heart that they are not the fundamental issue.

I'm not sure if I already mentioned that I'm almost thirty. Mention, mention, mention. Well, I think about it all the time. The Rat showed me this meme which said: 'Time isn't real, clocks are.' I beg to disagree, time is extremely real. This has caused me to take stock of my own life and I am finding there is not quite as much stock there as I might once have wished.

Chapter 12

On his way to work a young man drowns in his car. According to *The Guardian* it was his first day on the job, he was a Nepalese guy working on-call as a cleaner while also studying for a Masters in IT. He didn't see the water on the road because he had to go to work early while it was still dark, he couldn't open the window 'cos the electric locking system wouldn't operate while it was full of water. He was trapped in there for more than an hour. When they pulled him out, the inside of the car was totally destroyed. His parents are allowed into the country for the funeral, but not permitted to leave their car due to quarantine restrictions. Watching their son's funeral with the window wound down from inside a borrowed vehicle.

"It is of vital importance that all Australians listen to, and obey, the directions issued by our emergency services," says Katherine K. Kelly.

Kit is preparing mooncakes. The process looks intricate; they are entirely absorbed, like an animal whose whole body is given over to sleep. Hands moving with precision and concentrating tongue pushed to the side of their mouth. "I wish I had a stand mixer," they say, pointedly, when I come into the kitchen. With some foresight, to stop dough from getting everywhere, they have spread newspaper over the kitchen. Idly, I let my eyes rest on a full-page advertisement: 'Australians Say YES To Renewable Power'. Among others, it has been signed by multiple power retailers, Mark Miller from the Advanced Manufacturing Union and the Tiddaroo Foundation.

I pretend to study these names with interest. Then, trying to keep my tone casual: "By the way, I was just wondering, how do you know Park?"

"Park? Oh, you mean Alden? We hung out when I was in the US. We were roommates, for a while."

"Right – right, of course. And, um," trying to keep my voice casual, "have you been in contact since they came on set?"

"Ah, he messaged me once, I think. I can't remember what he said."

"Really? He seems like an intriguing person…"

"Yeah, well. It wasn't very important. I think I left him on read." Kit's face is as inscrutable as the stainless-steel countertop. I resist the impulse to ask how they might have known it wasn't important if they hadn't read the message. Absurd, given the relative differential in need and desire between us, to subject Kit to my silly obsession, this unreasoning passion for the truth.

As if unconsciously turning the tables, Kit asks, "How are we going with funding for *Red Jade Ravine*?" Surely it must be unconscious – the way they shake at my foundations like that. Careful not to betray myself, I say, "It looks promising... the network is just trying to clear up a few things. But there's a good chance."

Kit seems to scrutinise me for a moment, then laughs. "You say 'promising' with such a long face." Turning their attention back to the dough. "Oh yeah, I'm heading out for the evening, too. Gonna go back to my place, to see some friends and stuff."

"You can bring your friends here, if you like. It's not very spacious at your apartment." Trying to keep my voice casual. "It's also, uh... quite a lot of rent for you to pay, given that you mostly stay over here."

"Yes, it is quite a lot per week." The shutters fall in Kit's eyes. "But I still choose to pay it, because that is where I live."

"Of course," I say. I pause, waiting in undefined hope; when nothing else is said, I drift back into my home office, passing Kit's room where the door has been left open. On the desk a pile of stickers, a confusion of small trinkets, a purple wireless speaker that is shaped like a car. Which ones are gifts from me? I go back to the kitchen and remove a piece of chicken from the freezer to defrost on the off-chance I can cook it for our dinner later. Things we do based on the comforting assumption of a future.

Then I go to visit my old friend Kevin Nguyen; who thankfully for me, him and the world, does not work in the arts. As I do I feel a strange mix of trepidation and desire, that combination of pre-emptive humiliation and hope that always seems to come with the chance of being seen whole by another person over time.

The thing I appreciate most about Kevin is how he offers me permission to be my most unmitigated and worst version of self at any given time. It is rather refreshing, after the flattering delicacy of all of those sensitive, socially conscious types. This is balanced by the other aspect of Kevin, which is that he lacks either the desire or the capability to act out of true unkindness. No malice, only appetites. He enjoys snappy comebacks and practises them often, in the way of the aging homosexual for whom being a 'bitch' began as a defensive posture and has ended up as a gentle, subtle form of irony, directed in equal parts against the world, me and himself.

"Hello. Helloooo. So sorry, my Uber was delayed – would you believe, some fucking stupid people glued themselves to the road? What do they call themselves – 'Green Revolt'? Honestly, I can hardly keep *track* of all these groups. Judean People's Front, People's Front of Judea, ha ha ha. Well, *mwa*, I haven't seen you since, when – have some low carb beer? Oh I know, I'm fighting off middle-aged spread. Sorry to hear that your parents passed, how is your sis? Do you know who is going to get the house?"

A sense-image swims before my consciousness: my parents' house, the dank smell of rooms, unkempt and unoccupied. No-one to buy dehumidifier beads from Daiso – though there had been a problem with water ingress for a while, my father ran out of the energy for housekeeping well before the stroke. I think of the barely used exercise equipment, purchased in view of my mother's growing agoraphobia, now gathering dust.

"Oh, and you're still working on your show with Kit? After all these years – oh, I'm not *personally* an artist, maybe I shouldn't talk – but, most people, they make a show or two, put out a couple of books – then *bam*! Something just dies in them and it's all over. Finished. Kaputt! Oh, they're still living, formally speaking. Still making albums or TV or whatnot, but in creative terms, they might as well be dead. Hey, I saw Kit was nominated for the Best Of Teen's Choice end-of-year awards! Amazing news for them. You too, of course."

Kevin's apartment, like Deirdre's, is sparkling and white, yet somehow seems to exist in an entirely different genre of interior décor. He enjoys expensive things, but not entirely or primarily because they are expensive. Or if he does, he is totally and joyfully upfront about his own shallowness, such that the venality becomes elevated to a pleasurable form of camp. The place is very tidy, less a reflection of Kevin's own habits than of the Laotian woman who comes three times per week. Kevin tips and flirts with her, in both cases handsomely. Amidst the shining surfaces, there are small zones of human mess: Kevin's trackpants and grey workout hoodie tossed over the back of a chair, pushed hurriedly at a sideways angle beneath the table on which there is balanced a growing pile of takeaway containers. While Kevin knows a great deal about food, he does not cook, or indeed engage in any manual labour, choosing instead to outsource cleaning, removals and other such tasks. He is somewhat hilariously repulsed by any form of physical decay, even a bruised spot on a piece of fruit. He is not comfortable with any phenomenon other than sex having a biological basis.

It is hard to talk to Kevin without addressing all the different versions of Kevin I have known over the years – and of myself, as well. We knew each other young, when we both had similar reasons but different means of moving away from the communities of our birth, He was my neighbour and companion during high school, back when we were the only visible Asian people in the suburb. Later, he became my study partner and closest friend during university, two young persons in the process of inventing new personas for interacting with the society we were forced (in my case) or excited (in his) to meet. Always academically brilliant, he has completed two undergraduate degrees, a Masters and an M.B.A. from Columbia University, sponsored by the consultancy which was his longest employer – though latterly, he has eschewed the corporate life and now works for a non-profit called StandUp, a kind of pan-progressive lobby group with a finger in every pie from refugees to renewable energy to gay rights. It gets funding from private philanthropists, the state and federal governments, and the World Bank. They lobbied hard in favour of gay marriage, but Kevin himself has eschewed this route – despite the dog-eyed silent protestations of his partner, Alex, a white man who has adored

Kevin longer than I can recall. Alex visits twice a week, stays the night, and then leaves the next morning. They have persisted with this routine for eight years. As Kevin says: "I prefer to have my space, you know, my boundaries. I prefer to be sparing with emotional labour. My therapist says I give in too easily to other people... it all comes down to my relationship with my dad."

Right now Kevin is heading up a technical working group, exploring intersections between management theory, coastal erosion and applications of machine learning in non-corporate information processes. To my embarrassment, I do not really comprehend the overlap between these disparate subjects. But it fills me with awe how Kevin can work across these many realms, the mechanics by which he turns levers to effect tangible change upon the universe.

"Tell me, what have you been up to? How is work? How is life? I have been so *busy*, oh my God... well, how could I not, given the *state* of things right now. Oh, it makes me sick, just a shambles, from a policy perspective. The other day I was speaking to," Kevin draws himself up, speaking in a tone both casual and with an awareness of its own importance, "the Attorney General, you know. We disagree on many topics – well, I'm all about the human rights. You know they don't allow the torture inspectors into the jails anymore? StandUp made a submission to convey our most strenuous disagreement. Anyway, these differences aside, he is a smart guy. And when we're dealing with stochastic terror, whatever your personal views, surely we can all agree that resorting to violence is a hard line! Just between you and me, we've been liaising with the counter-terror group. When you have a situation like this, a threat to our democracy... counter-insurgency takes everyone. Even pen-pushers like me!"

Kevin simultaneously flicks his hair and snaps his fingers; a brisk, realpolitik gesture conveying both regret and a hint of satisfaction. I, too, experience a small pleasurable thrill of vicarious fear.

"But listen to me rabbiting on! Can't stop talking shop... tell me about *you*. Don't be coy, I want to hear about you and Kit. Come on, have you two gotten together yet? What are you waiting for? Wait, " Kevin's face takes on a look of grave concern. "Is Kit not *attracted* to you, then?"

"I told you, Kit is queer."

"Yes, yes, I know. But what *kind* of queer? Does that mean that they don't *like* you?"

"Yeah... no... I don't know, I think they... do."

How to begin to explain what I don't myself quite understand? And even more I sense in myself a resistance to understanding. As if it would be impossible to speak the truth of either Kit's or my emotional worlds without cheapening the reality of either. But who am I to speak for Kit? "I mean, our relationship is intimate. We work together. That's the main thing for us, really." As I speak, I feel the spark of incipient humiliation – a recognition, long denied, that I still do not really know Kit at all. Probably I'm just constructing them out of my own mind, my own fetishised needs and imagination. As if there were another way to be in love.

"Oh, all right then. Be mysterious. But you know, I was just *discussing* this with my therapist, the way we *defend* ourselves against our attachments, and you know, you and I... the way my *joints* are like, these days. We are not getting younger." Kevin is looking at me maddeningly, knowingly. For he has attended all kinds of therapy. He has approached gender, love and sex from every angle of study, both popular and scholarly; and now is the master of all he surveys, which is the whole domain of human feeling. All manner of affections are catalogued in his philosophy, there is no form of love of which he has not been latterly appraised. What is love? – a set of prescriptions about the forms of desire perceived as desirable. Which for all Kevin's sexual bravado, remain carefully defined, bounded and transactional. One should not invest oneself in another person without due cause, some promise of appropriate compensation in the form of sex, commitment or reciprocal emotional services. The heart enclosed, bordered off from unproductive extremities of feeling. I adore Kevin, but I do not wish to speak to him of love.

"Have I mentioned, I'm in line for a Lifetime Achievement Award? Sssh, it's embargoed, so don't spread the news… they're going to announce it at the Gala. Same time as I'm releasing my book, my memoir."

One can't help but observe the relative degrees of animation induced in Kevin by the words 'book' and 'Gala' – the latter of which causes him to perk up, like a fading phone plugged into a charger. "Oh, the award ceremony – amazing! Are you going to see famous people? And your memoir, of course. I cannot *wait* to read it."

Back in our shared youth, when I had just finished shooting my first, experimental short film and was riding high on the alternating waves of megalomania and self-abnegation, Kevin alternately offered and begged for me to let him view it in advance. Finally, undone by the intense fluctuations and reversals of these polarised emotions, I gifted him a pre-screening copy, inscribing the box, 'First film – first cut – first copy – and with thanks for dearest friendship – xxx'. Each time we interacted subsequently Kevin would, without my even raising the subject, apologise profusely for not having yet having watched the film, listing life events and circumstances which had prevented him from doing so. That was twenty-eight years ago. I don't believe he's watched it yet.

Being in proximity to Kevin makes me wonder if this going to be my lot in life: to be liked, admired; wanted, even, in a peripheral way, but never seen. Never to be known with the intense personal interest to which I persist, even after all these years, in feeling myself entitled to; in spite of a deep and sustained lack of corroboration from others on this point.

"Tell me about work, Kevin. Tell me about the world, help me forget myself. Let me be a disinterested observer of everybody else."

And he does. Oh, how he does. Kevin is an expert overlooking the whole field of expertise. He is unsurpassed in his capacity to name and to classify major events, the forces of good and ungood set innumerably loose upon this planet. "Well. Oh, my. Oh, *well*. It is great to have a chance to talk about remote technologies – often it sounds so dry, you know, one for the nerds. But in fact, what I am finding is that there are lots of uses – not just technology for its own sake, but humanitarian applications. For example, you might have heard about that riot at Mount Helliar Correctional Complex. Someone died of heatstroke in the cells – which is sad of course – not to be callous, but it is a *jail* after all. It was terribly dangerous for the staff. Whatever equipment you have, you're still outnumbered! You couldn't *pay* me enough to take that job. Anyway, it just so happens that via the working group, I have a relationship with Mark Miller. You know, the manufacturing union man –smart guy, kind of has a tradie look but don't let that fool you, ha ha. I was able to facilitate the supply of some semi-autonomous – well, let's use the normal word, *drones* – they sort of spin in the air above your head, give off strobe lighting and, you know, pepper-balls and stuff. Breaks up the disturbance without any staff having to put themselves at risk. And that put Mark and I onto a really good conversation – right now the machines are all imported, but what would it take to start producing them right here at home? I mean, you can talk theoretically forever about an open border, but if you can't get the support of the white working class… people need jobs, you know? And that's what I always say, the evolving nature of *security*, as a concept and an industry, integrating its human, governance and technical dimensions."

It is a comfort to hear Kevin monologue, as he has since we were teenagers. His knowledge is incredible, and I have never ceased to feel incredulous over it. It is like touring the control room of humanity.

"We've been trying to look at this from all sides, you know. Building relationships… we've been working very closely with all arms of government, from the security people right up to the Minister, Katherine K. Kelly. The minute I saw her, I felt it in my bones – she is the *boss*! Well, you know how I feel about strong women. Just another homosexual with mommy issues, ha ha. We're also trying to build relations with real, you know, *grassroots* communities. There is this one guy, Scott – very helpful fellow. We've been having a few little chats about, well, the lay of the land around there. What is going on in those kinds of alternative spaces. It really helps us out, just to keep tabs."

Kevin once again clasps his hands together, less a gesture of applause than denoting a close to the conversation. "Goodness me, I am exhausted. Alex wants to get married – well, how can I, when I'm already married to my work! I love working in policy, but it is so tiring! Gosh, I wish I could be like you, just making stories up for fun."

"Um, it isn't quite like that," I give in, surrendering to the momentum of Kevin's self-perceived importance, all the more maddening because it is probably real. "Oh, alright, Kevin. It absolutely is like that. Nothing I do matters. How I would love to be like you, to actually make a real difference. All I do is create silly escapism."

Kevin's eyes light up. "Well, here's the thing. You might just turn out to have one or two useful skills. Well, it's a big word, but sometimes I think it helps to see what we do in terms of *counterinsurgency*... it's not just brute force." Again the phrase, which carries a pleasing connotation of danger at arm's length. "Because, make no mistake, there are people who threaten the security of the rule of law, the ordinary citizen – and we will *hunt them down*. But, we also need to win hearts and minds, do we not? Here's an idea. If you want to find a way to make a real difference, why don't you go to this event my office is organising – the Festival of Resist-ARTnce? Ha ha, it's a mouthful, I didn't choose the name. A convergence of artists, activists, academics, sharing stories of rebellion – these spaces are so *needed* in these times. When people have nowhere for their voices to be heard, that's when they turn to violence. You know, I can't *wait* to watch your show."

Normally I experience a sensation of mild panic when I contemplate such issues but with Kevin there is only deepest peace. His political nous, his swerve and verve, combine to let me know someone is flying this plane, after all. While to the untrained eye the cockpit may appear empty, persons of competence and principle are leveraging the controls, performing intricate feats of calculation and balance.

"Thank you, Kevin. Good to see you again. It's a privilege to know you," I say rather formally, pre-empting our goodbye, for Kevin through certain movements of hands and through the clearing of the table has silently conveyed that though he has enjoyed our little visit, our meeting is now over. And yet the comfort remains. I will go to this festival, I will be in proximity to power and those who know how to wield it. They will tell me what to do, my latent idealism will affix to a series of steps, and everything will be all right.

When I get home Kit is gone and there are no visible mooncakes. Perhaps Kit has taken them as gifts for their many friends, none of whom I have met. I text them goodnight, as I always do of an evening, and a minute later they respond. Then I check my Insta-feed and see the mooncakes already staged and uploaded, with likes accumulating at great speed. In the background, I see my own kitchen – white, spacious, blurred. It looks like a space which could be owned by anyone. Anybody's kitchen.

Chapter 13

'ResistARTnce' takes place at the old town hall building, featuring a large wooden stage framed by scarlet curtains. Constructed during the heyday of municipal buildings. Old craft guilds, unions and professional associations meet here; ceremonies for new citizens are conducted. There was also once, I seem to remember, a spirited debate on the amalgamation of local councils, the upshot I cannot now recall. My own mood is anxious yet optimistic. It is pleasing to be here amid the real community, the grassroots. Here the intellectual noise will converge and clarify, revealing a small yet pointedly effective core of human idealism.

"So fascinating to have you engaging in that space," Kevin said. "Some new, off-the-wall thinking. Creating genuine synergies with the arts. You know, Joan Didion says, we tell ourselves stories in order to *live*."

The hall is already filling up when I arrive. Couples for the most part, either both of them white or a woman of colour paired up with an insipid white man, diffusing good intentions like an aromatherapy burner. While waiting for the event I pass the time by mentally organising them into typologies of dress. Some are bohemian-lite, wearing conservative styles rendered in mildly unconventional fabrics, like crushed velvet or crepe. Others aspire to be earthier, carrying cotton tote-bags, hair bound by rolled bandannas. They wear slack expressions and unclouded, healthy skin; they are not alert in the way of people who have experienced violence. A lot of them seem to be wearing *one* piece of leopard print clothing.

Kit's image swims before me, undesired and yet, as always, inspiring of desire. The intelligent alertness, like a young fox. A push notification on my phone says that four people have died from hyperthermia, this time in a WA correctional complex. I swipe the story with an automatic, mindless movement, and learn that tear gas was deployed and one building set aflame in the subsequent disturbance. The prison guards' union has called for extra staff to prevent future riots and secure the wellbeing of the inmates.

First on the program is a choir. Six women from the Pacific Islands, swaying and clapping as they sing a hymn: 'On Christ, our solid rock…' The atheistic audience smiles over-broadly.

Then the MC emerges. He is a middle-aged man who earned his fame as part of a comedy troupe of white schoolboys who did satire, or what passed for it when there wasn't much media available – there weren't memes back then – forcing us all to Stockholm Syndrome ourselves into believing they were funny.

"Hello, welcome everybody. Amazing, what a beautiful performance. That song was written by a refugee, by the way, a – um – Kurdish man from Iraq. No, from Syria. And, look how many of you took time out of your lives to show up today! What a way to give a big middle finger to the Prime Minister! We won't say naughty words tonight – there are children here, great to see the next generation. But we can say it together – 'Eff you, Bill Morrison!' All together now, put your hands up."

The audience looks happy, pleasurably titillated. They look cheekily around each other, as in unison they raise their hands into the air to say: "Eff you, Bill Morrison!"

"Thank you, everybody, for sharing that moment. And now, we have our first speaker for the evening – Karen Quayle, the chief solicitor for the Refugee Crisis Centre. One of my closest friends, she has worked tirelessly in this area for God knows how long and has the war stories to prove it. Please welcome Karen!"

A white woman in her late thirties or early forties approaches the lectern. She is wearing bright-rimmed glasses and a loose, bright-accented dress. "Last night, I spoke on the phone to a little boy who was in tears. He was crying because his family is a member of the Hazara ethnic minority in Afghanistan. Over the years, I have had the privilege of knowing many Hazaras. They are a gentle, beautiful people. All they want is to live here in peace with us – as hard-working, law-abiding guests in our country. I have no doubt that, as new Australians, they could make a wonderful contribution.

"I have been working with the Centre for almost a decade now. Over that time, I have seen and heard many incredibly distressing stories. Crying children, begging to be reunited with their parents. Innocent families, begging for our help. I have worked day and night to protect my clients as they go through these harrowing experiences, the result of the senseless cruelty of our asylum policies under this right-wing government.

"Last night I told that little boy – I would do all that I could to give him the best chance of being settled in this country. Under international law. The boy wept. He said, 'I love you, Karen.'

"This is the human face of the asylum seeker crisis. Innocent people, who want nothing more than to rebuild their lives and make a contribution to our community. It's so inspiring to see you all coming out today, coming together as Australians. Because in the end, we Australians are still a compassionate people. This is not in our name."

"Hear, hear!" says a woman in the middle row. She is wearing a black blazer with low heels in leopard print. Her husband also nods, but absently, as if the motion has been referred via a physical reflex like yawning or sneezing. He agrees, "Hear, hear!", but quietly.

"We are diverse, we are humane and we are democratic. And in ten, twenty years, when there is a *Royal Commission*," sporadic cheers go round, "well, we as Australians are going to stand up, and politicians will listen. Because this is not who we are as a nation! Thank you very much."

A union representative makes a speech, interspersing remarks about the ills of mandatory detention for refugees with exhortations to join one's union.

The MC re-takes the microphone. "And now, I have the honour of introducing one of my best friends… probably you know of her. Artist, activist, genre-defying… a woman whose work crosses all borders. The one and only… MANDY LO!"

'Lose Yourself' by Eminem starts to play over the speakers, probably ironically. People laugh and hoot. A Eurasian woman climbs the stage wearing an enormous grey hoodie, whose size seems to indicate that she moves outside normative standards of appearance. She is here to recite, or to declaim, a poem:

'FOR THE ONES WHO HAVE NO NAME': AN UN-AUSTRALIAN RECORD
Dirge for a refugee who perished in the care of so-called 'Australia'
My name is Mandy.
What is your name?
(I place my hands on my own rib-cage, caught within my own body…
My fragile, yellow body.)
I don't know your name.
I will never know your name.
Because you died there
in that place, perished
In that un-place.
You died right there, across the line that separated you from me.
Because this country would not give you safety.
Because MY country would not give you safety.
(My country?
White man's country.
Me yellowgirl, in white man's country.)
Oh, my darling
Nothing can cleanse me.
Nothing can make me different from what I am
Which is guilty, guilty, guilty.
For though I come from elsewhere, I am a citizen of Australia.
(An un-citizen of Un-Australia.)
I was there, you see…
We stood together, in the dust.
In the dirt of the desert.
The yellow, unforgiving desert.
(Me, sweatshop-girl

Massage-girl
#NotYourOrientalWoman).
Oh, my dear
Though you and I remain divided
By many lines
Of Capitalism
Colonialism
Imperialism
Still, you and I, we rise…
(FUCK CAPITALISM!)
Oh my refugee darling, I will never be you.
Yet, in that moment, the line was erased.
The line between you and I
Wavering away
Into un-being.
I AM
I AM
BUT YOU NO LONGER
ARE…
(While there is no transcript provided, this section of the performance seems most appropriately rendered in capitals. Mandy takes a breath, allowing the room's collective emotion to subside from its peak.)
Oh, my darling, you were there.
You are always there.
And from my heart, I bestow you a gift, I give you a name.
And the name I bestow on you is…

MANDY.

The room seems to blur with an intensity of feeling, as though seen through heat. There is a silence. Then, sporadically, a few people begin to clap. The applause builds in volume and duration, which the artist acknowledges from the stage with a low, reverent nod. Someone next to me nudges their neighbour and whispers, "Mandy Lo is so real... did you know, she was there on the ground at the Tuggerah detention centre breakout of 2005?"

The MC opens up the floor for audience questions.

"What can we do?"

Make a donation to the Refugee Crisis Centre, set up a regular transfer. Weekly or monthly. Leave a bequest.

"Can I buy T-shirt or a totebag?"

You certainly can, there are T-shirts and totebags. More T-shirts and totebags than can be appraised by the naked eye. I slip off to the bathroom and check my phone. A curation of images, what Kit likes to describe as the 'morning meme harvest', which does not arrive every day, or even necessarily in the morning, but with enough regularity to feel as though it does. Today's selection: a picture of a tennis ball being squeezed by a human hand, emitting orange juice. A frog labelled 'forg'. A piece of AI-generated art, in the style of an oil painting – a grotesque yet endearing, horse-like creature with elongated face and stubby legs. The caption reads, 'HONSE'. What meaning is conveyed here? Whence comes the hilarity which Kit so very obviously derives? It seems to me there has been an intensification and complexification of memes going on in recent years. Memes did not used to require so much context.

I message Kit:

It may amuse you to know, Mandy has written a poem containing reference to her positionality as the Orientalised downtrodden.

And receive the reply:

isn't her dad a mini-muffin mogul?

Kit's vibrating response nearest my heart, in my inner jacket pocket. All that is private between Kit and myself is tinged with joy. *It's been my dream to work for you.* It occurs to me that Kit and I do not, somehow, talk very much in person, but we communicate a lot through our phones. In their very mundanity there is an intimacy to these exchanges, although Kit very rarely initiates using words – always images, screens. Very rarely does Kit fail to promptly respond when I message them. There is a comfort to this regularity I find hard to overstate.

"How much money do you people give to the Labor Party? When they're the ones torturing refugees? When are you going to disaffiliate, when are you ..."

I can't see the questioner's expression, which is hidden beneath a surgical mask. The words seem unnuanced, gauche. Though I am aware they are convincing on an intellectual level, I feel a near irresistible desire to put distance between myself and their speaker. To choose different terms and a different location for this confrontation, though I can hardly say what terms or where I believe it should preferably happen.

"... yes, thank you, I'll take that as a comment!" The MC has found the right riposte. The crowd, which had begun to shift and murmur, bursts into a laugh tinged with our shared relief. I take a moment to appraise my own response, which is not simple. There is an uncomfortable sensation of having been manoeuvred, against my will, into the disagreeable position of being made aware of an atrocity – which, if truth be told, I was already aware of – while having no plan to act on the above, nor any sense of how I might begin to formulate such action. What is left is only inchoate resentment, which coalesces most easily round the person who brought the issue into our inconvenienced orbit.

Yet something unauthorised has swerved, the balance in the room has shifted. Up to this point our discourse has been akin to a musical call-and-response, the person on stage making a series of claims whose outline is pre-known though the specific elements are not. With this new remark, though nothing overtly hostile has been articulated, what was previously safe has now become unsafe. Uncomfortable, even.

"OK, but like, the unions. When will you stop sending the weapons – you're exporting missiles, bullets, bombs, when will you disaffiliate, when will you stop selling…"

"Oh, I see. You're one of those *divestment* people. Reform or revolution, eh?" The MC's voice takes on an insinuating slant. The crowd is laughing openly now, and the questioner shrinks back – even under the mask I can see they look young and flushed.

"Well, let me just say – there are a lot of people working in this space, lots of different stakeholders. Everyone on this stage has worked – excuse me for swearing – pretty *bloody* hard. Let's take a moment to thank them, why don't we. And thank *you* for coming. Because we're going to end this dark stain on our country. Future generations will look back and say, you were on the right side of history. There's a bucket at the door, if you want to shout a coffee for our wonderful volunteer artists. Giving up their time, their artistic labour. Oh, and one more announcement – please congratulate Mandy, because guess who is the newest member of the Order of Australia!" Sustained and heartfelt cheers. "Does that mean we have to call her 'Your Majesty' now? Death to the colony, ha ha ha. And, watch this space – if and when we get a Labor government, there is going to be a new arts policy – and I've heard on the grapevine, that means GRANTS!" A Pavlovian shudder of anticipated pleasure goes through the room. "Good night, good night."

We disperse, to purchase totebags and consume collegial dinners with fellow attendees. People with different faces yet identical opinions, interchangeable as leaves. I find myself reaching a pitch of frustration that feels impossible to articulate. In spite of it all, I must continue to believe that articulating what is true can serve some purpose. If not, what else? A central gap, a screaming lack at the heart of everything.

And then at the door, next to the 'ResistARTnce' poster, which looks hand-drawn by a child – a refugee child, as the accompanying text clarifies – I notice an unfamiliar corporate logo. Filled with spite, with compulsion, I pull out my phone to do a reverse image search on Google. And I learn that the Tiddaroo Foundation, the sponsor of the 'ResistARTnce' event, is a subsidiary of Nilsson Services.

Chapter 14

"Kevin, did you know about this – the sponsorship from Nilsson? What is going on?"

"Look, I understand. I absolutely see your point of view. In fact, I did raise the issue – still we have to be nuanced in these things, you know? It's not binary. Not black or white. Sometimes we need to find out what we have in common, even when we profoundly disagree. If we can find a point of collaboration, just this once. Hey, I just got the advance copy of your memoir! Thank you *so* much for mailing it. I'm so excited to read… well, I have one or two other books already in my queue. But once that's finished, I cannot *wait* to get stuck into it. Your book is totally the next book that's on my list."

Chapter 15

Somehow it is still raining. My parents in their new, ugly-as-fuck McMansion on the Warragamba floodplain – they are rich now, they have at-home exercise equipment, it's what you do – start sending nervous little texts in the family groupchat. Stuff about floodwalls and the insurance they don't have. In the end I just mute notifications. How our defeat is so total, we don't even see it as defeat. I guess that's unfair because what are you going to do, not live in a house? Always waiting for the revolt that does not come.

Because of the humidity after the rain, the mould in our house sends my foggy brain into a fugue state. In my boredom and loneliness, I read a news story about an Indian international student who stalked a girl, then got off from the trial on the basis he had learned all he knew about sex and romance via Bollywood, and had thus come to believe that stalking was OK. I feel some identification with this student – having watched a lot of Bollywood movies, I can see how you might reasonably draw this conclusion. Then I log into the groupchat with some overseas cousins, only to learn of a furore involving student activists who have decided to eat only beef in solidarity with Dalits targeted by Hindutva fascists, who won't allow them to eat beef at all. So far, this campaign has caused no problems for the fash, only massive constipation for the activists. Truly, how is a person meant to know how to be? No-one tells you anything.

Finally, I go out for some cheese and find that there is not enough cash left in my account. This wouldn't be so bad, except when my card gets declined, the machine makes a really depressing sound. 'Duh-deuuunnnnw.' No cheese for you, loser. That's what the machine sounds like it's trying to say.

"You can get an advance if you need one," says the shop dude. "You just need to use the Tidcard." He looks pretty exhausted by the process. "Tidpay – it's automatically enabled with your bank. You just have to choose a PIN to start off."

"What's the catch? Do they charge a fee?"

"Um, I'm not sure…"

"Wait!" says Brian, who has joined us to get gum and juice. "I think I heard about this, it's from the Tiddaroo Foundation. They charge a bunch of interest and pass your details to job agencies and stuff. Ya know what this is?" He looks around meaningfully. "It's surveillance capitalism, man. The mechanics of control in the colony. First practised on Black people, then expanded to the non-Black underclass. That's us, bro. It's totally us."

But we want the cheese so we still sign up.

"You shouldn't eat cheese," says DojaCat!!! when I get home. "Do you know what those people do to the poor cows? They are forcibly impregnated. The farmers steal their children, then they clamp a machine on their nipples to suction out the milk. Cheese is sexual assault."

"Stop talking like a racist vegan, whitegirl," I say. "I was looking for sympathy. For collective outrage at the unfortunate nature of my predicament. As my friend, you should just give it to me."

"But cows are innocent moos," Stickie interjects. "You shouldn't blame the cows for what whites did to you. That's lateral violence."

Then Bombadil wanders in and I am ready for my moment. "Hey Bombadil," I say. "I was wondering, I had an idea that I wanted to run past you. I feel like we don't do enough about green imperialism. You know, green steel and stuff like that. I've been reading about the Black Panthers, I was thinking, why don't we start a working group? Maybe, if it's OK, I could borrow some space at your zine palace."

Probably it's my own fault, 'cos I just wanted affirmation, but Bombadil seems less enthused than I had hoped. "Look, I see where you're coming from," he says. "But the Panthers were a long time ago, you know? Very easy to get insular. You've got to learn to build coalitions. Think of Jack Mundey and the Green Bans."

"I totally support parallel organising, love that for you," chimes in Doja-Cat!!! Both of them smiling with vibes of powerful, yet somewhat vacant, affirmation. The whole thing leaves me with an unsettled feeling; because I want it to dissipate, I go on the apps and end up hooking up with some white chick. She's cool, I guess. Lovely and sensual and thoughtful, although she does laugh out loud at the micro-aggressive jokes on the podcast which we listen to as part of our pre-coital entertainment.

Sometimes I look back on my own intimate life and think that it's the same feeling, subdivided between different, yet fungible personalities and bodies. Nice white boys with their untested niceness, nice white girls on that pedestal you just want to pull them down from. Well, beggars can't be choosers. And there is something comforting about coming back to another version of the old betrayal. Going back at 2am for more racial trauma.

When I get back, I start to go through the NGO-guy's mail. An experience both depressing and voyeuristic. A bunch of bills, a couple of postcards, Christmas cards, one birthday. I keep the bills and enter the details into a file just in case this ever helps us steal his electricity somehow – I live in hope. I also start making a list of all the people he communicates with socially, because you never know when this might come in useful.

I'm still absorbed in this task when I get a call from The Rat. "Have you heard about the leaks? Omg, it's the coolest thing ever. There's been this big release of data – huge hack of the main servers at UberGoogleDinnerlogNetflixAGLChevronTimeWarnerTinderSkynetAdani. Like, incredible stuff. Names, addresses, who people visited and when. What movies they watched on a date, who they're sleeping with. Also their dinner orders. Anyway, you should come and check it out."

Part Two

ACTING

Chapter 16

"We do require a response sooner rather than later," says the rich guy. "With regards to the sponsorship from Nilsson."

"We do," says the assistant.

"There are timelines on these things, as you know."

"And the offer will not remain in place indefinitely."

I say, "So there is absolutely no prospect of us being renewed without Nilsson sponsorship?"

"I believe we have had this discussion," says the rich guy. "We have had it more than once."

"But circumstances change."

"They do."

"They do," agrees the assistant. "But not in this case, unless I am mistaken."

"Please," I say. "If you can, just a bit more time."

The rich guy sighs. "I will speak to the network."

"An unusual measure."

"A highly usual step, premised on our great admiration for your work."

"Your very culturally important work."

"Thank you," I say. "I can't express, how much I truly appreciate…"

"We'll get back to you via email," the rich guy says.

Chapter 17

As long as I can recall I have wanted to be a performer. This is because I want to be seen, and also because I want to disappear.

It's a bit silly, really. Wanting to be looked at so much. And just wanting in general. Desire: which falls on you like a mountain, which simply *is*. I have looked for this feeling. I've looked for others to feel like this when they are thinking of me, as well.

I have felt this way before on exactly two occasions. Once was my first ever professional gig. I was seventeen, if you can believe it. This guy who was a Name, he wasn't just making entertainment, it was Art. Real writer/ director/ producer kind of thing. And I was very romantic about Art back in those days.

He told me how wonderful I was, that I was beautiful and gifted, the only really living person in the world. Words words words words. Then we went back to his room and it happened just the way you think it did. I told myself it was fun, and the shameful thing is, it kind of was. Afterwards I felt like I was magic. Walking round with a secret no-one else could share.

When I finally said I didn't want to do it anymore, he seemed OK with it at first. He seemed sad but accepting. I thought, there goes that. Then the next day he tried to throw me from a moving car. There was a driver there too but no-one did anything, I'd like to say I wasn't begging but I was. Eventually they slowed down and let me out.

After I got fired I had to fly back home and crash on people's couches for a while. The worst part was, everybody knew or they inferred what was happening but they said nothing. Some of them messaged privately and said, *We are sorry*, or, *We've seen this before*. But nobody said anything to him. That's how I learned they didn't actually care for me, not really. On set we were like a family, we said so all the time. Everybody-fucking-knew, nobody-fucking-said. That's the law which governs this whole universe.

Let me tell you a bit about my work. I take my craft very seriously. The trick is to be honest and to make fuel of your emotions, but not just to emote. It is not how they portray it in *Dead Poets*. You start off with the script and take in every single detail, every bit of punctuation. Down to each semi-colon, you treat it like a thing that was put there on purpose. Nothing is by accident, everything is chosen. The thing is, the ending has been pre-determined but you act like it's not. And I love being famous but every now and then this whole business just disgusts me and I think I will walk. But as I turn to go, I catch a glimpse – I know there's nothing there, I don't have to look, if I look around it will be non-existent. But I still want to look.

You get prepared, you read everything. Introject everything so all the moves and movements are in your muscle memory. And then at the last moment, take your hands off the wheel. It might not work but it might. That's what the skeezy director said, which is hard to admit, because but he really did teach me things, that guy. I wouldn't be where I am today if it weren't for him. And I think I may have experienced something very special recently, but I don't want to name it because if you talk about a thing you might jinx it. And there is nothing which illuminates my days more than the possibility of… oh, never mind.

Do you know what I want? I want someone to spend hours telling me terrible things about myself. Insights that only a true friend could possibly discern. But just for me to know, not with a will to make me different. That's my ideal relation with another human being.

Do you know what I want? I want to have everything and not to give up one single thing. How is it possible to want something so much and still not have it?

The thing about performers is we're for today. It's not going to make sense looking back at what I do in fifty years. Maybe not in ten years, even. Realism isn't real, it's just what people have decided to pretend the world looks like at a given moment. And when I say 'people' I mean writers and directors, not bodies for hire like me. It's not even my own story – I say *Yes* to everything – I am a dog that is answerable to someone else's whistle.

When do you lose the sense that you are LARPing your own life?

But when you do it really well, it just feels like forever. The thing is you make fuel of yourself, burning yourself in service of someone else's imagination. That's what I want – all my feelings, my personality, to just disappear in that beautiful conflagration. And at the end of it – oh my God! – I step out of the ashes, still alive. Man, it's the worst job in the world. I feel sorry for all the people who *don't* get to do this.

Chapter 18

It wasn't hard to get away from that skeezy director because I'm used to leaving people. Kind of comforting, really. Like pulling the same familiar old jumper over your head. Each time the same apprehension; the same bereft, desolate drop. But the surprise gets less.

The thing about growing up with abusers is, they give you cruelty and kindness sometimes, but no access to the truth. You do not have the rights to your own story, it can be changed in an hour or a week. That's how you learn to be helpless, you are not really helpless but you can never really get purchase on just what is going on.

I am Chinese and sometimes this matters not at all and sometimes quite a bit. I think the way I was abused was specifically Chinese, but it is hard to say this around other people. Of course, each culture has its own specific way of being totally fucked up, but most of them are not capable of seeing this about themselves. They will use your unhappiness as proof of your peoples' particular civilisational dysfunction. And so the boot of your family is replaced by a different boot.

One thing my mother used to say is that no-one would love me if they knew what I was really like. Other people – teachers, classmates, friends – might *believe* that they liked me, but this was only because I had tricked them. They did not know me wholly, as my family did. My family, of course, would always love me; but that was just because they didn't have a choice.

She hit me often, not causing major injury but with sufficient force for humiliation purposes.

It was a terrible shock when I first realised there are people in this world who don't walk around catatonic with dread all of the time. I still haven't quite recovered.

Gender, orientation, biological sex – none for me, thanks! Although I do like the way I look. There are so many things about me which are wrong but in terms of appearance, I'm really quite satisfied. Dysphoria's not my style. Sometimes I don't appreciate how other people treat me because of it, but that's another story. And I've been very lucky to be able to parlay my specific chromosomal nature into a career where it comprises an advantage. Every actor is a shapeshifter, but I can shapeshift more than most on account of how I'm built. Masc roles, femme roles, whatever. Anything is possible with a little help from hormones, the cosmetics industry and science. And I just love being looked at. I love luxury stores – I know you're not supposed to. A single bag uplifted in a pillar of warm light.

The trouble with running away from a place which is bad is there is pressure for the next place to be perfect. Otherwise you are left wondering if it was you who was the problem. The thing is, lots of people can be wrong at the same time. Your mother and father, cousins and siblings. Colleagues, family and friends. All of them could be wrong and you could be the one who's right. Pretty crazy, hey?

I am not sure when it first became clear there was something atypical about my developmental process. Around the time I turned twelve, it began to be clear that puberty was not happening the way it was supposed to. My torso was not thickening, hair was failing to appear on my face and arms. And (though this was not something I shared) I was not having the requisite sexual thoughts and feelings. While this wasn't an issue for me, even then I could see it would be an issue for everyone else.

Oh, sweet mother of mine:

She used to rage around the house, driving herself into increasing fury about things I had not paid for – electricity, gas, water, car, dancing lessons, mortgage. Sometimes she would physically grab and try to wrestle me outside. 'THIS IS NOT YOUR HOUSE,' she would scream. 'YOU DIDN'T PAY FOR IT'.

But when I finally left home she threatened to kill herself, several times.

They teach you to be frightened of everything, your parents. They cut off your legs and then say you must be grateful to them because you need their help to walk. They say they love you the most and the scary thing is, it might be true. Such experiences have entirely ruined my emotional palate. These days I can't recognise a feeling unless it's been dialled up to the wazoo.

My parents booked a consultation with an endocrinologist. She was fine, I guess. Like, she was friendly enough. But I would not consent to being rendered normal.

I had to wait for her to go out of the room. Maybe to get a pen or a printout, I don't know. And I just climbed right out the window. Yeah, I really did. I suppose I could have snuck out through the corridor, but whatever. I like to think this little dramatic flourish presaged the shape of my career to come. My body just fitting through the gap, feeding myself through the space like a belt passing through a notch. Falling headfirst from that prison place, all made of gravity. I landed at a bad angle and there was pain like it was fired from a nailgun. I remember looking up at that blue square full of sky. "Oh wow," I said. "Oh wow."

I did not know a lot at that moment in life, but I knew some things:

I knew that I was aggressively in love with the world and would keep being so, always.

I knew that I did have access to some talent of my own but that I was an interpreter, not a creator. Therefore, I would need to find someone else to be the container I could pour myself into.

Looking up at the patch of sky, I knew that I would escape, that it was already happening. That in some important respects this had already occurred. I would find a way to go away from this place and keep a hold of my essential body, my own self. This I knew with total certainty.

I don't love my work all of the time. But it has been the velocity that has taken me out of my own life and for that I am grateful. Keep on running till the day that the power is taken from me, which is not today and I won't let it be tomorrow. Just keep running, there's a road out there. Get up and dust off your dusty heart.

Chapter 19

But you see I just want so many things. Desire like an open flame upon your tongue. I don't have enough lives to learn all of the things I want to learn.

The thing about acting is, you're always playing the writer on some level. No-one knows you better and no-one knows you worse. Though I am obviously a professional, I am ashamed by how many feelings this causes me to have. Like being taken in by a joke Valentine. I want someone to care about me, even negatively. I want someone's behaviour to be affected by whether and when I am coming home. Being a person without other people is like living without skin, but fake relations are like skin that is poisonous. They corrode you from the inside. You have to choose your way of death, death by exposure or being poisoned by your own skin.

I would like to feel just as much as I want to feel about anyone and anything, to feel extravagantly. But that doesn't seem a viable option, not in this economy.

I haven't found it hard to be loved but I have found it impossible to be chosen. And that is quite unfair, in my opinion, because I think I am incredibly easy to love. I am talented, electric with feeling, and not to put too fine a point on it, totally fucking gorgeous. To be wanted the most, except for one other thing. Of course, you don't need other people's help to hold onto your integrity. But then there you are left there on your own, just you and your integrity, and what the hell kind of use is that?

Sometimes I want to hurt other people. And then I just say things. It's not that I believe what I'm saying, exactly. It's more when I get to that place, I can't remember what I'm like when I am normal.

Maybe it's obvious how this is going to end but I can't not feel it.

One day I went to the foreshore and took a long walk across the bridge. Buildings arranged on the other side. Empty resting boats. And the conjoined shifting blanket of sea and sky.

I stood watching the sky until it darkened and merged inseparably with the water. Commuters on the bridge. And I, too, wished only to merge and disappear. This scene, this environment would still be here whatever I chose to do. The thought did not bring me joy. It brought me peace.

There was no-one to share the observation with, but I didn't mind. It was so perfect and unchangeable. It was exactly what I needed to know at that particular moment. All the best, the most ecstatic moments of my life have been alone. I don't know how to square this with how much I want someone else to love me.

Chapter 20

There's an explosion on the dam for one of the cotton plantations on the Murray-Darling. It is kind of amazing, seeing footage of the water gushing out. Guess the eels must be happy, as are Mob living downstream who get to swim and run dialysis machines and stuff. These underappreciated small pleasures.

No-one knows what caused the blast, although there are some rumours it was sabotage by this new Black power crew who call themselves, appropriately, BLKPWR. All the vowels removed for ease of googling purposes. To be fair, this could be wishful thinking – the way our necks are craning, thirsty settlers and our emotional needs. For the obvious reasons, no-one is rushing forward to claim credit for the blast. The funny thing is, it could just have been incompetence. A fuckup with the fertiliser or something.

"The markets don't think it was an accident, though," says J in his quiet tone. "The price of Nilsson shares has dropped. They have the contract for security. If there was a successful action on the dam, that means they fucked up."

"Your brain is so big!" says Stickie admiringly.

"Hey, what do you think," I say. "Maybe this is a sign – we can raise our sights a bit higher than a bloody nose for some individual imperialists. You know, infrastructure, pipelines and stuff. I read that Nilsson was gonna invest in a new data centre. Either way, things a bit less replaceable, less fungible than people…"

J looks bored and aloof, he doesn't even answer. God, the guy is so weary with the world. Just then DojaCat!!! comes by, munching from a family-size pack of generic corn chips. Her look today is slutty Gothic nun – ripped black tights, a black and white habit with a skirt made of false leather.

"But pipelines are out in the middle of nowhere," she says. "And in case you haven't noticed, none of us can fucking drive."

In the end BLKPWR put out a statement saying they support 'any and all actions in resistance to colonial capital', which is as clear as mud.

One of my particular and personal deficiencies is that I just can't deal with stuff to do with computers. Nor do I possess the attention span to learn. It's not that I don't work at it – I swear I do – but whenever I try, my mind just seizes up. Personally, I blame the lead.

It is to rectify these and other shortcomings that I turn to my erstwhile friend and comrade, The Rat. To be honest I don't know what 'erstwhile' means, but it doesn't matter. They are someone I feel I've known forever, though I don't know where they came from or where they are going – they just appeared in our lives one day. Doing things with them is always a whole thing, they are so very hype. They were born with the name of Aamir and took up the Rat-moniker around the age of fifteen or so; they have also cycled through the pronouns 'he/him', 'ey/em' and for a while, 'null/void', which I respected very much. Honestly, I wish I had as much lifeforce in my whole body as The Rat has in one finger. It is as though they have Gatorade in their veins instead of blood.

"Hey man, how have you been? Oh my God, you would not believe what people have been posting in Asian Bakery Obsessions… Air-fryer pork. Yes, that's right, pork that was cooked in an air-fryer. How the fuck is that appropriate? They're trying to argue you can sometimes buy crackling in a Vietnamese bakery, at the hot bar. Well, I call bullshit! You can buy a can of Coke at a Vietnamese bakery, does that make it a baked good? Anyway, I put in a complaint and the moderators took the pork down. But then, if you'll believe it, one of the pork posters complained about my cake made of jelly. They're trying to argue that it's not really a cake, just because it's not baked and doesn't have any flour. I mean, this is obviously retaliation and bad faith. Clearly it's a cake, it's round and you can slice it! This is practically Islamophobia… hey, sorry that I've been so MIA lately. Man, this fucking job – can you believe there are people who work *every single day*, five days per week? Don't let me do this again, OK? If you see that I'm about to do something like this again, you have to stop me."

The Rat has been employed at a warehouse for a total of one month.

"So, let's get into it. What are we trying to do? Match this NGO guy to the leaks? OK, let's have a go. This is the food delivery history for his account over the past three years. See, I think you were right about the energy, the guy just got divorced. It makes sense, look at his order history – he used to get Pad Thai and Pad See Ew, but now it's just the first one. And he's just stopped drinking Diet Coke. Not to be all heteronormative on you, but lmao."

While The Rat is working I don't do very much, just twiddle my thumbs and think a bit about life. It feels good to be with them, warming my hands on the heat of their competence. All of these skills, like using the command line and coding in Python, it just feels like witchcraft, to be honest. The house itself, though, makes me kind of uncomfortable. It's one of those old activist sharehouses, where no-one remembers who is on the lease. Robbie and his wife Krissa have been here for ages – the house has absorbed their preferences and their décor, throws on all the couches, very clean but with a slightly fussy vibe. It doesn't feel like The Rat really lives here yet.

Feeling, as ever, vaguely guilty for being insufficiently radical in my aesthetic tastes, I open Robbie's Insta. That's right, my daily dose of Soviet worker-caps. Here I am pleasantly surprised to observe an image that not only is different in style from those I've seen before, but actually bears some relation to our contemporary lives. It's in a kind of meme format: 'Poor person:' [indication of speech] 'give me a normal house please.' And then a pic of a poor person, for diagrammatic purposes. Followed by the words 'Rich person house', which is illustrated by a photo of an ugly, asymmetric, Rubiks-cube-like building, which looks kind of familiar. Actually, it looks a lot like one of the pics I took of the fossil imperialist house, which is weird, since I passed them on for just Tamina to use. Probably just a coincidence. That's the thing about sleuthing, you become so obsessed with joining dots, you start to see a pattern where there isn't one.

"Hey, Rat. How do you deal with it? How messed up people are. Even people who were meant to be on our side. How do you cope?"

I don't even know where this came from. Well, I sort of do, but not why it had to come out in this particular moment. Pain that can have no answer and is so mysterious. The gap left by the unspoken truth, which grows into a void, which changes shape over time into a yearning. Shows itself in your life in all these fucked-up ways and inopportune moments.

"Well," says Rat. "Depends on what you mean when you say, 'messed up'. If you mean in terms of politics, obviously none of us is totally solid. In fact, I hate that word –it's just clique behaviour. I don't trust anyone completely. Nor should you. The moment you start seeing 'trust' as something somebody just is, as opposed to something they have to keep on doing, ya know, in their interface with other people – that's when you're fucked. Like, I don't mean we should cancel people for each little thing – we're not born knowing everything – we all have to come from somewhere. And all of us, you gotta remember, act out from a place of trauma. Like, you store it up and them Boom! – it just comes for you. What was I talking about? Barely have a memory these days, bloody psychosis. All I do is eat Dexies, look at my face in the mirror and cry."

"It's OK," I say. That's how it is with The Rat – listening to them is like a waterfall of sequins. You can't possibly hold onto each sparkling piece, but it's exciting. "Oh hey, so, Rat. Let's say that you're right, and people doing fucked stuff are acting out of trauma. What does that mean for how we deal with the result?"

The Rat's face lights up. They love a challenge, love it when their theory gets taken to the limit. "Can you give me an example?"

"Sure. Take SwiftBoi for instance. I guess that it's good he keeps on organising those rallies – something must be better than nothing, yes? But what if it's not? Like, each week he just shows up at Town Hall with the same speeches, the same route, and just a slightly smaller crowd… it's diminishing returns. And then they get pepper sprayed, or whatever and then you can't say anything about their dumb strategy, because they're hurt and if you say anything about it you're the enemy. And then you have to give money to their fundraiser to pay the fines… like, we are literally fundraising for cops. And, dude can't handle any criticism – even if it's the smallest thing, he just starts blaming himself. Saying how he's the worst in the world, etcetera. Then everyone else starts going, no, no, we love you so much Swiftboi, you're the best, and the actual problem just gets lost until the next time they fuck up. Sure, it's probably to do with some shit that happened in his childhood. But who cares, ya know? Everyone had a childhood."

SwiftBoi is this dude who has been hanging round 'the scene' since forever, so it feels. Loves holding rallies, also really good at raising cash. The trouble is, all the 'activism' SwiftBoi does just seems to circle back to himself. If there's any kind of public event you know that he'll be there, the Generalissimo towering over us like Jesus in Rio. Always in a high-vis vest, so nobody can forget he is the real working class. Even though these days I'm pretty sure he works in a library.

"Ah yeah, SwiftBoi." SwiftBoi really gets on The Rat's nerves, which is why I brought him up. "Yeah, I'm not saying we just sit on our hands and do nothing when people are acting toxic. But there's a way of doing that with love, also everyone in this entire world is not fucking SwiftBoi. I hate this thing where we take the worst possible construction on each thing a person says, jumping down each other's throats over random shit. Or stuff that is bad, but also totally fixable... speaking of fixable, did you know that I managed to repair my Instant Pot? The power shorted out when I was trying to make gulab jamun and the syrup boiled over. Also, why do East Asian people like air fryers so much, and South Asian people like Instant Pots? No, don't answer that. Some things are not meant for us to know."

"Yeah... Bridget used to love gulab jamun."

And we go quiet, because we remember we are not supposed to talk about Bridget.

"Hey, Rat," I say, trying again. "So, something weird happened recently. I tried to talk to Bombadil about having another working group at the zine palace. You know, for the green NGO stuff, green industry bullshit. I think I just assumed that he would be supportive. Probably I'm being oversensitive, but, it sort of felt like I was being brushed off, somehow…"

I'm hoping for a touch of solidarity, bit of sympathy here. Instead The Rat gives me this supremely irritating, psychotherapist-on-the-couch look. "And how did that make you feel? Look," they break off and laugh, not unkindly, "Bro, I have been around this place for a hot minute. Not super long, but I've had the time to think, to learn about a few new things. Complain all you like, but that is how it's going to be around here."

"But if they're our comrades and our friends, we can work this out together, right?"

And The Rat just looks at me.

"You have to understand," they say at last. "I'm a keyboard warrior. The only thing I shoot off is my mouth. Here, take this zine and have a read." I look at the title: *To Hate The Ones Closest To Me*. There's no name for the author. Intrigued, I flick through, the first snippet sticks with me, but the edition as a whole blurs through my mind. Images overlaid unevenly on each other, different fonts in different sizes – the zine evokes a kind of cut-and-paste, DIY aesthetic. It just doesn't feel like it came directly from real life, it's like a photocopy of someone else's photocopy. Lightly ashamed, I fold the pages and put the zine away for the collection I keep under my bed.

"You see," says the Rat, as if talking to themself, "There is a difference between personal bullshit and structural oppression. If it's personal, it sucks, but if you didn't care about it anymore, you wouldn't care. You could just turn round and ignore. If it's structural, you can turn away, but it's still there."

At this moment the fan on Rat's laptop starts to whir: a grating, unpleasant noise. The sound makes me jump, then it makes me annoyed, then the fact I'm annoyed makes me even more pissed. For someone who spends the better part of their life fighting climate imperialism, I shouldn't be so surprised each time it's hot.

As if to clear the tension, The Rat claps their hands. "Enough gossip and diversion! Let's get back to work. Hey, look at this address the non-profit guy's been going to. He ordered forty-five spring rolls. That sounds like a catering order, don't you think? Weird, it should be an office building, but it looks too expensive to be his office. I think we are going to need some help to work this one out… to be blunt, we're going to use Robbie's login. That should be him at the door. Follow my lead and I will sort it out."

Chapter 21

"Oh, hey," says Robbie. Most days I don't really mind him, though we are not exactly close. He has a way of looming which I find intimidating. Today he has a dour expression and some facial hair which he has not been taking very good care of, in my opinion.

"Oh, hey," says The Rat. They perform a series of infinitesimal physical adjustments which acknowledge the incursion of masculinity into the room. When there are men around, Rat tends to go more masc in their self-presentation, whereas I go femme. These small subconscious tics.

"Oh, hey," echoes Robbie's WIFE, Krissa. Yes they are married and I won't let them forget it. Like Robbie she is white, and I can't help how my body reacts, which is to tense up. Two of them on two of us now. If something goes wrong and we have to eat each other, they'll probably win.

"Hey, Rat. Hey, um... anyway, it's good to see you. How have you been?"

"I've been well, thanks, and you?"

"I've been well... yeah, busy, yeah." That's how it is with me and Krissa. Known each other for years and still less spark than two pieces of Ikea furniture. "Same old, same old. Working at the café, it's not a bad gig, Robbie and I have been living off this wage for sixteen months now. We get free sandwiches, would you like to try? They're a bit stale but I've re-toasted them."

I eat the sandwich Krissa proffers in a state of deep shame and alienation. Like someone learning how to eat a sandwich based off YouTube tutorials. These days I don't really have friends, I mostly eat alone and the way that I do tends to be quite disgusting. Just shoving it right in the hole. Horrible to think about and horrible to look at. "Thanks for the sandwiches, Krissa," I say. "This is really nice."

Krissa laughs charmingly. She can really do that – she's someone who charms and expects others to be charmed. "No problem, you're very welcome, thank the café! Without it, Robbie and I would starve, ha ha ha… Robbie, did you remember to pick up the tarp?"

Robbie's whole huge being forms into a shrug, which looks kind of defensive from where I'm standing. "I did not."

"It's just that I thought you were going to pick it up after the meeting."

"I was, but I forgot. It's no drama, OK? I'll go pick it up tomorrow."

Both of them have this little look – Krissa still smiling, looking so NICE but also pass-ag and resentful, Robbie apologetic but not really. Couples, man. They all make up their own pocket reality. Either the man does fuck all but still gets doted on, or the woman is perpetually anxious and the dude ends up remodelling himself as a human-shaped pillow to absorb her neuroses.

To get away from it all I excuse myself and go into The Rat's room, where I try to play some Cardi B over the Bluetooth speakers. Somehow the Bluetooth is connected to the radio and I end up listening to Tamina's mate, Scott H., interviewing the guy from the advanced manufacturing union, Mark Miller. "Tell me Mark, normally we see this kind of antagonistic relationship. Unions versus businesses, bosses versus workers. But the way you describe, it kind of sounds like your approach is a new way through this kind of standoff?"

"Yes Scott. Yes, it is." Miller sounds blokey but polished. "What we want to break down is this decades-old standoff between jobs and the environment. I always say, we've got to stop seeing climate as a moral issue. The transition is about all Australians, the hip pocket. We want to be leading the manufacturing of the future – batteries, electric cars. And the more sophisticated technologies, like drones and er, data centres."

From the way he says the words, I get the impression Miller's mental model of a data centre is a cartoon building with a sign that says 'Data' out the front.

"Anyway, keeping things local keeps the costs down and the quality up. Like paddock to plate manufacturing, you might say. Just the other week they opened up a new facility at Tannehill, a pilot project facilitated through the Alliance. We're very happy to see how that has panned out in terms of investment in the local community. Not to mention the national security benefits! Before, if you'll believe it, we had important data, information from law enforcement, surveillance, from our correctional centres being processed through places like China."

"Right. Riiiight." Scott H. has a voice which is bland but soothing. It reminds me, somehow, of a paddle pop that has been left too long in the refrigerator and is covered with ice crystals. Not poisonous, exactly, but hard to identify the flavour. "Breaking the standoff, right. We've been stuck here too long."

I start to feel like I should go back to the others. When I get back I find The Rat and Robbie with their heads bent together over The Rat's laptop, and Krissa nearby and observing. I sit down very carefully on the couch. There's a bowl of fruit on the table, but it doesn't make the space seem welcoming, it makes it seem like a parody or simulacrum of a home because you know you're not allowed to touch the fruit.

"OK, let's use my Street View subscription," Robbie says. "You're right, this place was purpose built. See there, that looks like an alcove for security cameras – they didn't just lease out a pre-fitted place. And here, if you zoom in…"

"Bars on the windows," Krissa chimes in. "But fancy ones – it looks nice, like it could be a trellis for plants instead of just a grille. They don't want people to work out that they're here."

Weird, how couples can transform into this dual-knowledge repository unit. I guess they have their uses after all. "That's amazing!" I say. Sounding a bit too cheerful, because I want to remind us all that we are on the same team. "Good work all, finding climate imperialists!"

Somehow that wasn't quite the proper thing to say. Robbie and Krissa seem to stiffen. "Yeah, there's been some stretching of the term 'imperialist'," Robbie begins.

"You know, it be great to find the name of the company!" interjects The Rat, saving me from my faux-pas. "But, oh no! My subscription to the corporate register search-tool just expired… you know, J is the expert on this sort of thing. Maybe we can ask him about it, he knows a lot of stuff…"

"Ah, yes, J," says Krissa. She and Robbie exchange meaningful glances. "I think you should know there are some issues with that man. With respect to interpersonal relationships."

"Oh no!" says The Rat. "Sorry to hear that. Like, can we be more specific. Is it sexual assault, is it DV?"

Krissa inclines her head gravely, as though determining whether to entrust us with a weighty secret. "There is a pattern," she says, "of imbalanced emotional labour in his romantic relationships. I, personally, would not choose to participate in any space that he is in."

"Oh no!" says The Rat. "Yeah, no, totally see that. Yeah, no, that makes sense, Krissa."

"What, specifically, did J do?" I begin.

"Oi, Robbie, mate!" says The Rat. "Did I tell you, I did another run with your posters? Round the Bankstown, Cabramatta area. Amazing stuff, man, really good reception. Yeah, everybody loves them… no, don't thank me, I'm just doing the work. You're a master propagandist, dude. Speaking of which, how's the Ph.D. going? Man of books and of the people."

Robbie seems to swell physically with pleasure. "Yeah, thanks mate, it's going well. Just getting my head around some things, don't see why we have to import all these Americanisms into our own politics, you know. This obsession with terms like, 'white supremacy'. Well, what does a word like 'black' mean, really? Aren't some, you know, Tamils blacker than Aboriginal people? Course, I'm very sympathetic, that young BLKPWR crew, I mean sure, I support Indigenous sovereignty. But when you start going down this route – kind of awkward to say, but you get pretty quickly into, well, blood and soil territory. If you read Badiou…"

The Rat is nodding along, seemingly rapt. I can never quite tell what is happening when they and Robbie interact. Can't quite tease out what part is info gathering, and which is the impulsive, unpredictable swerve of a human exchange. Sometimes it weirds me out, how instrumentalised we've become. "Totally. Totally. Oh and Robbie – mate – do you mind if

I just quickly borrow your login? Aw, thanks, you're a legend, let's have a look. Actually – listen mate, I think we've had enough for the day, don't you? How about we crack open a few cold ones?"

I have never, not once in my life, heard The Rat refer to 'cold ones' when not in the presence of Robbie. Nonetheless, the suggestion is taken up. The social volume goes up, even The Rat seems drunk. I notice, though, that on their laptop they have not yet logged out of Robbie's account.

Krissa, who is not drinking, goes out of the room with an air of being forced to take care of things that no-one else has noticed, then immediately comes back and starts to clean around our feet. There isn't any dirt there, but she does it anyway, pushing the mop literally in between our ankles, so we have to move our feet.

"Sweetheart, does that really have to be done right now?" Robbie asks.

Krissa sighs deeply, a sigh to excavate the earth. "If not me, then no-one else will do it."

I have this theory: women who have been partnered for too long to a guilty man tend to regress into a childlike state. It happens step by step, they lose the capacity to self-soothe. When you meet them, you can feel it right away – just this ambient vibe which tells you that the Lady Of The House Is About To Crack The Shits. Then the man goes into placatory mode, in recompense for shit stuff done by him and men everywhere, while everyone else has to pretend nothing is going on. If it works for them, then cool I guess. The trouble is, this settlement has not been agreed on by anybody else. Yet bit by bit, it expands to take over the whole emotional economy of the household. Word from the wise: never live with a couple unless you are very, very prepared to look out for your own interests. No matter how good you are as friends, there are still two of them and one of you. Though it may seem fine at first, once it comes to a conflict you will have no defence. You just have to rely on their integrity, that they will value this more than the privileges they accrue via in-group silence about each other's cruelties. I mean, good luck with that.

Sometimes I resent the nice white women so, so much. I want revenge on them, for reasons that are their fault but also not. Even when they are nice, they are so clean and oblivious. I am ashamed but I also know via pop culture that I am not alone in having these dark feelings. I mean, what else is the video for 'Bitch Better Have My Money' by Rihanna meant to be about. Oh, and obviously Killmonger in the museum. Also the bit in *Django Unchained* where he blows away Leonardo DiCaprio's sister, also the start of 'Partition' by Beyonce where she drops the serviette on the floor and the white girl runs to pick it up. Also the end of *Get Out* where the Allison Williams character looks into his eyes and says 'I love you' and he strangles her. He doesn't finish, though. I reckon that is a cop out, I reckon he should have finished, it would have been a better ending for the movie…

You can probably tell I have some history with Robbie and Krissa.

Krissa's voice breaks through my reverie. "Rob, have you paid the electricity bill?"

Robbie, who has a beer in one hand, waves the other irritably. "Krissa, I'll deal with it."

"Well, that's what you said last week. Now we have to pay a late fee."

Something brushes my hand. Looking down, I realise the red cord around my wrist, which has progressively been fraying, has finally snapped. I loop it through my hair and retie the knot.

Robbie makes an exasperated *tssch* noise. "It's not the end of the world," he says. "For goodness' sake, Krissa, give it a rest. It's ten dollars, OK? People forget things sometimes, it happens."

Krissa grabs Robbie's glass from his hands and hurls it onto the tiles. It explodes in tiny shards. The Rat jumps backwards and yelps.

"What the fuck, Krissa!"

"What the fuck to you!" Krissa is shaking and crying. "I do everything around here, everything. You do nothing for me, nothing!"

"Fuck off."

"You don't tell me that!"

"I said, fuck off, Krissa, you don't get to smash my fucking stein!"

I don't know what to do, I am frozen with a silly little smile on my face, trapped in this zone of social nicety. The Rat is smiling in a fixed way which means that they are completely spaced out. I guide them to their bedroom, holding their arm at arm's length. Their warmth an elbow's length from mine. I'm glad that, at least in this moment, I'm the one who can be strong while they are weak. That I can do this much for them, at least.

I've never seen Krissa injure Robbie physically, although I have noticed bruises. Once I saw her grab Stickie's ponytail during an argument. Stickie's head was jerked back and she fell against the wall. I don't know why I didn't think to mention this before. Blanked it out, I guess.

"This place," says The Rat later, while we are sitting on their bed. Through the door we can hear still hear Krissa screaming her head off at Robbie. "This whole fucking scene is just a cottonwool palace for white women."

And there's not a lot that I can find in my heart to say to that.

I stay with the Rat till late, waiting for Robbie and Krissa to stop fighting so I can sneak out through the living room. When they finally fall asleep I walk home, taking a detour through Tannehill. It's drizzling and still dark. One of the buildings has been recently refitted, and my eyes trace the lines of the metal fire escape running up the side. Could be the facility Miller was mentioning, or maybe not. My umbrella held low over my head, less for the rain than the CCTV. While I'm leaving the industrial area, crossing the bridge on the pedestrian side, a car slows to avoid splashing me as it drives through a puddle. Looking back, I want to nod to say thank you, but the car's already gone.

Via some alchemistic process, clout.

There is an unspoken formula with respect to getting 'cancelled'. It is less to do with the severity of the offence than how integral to 'the scene' you are. Which is itself the cumulative product of various factors: how long you have been around, how many friends you have, who you are dating or sleeping with, and of course – almost too obvious to state – what you look like. Nothing so uncancellable as a white man dressed in black. It is the interaction of these variables which, via some alchemistic process, combine to make clout. No need for gravity, clout is the force that makes this world go round. And for those who don't have the appropriate clothes, friends or social histories, well, you might as well keep on dancing, tap tap tap. Performing out your usefulness till you collapse like an old horse and so much for that.

Chapter 22

"Wow!" says Kit, looking at the pink KitchenAid which they have just finished unboxing. "This is just what I wanted. Oh my God!"

I watch, mostly quiet, as they exclaim and make noises, hands flitting around as they explore the various fittings and add-ons of the new contraption. Whisk, dough hook, paddle attachment. The way Kit's expressions chase one another. A flicker of engagement and an answering shadow of future boredom. My phone shivers on the countertop. I register the ___@ozflix.com.au suffix on the notification before being fully conscious of it.

"What is it?" Kit asks. "Is it from the network?"

I open the email.

We are proud and delighted to have worked on _____ these past years. Over that period, the writers, cast and crew of have become a valued part of the Ozflix family.
Unfortunately, budgetary constraints...
... declining viewership...
... a regretful decision...

"What do they say?"

I say, hardly skipping a beat: "Well, I'm not going to say the situation looks ideal. But nothing's set in stone, there is still a decent possibility that we will be renewed."

Kit laughs. "I feel like I've heard you say that before." Packing the instruction manual carefully back into the box, laying the foundation for a modest settlement against the unknown.

As if to regain an advantage, I say: "You know, I've heard on the grapevine I'm going to be given Lifetime Achievement Award. They're presenting it at the Gala. It's supposed to be embargoed, though, so don't spread it around."

Kit's sideways, significant look – is this admiration, or a covert appraisal of an asset changing value? When they do speak, the words are unrelated. "Hey, are you going to be around tonight? There's this Zoom event that Deirdre asked me to."

"Got a meeting, surely you can handle Deidre on your own?"

"Of course I can. Who are you meeting with, anyway? When do you reckon you'll be back?"

"I'm not sure yet, I'll text when I finish up. Or, you know, I could call." Almost laughing out loud at the barely concealed panic on Kit's face at the suggestion. For all their studied insouciance, they don't answer voice calls; it has taken me a while to work out this is not due to an aversion to my voice, but because they are barely capable, in social terms, of answering their phone. This knowledge fills me with endearment. It levels the playing field between us, until I recall which one of us is telling the lie of greater consequence.

I say, "I'm just heading off to see Alden Park." And then, my turn to be casual: "An odd person, isn't he? You haven't heard from him lately, have you?"

"Ah, we haven't messaged for ages."

It is beside the point to question whether Kit is being honest. Absurd to subject them to my non-reciprocal obsession with the truth. Instead, I go out to the balcony to be surrounded by air and pre-emptive loss. There I rummage for a plan and come up with only blankness, my mind a consortium of empty shelves and disassembled furniture.

Alden – without precisely meaning to, we have arrived at our own cautious settlement of first name terms – has invited me to spectate on his talent-seeking expedition, a day out at a dance centre in the middle of the Sydney CBD. Since our tour of the set we have kept in touch sporadically; in spite of my misgivings, I have come to look forward to his cool, carefully punctuated messages about the logistics of his Australian trip, auditioning young singers and dancers at varying levels of promise and performance.

Kit rides the lift downstairs with me on their way to the supermarket to buy a block of Philadelphia so they can make mooncakes filled with cheesecake, a process to be filmed for their TikTok channel. As provisions for this journey, they have brought an entire family-sized bag of popcorn, from which they are assiduously munching by the time we part ways.

The dance complex is on the eighteenth floor. Waiting at the reception I realise how high up we are. The wind, moving against the windows sounds like somebody talking.

"Windy," says the receptionist, as if delivering a pronouncement.

"It didn't used to be this windy when I was young," I say. As if this were profound. As with all talk that concerns the weather, an unarticulated path of foreboding weaves its way through the conversation.

Alden meets me in the waiting area and, in a gesture which should seem incongruous, offers me a can of Coke, which I accept. There is something oddly disconnected in his physical presence. One gets the sense that the vulnerability inherent in cultural production is both something to be coveted and a bit beneath his notice.

The first class we see is JFH, which stands for jazz, funk and hip hop. The dancers are all aged between fourteen and seventeen years old, mostly of South or East Asian ethnicity. All are women or AFAB, except for two white gay boys who are probably a couple, based on how they move and keep touching each other. All of them are beautiful, though far too young to know it.

"Hmm," Alden says. "That girl over there, she is very good. Movements very crisp. Her face is overly round, although maybe it will become thinner as she grows up. She has that girl next door look, that can also work for us." Inputs a note on his phone, marking her as a possible candidate for an audition.

The class after that is K-pop Girls' Style. It is a children's class, all under eight, and frankly quite adorable to see. These dancers are too young for even Alden to evaluate for star potential, but we watch anyway. The girls follow their teacher with deep concentration, staring at their own feet with an absorbed inward look. Some of their moves are, strictly speaking, sexualised, but in context this is not really the meaning that is conveyed.

I say, "This should be uncomfortable – seeing little kids doing adult dances, adult, ostensibly sexualised moves – but it's not. Perhaps because it's images based off other images. It started off being about sex but now it's not, not at this distance. The fantasy isn't fucking, it's competence and mastery. You know, I read once that the best pop performers are those who are trying to escape something."

Alden smiles. "Very philosophical. I'm just looking for some beautiful children who can grow into good singers and dancers... and actors." The way he says the consonants seems to function as a threat.

The class finishes. There is a confusion of young people in the corridor. Alden and I go to wait in the unoccupied studio, and I try to avoid the sight of myself in the dancers' mirror.

Alden says, "Out of all performers, I admire dancers the most. They are the most exposed, bodily speaking, and have the shortest careers of all the artists. As a result, they have a kind of neediness about them – this desperate speed, and fear of being judged. Because when they make a mistake, everyone will know. But money lasts. Which is why," he gestures vaguely and broadly at the studio, "I want to talk to you about Kit."

"I see." Trying to tamp down my defensiveness and panic. "Well, everyone gets old eventually. But Kit doesn't break down like you describe. Maybe physically speaking – but on another level, Kit is not like us."

"What do you mean?"

"It's hard to put into words. Kit has a lifeforce about them. They will scratch but won't tarnish, bend but not warp or break. Which doesn't mean they won't suffer – there will be bad sets and bad scripts, money problems and failed relationships. But at a base level, Kit has this essential flare of responsiveness, this access to forms of desire without limit, without qualification. They're not the sort of person who needs other people." Even as I speak, I marvel at my own easy access to falsity. Perhaps I am inventing a character, just as much as Alden does with his idols. "Alden, please be honest. Do you plan to get Kit to sign up with your agency?"

"I would like Kit to undertake training with us, yes."

"Even though… are you crazy? That's ridiculous. You're setting Kit up to fail. They're not a dancer. They're not that good at it." I pause, hating the ugliness drawn out of me by fear. "They're too old."

"I believe that is for Kit to decide, not you. As you can tell, I am doing my best to be honest with you. We are professionals here. I don't wish to go behind your back. By the way, did you resolve the question of Nilsson sponsorship?" Alden pauses in a way which could reflect either mockery, or genuine delicacy of feeling. "A difficult position, isn't it? With so many people's jobs now on the line."

"How do you know about Nilsson? Anyway, it's none of your business. You know, Alden, it's a kind of hypocrisy, being in love. Narcissism – playing a role for an audience of two. It's not morality which motivates me with respect to Nilsson, not for the most part. Fidelity – not to a principle, but to a certain conception of self. But when you lose that you lose everything. You wouldn't understand."

Alden says nothing, but smiles – either from nervousness, or from the shamelessness of his unassailable position. I find myself still talking. "Anyway, you'll be happy to know that our show has been renewed. Yes, that's right. Even without the sponsorship. So, your little hunting expedition can end right here. There isn't any point in asking Kit. In fact, I would advise that you didn't. It will give you a reputation in this industry, trying to poach other people's talent."

"Oh, I had no intention to offend."

"And you can tell that to Kit, too, if they ask. Don't try to hide it from me – I know the two of you have been in touch." I get up to go and Alden follows suit. "Thank you for this interesting day out. I hope your little trip was worth your while. Pity nothing will come of it, as far as Kit is concerned. Go home, Alden. And don't ever try and speak to either of us again."

Chapter 23

There is a blank, there is time passing. I am in my car. There is a blank, there is time passing and I am in my car which is hermetically sealed, the smell of air-conditioning. Within this space, all the world around is safe, and I can do as I please. I control the order of all operations. Don't know how long I have been here. There are suburbs, there are pavements, there are trees.

There is a blank, there is time passing. And I am still driving, it's long since I have left Alden and the children at the dance centre and I am still driving though I am unaware as to where. To be in motion is to look for a release. It must have been for some hours: the tenor of the light has changed, from fading sun to the deep colour of the evening. I stop the car. Here are places familiar. Yes, here is the suburb I lived in when first moving from my parents; here is the street where I drafted the screenplay for my first film. My mother cried when I left; since her death, I have not once spoken my native dialect. Vision of myself, same age as Kit. Where are we now? Alone as you can only be alone in a car. Words words words words. I've made a name for myself. And when I myself am gone, that name will continue to walk the earth without me, doing what it likes with no volition of mine.

I slow down on the bridge. Those shining streets, aftermath of rain. A solitary figure walking by on the pavement, wearing nondescript clothes. But when I look back, a singular glimpse of personality like the chime of a triangle. Just visible under the umbrella, I see their hair is twined through with a length of red cord.

On the front passengers' seat my phone brightens for a moment. A small, specific chirp. Did Kit message me, did they message not. That simultaneous lilt of fear and hope, when someone else's words arrive fully formed into your evening. I stop the car and find no word from Kit, though I do notice a new reel on their Tiktok – a compilation of reactions to some memes they have collected. Their expressions flit across the screen, artificially sped up and ironically jerky. I notice, too, that the reel has been shared by Mandy Lo, whose own account is decorated copiously with Kit's likes.

I had forgotten how empty these suburbs can be. The tenor of the light has changed, early morning deep blue. How long have I been circling these streets? Exhaustion deep as the ocean, rest my forehead on the steering wheel. Outside a house for young people, you can tell, it has that look. Curtains left undrawn in the front room: a rack for clothes, an unframed poster, several pairs of shoes. I am untethered in time, it is a book whose pages flick without intention between the past and now. And then the nostalgia parts like curtains in a theatre, and I see three unmarked vehicles draw up next to me on the silent street.

There are men in dark clothes exiting the cars. How many of them – three – no, four – five. They are wearing no insignia, but even in the dark with civilian eyes I can see the recognisable bulk of police. Large torsos, with the heavy squareness of body armour – like they are mecha-people. Weapons in their hands. How do I know? I've never held a gun in my life, but I know. Lethality has its own, instinctively recognisable mark.

One of the men walks quietly and fast round the side of the house, next to the wooden paling fence. The others mass on the front doorstep. A sudden, intense beam of light, like an injury. Suspended moment of silence. The order of events in my mind seems reversed – the door caves in, and *then* he kicks it. A confusion of people and of screaming. The blue of the dawn growing ever lighter.

Someone is being dragged out from the house. Much smaller, limp next to the bulked figures, one of whom is standing on them. Wait, there are two. They look dishevelled and young, as if just pulled from sleep – disordered and disoriented. One young man and one young woman, cops standing on her too. More mecha-figures emerging – they are not exactly human – wearing goggles, so that you can't see their eyes. How many must have been waiting in the vehicles? Now more people are coming from the house, and somebody is screaming. A confusion of movement, a cry of pain. Animal, lunging shapes – my God, they've brought out the dogs. And I come back to myself. I sit up, turn on the ignition and drive off.

I drive and I drive, for an uncertain length of time, and then I stop. The scene is familiar, the roads are familiar, but the circumstance is not. And there it is again – that sudden exodus of feeling, de-personalisation. I am not so much ashamed as I am simply not, in any meaningful sense, present. Helplessness evokes embarrassment, embarrassment with nowhere to go turns to disgust. The machine stops – the cocoon of routine, of repetition falls away, and there is silence. The face of my own shame, my own shameful irrelevance juxtaposed to overwhelming force.

I don't know what I saw, but as I was reversing from the cul-de-sac, I recall one of the mecha-figures leaving the house. I believe they were carrying a draped, trailing flag. The sky was blue tinged with orange, the dawn intensifying round my ears. In the growing visibility, I recall I saw a flag that was dyed green, with a symbol printed on it – not very complex, a Microsoft Paint-ish job. And in my memory I see words on that flag, in amateurish bold letters: 'JOIN THE REVOLT'.

Chapter 24

In which Kit dreams some electric dreams about becoming a K-idol.

Sometimes I just long for a clean slate. In terms of everything – who I know and what I do, where I wake up in the morning. I want to sweep the pieces off the table, like wreckage from a bad meal. Or a board game I was already bored of hours ago, but somehow is still going.

I've been trying to gather some thoughts on some career opportunities which may or may not lie before me. The other night I wrote some lines down in my notebook. I call it 'writing in poetry,' though it is obviously not.

Realistically, nothing will happen for me. But unrealistic things do happen. That's kind of the whole point.

Sometimes I just want to quit this whole fucking world and spend the rest of my life making TikToks which I upload to **understated** asian baking. Yet even that is no haven – I guess that it was never perfect, but lately it has turned into a hellspace. And do you know why? It's because, in what was ostensibly a space of ethnic pride, they have let in white people. And it poisons everything. Not even necessarily because of what they do, just the dynamic that they bring.

Let me give you an example. Exhibit A, a post from Edwin Chan, a group regular and **understated** asian baker right from the start. See here – he has painted a replica of Monet's lilies, on a slice of toast, using Greek yoghurt. No, let me clarify. He has posted a replica of Monet's lilies, on a slice of *homemade* bread, using *homemade* yoghurt. I mean, look at the state of it. Observe the response: four hundred love reacts, five hundred likes.

Now, for comparison: Exhibit B, a post from Paul Davis, a white man. More specifically, a white man who looks like his profile pic was generated using an AI that crawled through LinkedIn. How, may I ask, did he come to be a member of **understated** asian baking? Why did he ask to join, why was he accepted? I have no idea – yet I have every idea, if you know what I mean.

Anyway, as you can see, he has posted a picture of a slice of cake he saw at a Kyoto Starbucks. Alongside a matcha latte… also purchased from Kyoto Starbucks. What, pray tell, is the point? Did he bake that cake? Did he even eat it? Neither of the above – he simply photographed, to post. If you saw him on the street, you would know in the first moment he knows nothing of patisserie. And yet… five hundred love reacts, six hundred likes. Do you see what I'm saying?

And the worst thing is, who is admiring this visual and intellectual slop? Asian people. Yes – and to be more specific, *Asian women*. Yellow ones, to be utterly frank. Let's take another example, Agnes Tsai. That woman is so brilliant, she invented meringues in predicaments – these are meringue animals stuck between two Ritz crackers, trying to get out. Genius, no? And yet! One flash of white dick, and she forgets all that she cares about and values!

I don't want to go.
I don't want to go, but.
That sentence has always contained an implicit 'but'.

I want to run away, I want to go far, far off. Get on a train and keep riding forever. I want to go where phones can't reach me, and where I only partake of the internet on my own terms. Where no-one owns an air fryer. Hate making trade-offs, why do I have to choose? It is so fundamentally unfair that if I have A I can't have B.

He threw me out of a car.
The thing is, I could leave.
But I did not.
I still miss him, though.

As a diaspora kid, I have some thoughts on Hallyu culture. 'Representa-tion', 'visibility', whatever. Blah blah blah. If you want to win at this game, you do not beg for inclusion. Just come right in there with an alternative hegemony of beauty. Remember how it was when 'Gangnam style' came out? I was just a kid, but I remember how they laughed at Psy. They love us to look comic-relief, desexualised – they laugh at us, we pretend that we're laughing with them. Well, no-one was laughing when Jungkook came along. His beauty moved them to silence. Yes I know the training schools are meant to be super abusive, well, what isn't? There's no war without blood. Hallyu culture has redeemed our collective psychosexual honour. Support our troops, I say.

You know I could dance, I could learn to dance. I used to dance with a crew outside the convention centre at Sydney Harbour. Every now and then some older white guy would come along and say, 'Now now what have we here.' I'm not telling you this because it's racist, I'm telling you because it's funny.

You know that No! One! Was! There! For me!
Tell me what to be, and I'll be that.

I want everything, I want nothing, I want to be famous, I want to be a hermit and live under a bridge and perfect my craft. I don't want to have to make any decisions at all. You know, people go for surgery to look like a K-idol – people who aren't Korean, not even Asian. That's how you really know the truth of their desire. The knife doesn't lie and nor does the cash.

We don't need it, we want it.
There is a difference.
Could I be wanted like that?
Would I want to?

HE PAINTED MONET'S LILLIES ON HOMEMADE TOAST
USING HOMEMADE YOGHURT!!!

Chapter 25

I'm late dropping off supplies at Tamina's place. When I arrive through the back gate I see that Stickie is sitting on a crate in the middle of the garden, surrounded by Tamina, Robbie, Krissa and Scott. People's faces are stony. It looks like an interview or an audition. Instinctively I turn and go to sit on the porch, listening to the trains go past – we're a few doors down from the rail line, the sky is buzzing with noise and heat. After a while Stickie comes out and stands dazed in the sunlight, almost in tears.

"Oh hey, Stickie," I say. "Is everything all right?"

Stickie, wiping her eyes, says, "No!" She makes a gesture in the air, as if to describe an uncertain shape before us, and then drops her hands. "I fucked up, I hurt Krissa, I had to be accountable," she says. Head bowed, she makes as if to go and then doubles back into the house. "Tamina needs her stuff," she reminds me before going inside.

Obediently I lug the bags into the house. These are heavier than normal – apart from Tamina's normal groceries, she's asked for mini corkboards, a whiteboard, whiteboard markers and a block of index cards. Apparently she's going to host a seminar on rad politics. When I finally finish setting the stuff down, I find the others have dissipated – only Tamina remains smoking in the garden. I can't help looking at her with an implicit question, even though I know it isn't any of my business.

"We're exploring new ideas," she says, in a way which makes clear no explanation will be forthcoming. "Thanks for helping me out, dear, you're a treasure. Would you like some soup?"

To be honest, I don't really feel like it – it is kind of warm for soup. Actually I'd sort of hoped Tamina would re-imburse me for the supplies, since I haven't had a shift at the toy shop in a while. But she needs the cash more than I do. I wish I could learn to be less selfish. To silence my un-cooperative mind, I turn my attention to my phone, where I am drafting a character reference for Leaf under a fake name. She got arrested for putting up posters saying LOVE PIGS KILL COPS on a Hungry Jacks, a pharmacy, a dumpling restaurant, an indie music venue, a 24-hour McDonalds and a Korean store that sells novelty umbrellas.

Then, Tamina sticks her head out the window to call me in. "We're getting together for a meeting now, can you come back?"

To be honest, I get anxious about doing social or semi-social shit without much notice. But I'm looking forward to chatting with the others. It's been a while since we last did an action – I'm sort of spoiling for it. You feel better that way. Less like a ragdoll tossed around by the insatiable fucked-upness of the world.

Out in Tamina's garden, everyone is sitting round on milkcrates in a circle. It's not great for your butt but you can fold a towel if you have one, which I don't. J is here, and Stickie and Leafie and The Rat – they must have come in the back entrance. Robbie and Scott have stuck around, though Krissa has disappeared – I feel a bit iffy about this, I'm not sure if they are officially part of the crew – but they are friends with Tamina, so I guess this means they are OK.

"Are we waiting for Kabir?" I ask.

Robbie and Tamina swap glances, and Tamina gives a small shake of the head. So here we are, avengers assembled. Climate imperialists, quake in your little boots.

"So, to update you all," says The Rat. "I went and did some digging. Wanted to find out the name of the company the non-profit guy has been visiting, by going through the UberGoogleDinnerlogNetflixAGLChevron TimeWarnerTinderSkynetAdani leaks. Nominally it's called Tiddaroo, they have an office in the city. But I checked out who else is registered at that there, and basically it's the same as those security contractors, Nilsson. There's a couple of board members in common too. Which makes me think that in effect, they are the same people."

This revelation is greeted by a series of realtime live reacs from the assembled polity. "Wow," says Stickie in unfiltered admiration. "You guys are amazing."

The Rat does this smiley little nod. God, they're so cute sometimes, like a living emoji. "Yeah. The question is, what does this imply? Why would some non-profit peak body dude be hanging out with them? Well, I checked out what Tiddaroo is nominally about. They're meant to be this Traditional Owners' corporation. But they only got set up a couple years ago, just after…"

"…after the BLKPWR crew put out that manifesto," says J. "I see. So you reckon it's an op."

The Rat nods. "Yes, I do. So, I had a look at the board members at the time Tiddaroo first got set up. There was quite a bit of overlap with Nilsson – it's kind of hard to get info, 'cos since that boycott, Nilsson have become a lot more secretive about their contractual relationships. But Tiddaroo, people want to brag about it, you know, the Indigenous aspect. They tend to be pretty public about the connection."

Because our collective wits have been so dulled by lead exposure, it takes a while for us to register the significance. "Interesting," says Tamina. "You know, I still remember, people used to be much more open about working with companies like Nilsson. Promoting the connection for investors and so on. Now they're much more secretive, they can't talk directly about what they have been doing. They are scared of us, it's annoying for them and it's expensive, and it's us who have achieved that! Remember this."

And just for one hot second we all feel nice together.

"This is brilliant," says J, usually so contained within himself, you can forget that he is there. "It seems it might be time to move beyond these sorts of rear-guard actions… I've been thinking about this for a while. How to move beyond a position of marginality. And one of the things is to scale up from targeting individual fossil capitalists to shutting down the whole supply chain. And not just personnel, infrastructure, data centres, pipelines. Something a bit less fungible than people." I look up in pleased surprise, but J ignores me. His words are directed towards Tamina, Bombadil and Robbie. "One thing, though – this is an expansion in our project. If we are going to shoot for something like this, we are going to need to find other people to work with."

"What about SwiftBoi?" asks Stickie. "He has his issues, but he does show up. And he gets people out, people get behind him."

The response is instantaneous.

"No."

"No fucking way, man."

"No."

"His posters are moronic," says Leaf, surprising me – she isn't normally so direct.

"Unlike our own posters – which are entirely current and relevant, heart-breaking works of staggering genius," says The Rat, *sotto voce*.

Automatically we all turn to Tamina. Kind of assuming she has the status and wherewithal to adjudicate disputes between us. "I veto working with SwiftBoi," she says. "He's a cosplay communist, no real strategy. Everything he does is for the clout."

"What about Green Revolt?" suggests Bombadil.

Tamina gives him the side-eye – I've never worked out what precisely went down between the two of them. "Green Revolt are radlibs," she says, not looking at him directly. "Middle class saviours – they have no links with communities, no systematic critique of capitalism. All they do is inconvenience working people, sitting down there in the middle of the road like clowns. Instead of disrupting logistics, circulation."

I say timidly, "Um… aren't roads a part of circulation?" No-one deigns to respond. Great. Here we go again, me and my inadequate knowledge of Marxism. This is what happens when you haven't read Badiou.

"Hmm, this is just an idea," Robbie says, in the way of white guys who say things like that, and then just bludgeon you to death using words. "But there are some interesting things going down with Mark Miller, the manufacturing union man. No, his politics aren't identical to mine – well, of course, *I'm* an anarchist. Been that way for decades, ever since Tuggerah, you know. But Miller's people, they've been really going out there into the communities. Mums, dads, farmers, steelworkers. So, if we want to be pragmatic…"

"I won't work with Miller's people," says J. "Others can do as they like, but I won't fuck with these people. Don't they literally share their funds with cops?"

DojaCat!!! comes unexpectedly out of the external toilet. He – I think it's 'he' today – is dressed as a comedy nun and wearing a nametag which says, 'White Sharia Now'. "No one baked a cake for *my* birthday," he says in a dejected voice. "Depression is a shitpost," he adds, walking past us cradling a bag of dirty clothes, to the laundry.

"Do you think, just as a suggestion, we could maybe reach out to the BLKPWR people…" I begin.

"They're tankies," says Tamina in a tone that brooks no response.

Scott says, with a little prefacing giggle, and a smile: "Personally, when you talk about Miller… I think we need to be moving past sectarianism. A broad coalition, you know, being grounded and accountable to people who are really around us, our families, our neighbours." He looks around us, very cheery and helpless, with his big smile and his good skin. I feel annoyed with him somehow. Robbie and Tamina and he exchange a little glance, a charge of shared experience, and I am chastened, and remind myself to take Scott more seriously. He was there and I wasn't – he must know so many things which I just don't. He's done the work for years.

"Scott, I think I see some part of what you mean," says J. "It's this question of – not consent or legitimacy, in terms of a liberal framing. But that majoritarian thing. I suppose it comes down to how we understand international solidarity. There doesn't seem to be a way around it – when we do this work, we are not accountable to anyone in particular, not in a direct sense. Rather, we are accountable to what we set out to do, which is to shut down the imperialists…"

"Unless we grow movements and organise out of our actual communities," interjects Robbie in this way which is just on the edge of being aggressive, without being obviously so. "That's what community means – people we live amongst. Not just abstractions, people who share some kind of ideological or identity grouping. Look, you can be as pure as you want. Degrowth, land back, anti-colonialism. Obviously, *I* believe in these things too. I was at Tuggerah, remember. But let's just be practical – in the immediate term, the nation state is here to stay. Workers need jobs, they need to feed their families. Ordinary people, not just a minority of hyper-politicised ratbags like us! And yeah, I know this is *personal* for you, J." Robbie hesitates. "Actually, while we're talking about this, I wanted to tell you, mate. I was pretty put out when I heard you had a go at our man from the Renewable Jobs Alliance."

J smiles without real light.

Robbie continues: "it seems un-strategic, at best, to come after the one org that is trying to bring some semblance of a green economy to this country. Breaking the jobs versus environment standoff that has lasted all these years. Actually," Robbie pauses, clears his throat, "Mate, let me be direct with you. Un-strategic is not all I would call it. It's bone-headedly stupid."

J seems to have become even stiller than usual. "Tell me more, Robbie. I seem to recall your man at Renewable Jobs Alliance signed off on that lithium mine in Mali. The one which poisoned the water – and they're sending troops over there, aren't they? 'Peace keepers'? Aren't there members of your alliance who are selling the bullets? Oh, you can say it's a trade-off – if African lives are a thing you like to trade – but, remind me, have they actually stopped exporting coal? Or is it just a bunch of imperialists getting rich off two industries simultaneously? But hey, so long as your beloved Aussie workers get their electric cars…"

Bombadil looks very uncomfortable. He looks stiff, avoiding everybody's gaze. A sense of expectation seems to pass in between him and J. A question in the air that hasn't yet been answered.

Robbie raises his large palm, placatory and defensive. "Look J, mate, there's no need to talk like that. All of us here, we're all on the same side…"

"Are we?" J raises an eyebrow. "Who is your 'we', Robbie? I don't think that it's the same as mine."

Tamina laughs in that way she has which says she could intervene to stop the conflict but won't 'cos she's enjoying it too much.

"Who is my 'we'? Yeah, good question." Robbie rubs his hands together, a blokey, uncomfortable gesture. "It's normal people. People who we meet organically, have conversations with, relationships…"

"Yes, but what does 'organic' specifically mean?" I realise J is way, way more pissed off than he appears. He and Tamina are about the same age; every time there is an argument among our number, you sense the shadow of an older and much longer-running dispute. "Let me remind you, mate, that you live in the imperial core. All of us do. So if we define as 'real' and 'organic', only those relationships with people who are physically proximate to us, that is solidarity with imperialism. You say 'feed their families' – well, romanticise Australian manufacturing all you like, but in Madagascar there is a non-metaphorical famine. It is not my aspiration to live here the way, like, five white people used to do in the seventies. If your solidarity just means defaulting to the priorities of whoever lives closest to you, that is imperialism whatever you choose to call it. Fuck your ordinary Australians, fuck your 'communities' and *fuck your unions*." He pauses, seeming to deliberate whether it's worth crossing a line beyond which there can be no return. "Let me be direct with you, mate. With all of you. If that is your primary solidarity, I don't know if I feel inclined to hang around with this crew much longer."

There is a silence. I try to catch J's eye, but he won't look at me.

"Just personally, I don't like the idea of permanent jobs," says Stickie, in a small voice. "Saying 'permanent' makes me feel like I'm going to die."

"You are going to die," says The Rat.

"Thanks Rat," says Stickie.

Robbie has this look on his face – pleading, belligerent, aggrieved. "So, J, answer me this. You, personally, are just going to decide who is an imperialist? You and your friends, or your identity grouping?"

"Yes."

"And once you've decided? What will you do then?"

"Then we will kill them."

Tamina is watching with a faint smile on her face. "All right, you two. That's enough with the philosophising. Let's see, where do we all stand. Scott, Robbie," a small pause, "and Bombadil, what do you think?"

Robbie shakes his head gruffly at Tamina with a flat-mouthed non-smile. Scott smiles brightly and half-nods in his loose, silly way, conveying agreement with Robbie. Bombadil seems very uncomfortable, rubbing his hands, smiling in a way which disseminates blokey, can't-we-get-along intentions. He, too, gestures towards Robbie, shifting in his seat and not speaking, but letting it be known that he supports the majority view.

"Ok, that is settled," Tamina says. "J," she shoots a sharp look in his direction "made the decision on his own to target a participant in the Renewable Jobs Alliance. He was acting autonomously, although he was helped, without our collective agreement, by those two." Her eyes skate over Stickie and I. Both of us flinch. "They did not know, they believed the action had been agreed upon by the collective. This choice did not have my approval. It will not happen again."

J says nothing. He appears to have retreated to an interior point of the deepest stillness. Bombadil smiles awkwardly and vaguely, in the direction of the fence. I feel bad that I haven't said anything. Sitting here like an admonished teenager. Then I remember the thing I had wanted to ask. "So, are we going to do more actions?"

Tamina looks at me as though I am a child. "You know, the surveillance environment is intensifying," she says. "If we keep it up like this, we could go to jail."

And I feel a small twinge of un-recognition. Weren't we all risking this already?

"What about the Dragon Philosopher crew?" interjects Stickie, very humbly. I feel proud of her for being able to share her ideas with the group, so soon after an accountability process.

Tamina laughs. "Oh, that idpol crew," she says. "All talk and no action. Robbie gave them a whole stack of posters and they haven't even put them up."

Bombadil smiles at the sky but doesn't speak.

"One day," says The Rat, speaking slowly and with long pauses, as though in a dream. "You know, there is only one revolution. One day we will say to them, 'shut it down' and it shall be shut. Our will be done. That is the power that I build towards, every day."

"Well that's settled, then," says Tamina.

We continue talking in a circle. All these different beginnings of plots and plans, but nothing really landing. Normally I feel better when I gather with my comrades, but today I don't. Maybe it's just my mind, so noisy and disordered, but it doesn't feel like much has been settled here at all.

Chapter 26

The night goes on, we start drinking. Some other friends and friends-of-friends, comrades and comrades-of-comrades, show up and we tone down the red-hot stuff. The diaspora kids show up, they are developing a powerful cumulative pan-Asian aesthetic. Costume jewellery round the hands with vaguely Tamil/ BDSM connotations. Super shiny trackpants, very low-rise, lots of dragon insignia which would be tacky on anybody else. George Jackson vibes. A printed dragon rides above a square of midriff, fuck my life.

"Hey, did you know Brian has a gig tonight? It's meant to be, like, post-experimental-climate-punk or something."

Brian is sort of a wildcard to be honest. Some people say he's a narcissist but I think that's not precisely the real issue. More, he was born with a hole in his heart and nothing can fill it, he's tried alcohol and Dexies and clout clout clout. God knows he loves that shit, pumps it straight into his veins. What is so obvious to everyone but him is that it can't be fixed, but this will not stop him trying. That's what makes him so compelling as a musician. Nightmare to organise with, but whew, what a performer.

The gig takes place at a warehouse, it's the gentrifying side of Tannehill even though the ground is probably lead-contaminated. Couples dine al fresco left and right, heads turn discreetly as we get off the bus in a posse. Mouths stretched in lines of pale dismay. DojaCat!!! saunters deliberately past them to the ATM, each table averts its eyes successively, like they are watching tennis. Tamina watches from across the road, peeling a banana. She always seems to have one of those on hand, that and a Ziploc bag of nuts.

Kabir, who has linked up with the diaspora posse, wants to jump over the back fence. "Fuck those guys! I bet they all have rich parents!" He is so enormous but moves with the grace of a comradely elephant. I appreciate the size of him, his heft.

"If they check stamps they'll throw us out."

"Ah, they'll throw us out anyway."

"Not necessarily."

"Oh yeah? 'Not necessarily'? Look over there."

We look over to where Leafie has commenced to interact with a bunch of aggressive looking men. One of them is wearing an 'AFF' T-shirt, the Nazi guys. Almost all of them are men and they are almost all losers, but not quite; they move beardedly and in groups. Most of them are white but there are always a couple of self-hating POC on the side, two of whom are in evidence today – this Chinese guy who I think grew up in Tamworth or something, who talks with this super fake ocker accent, inflections of the Cantonese that is his actual first language. Then there is this Indian dude who is technically quite smart, he got into this through computer science or something. You know, rationalism. One of these days someone will explain a thing about how race isn't real, it is just your relationship to power which is inherently fucked, so of course there are people who develop a fucked-up sort of relationship with themselves. Yeah, that was me doing my Critical Race Theory bit, do you like it? I'll be here all day. The Indian guy wears this supercilious look, like he can't even talk to you because his brain is just so big. Thoughts which are way too rational for you to understand.

"Ah no, not those cunts," says Kabir. "Inshallah this is going to be a good evening."

The gig is great, all bouncing round and crashing into each other. I am a bit hazy on the actual music – for me, the velocity of Brian's charm goes just a little bit further than his talent – but the vibe is enough to keep us going. Then I hear voices and the beginnings of a scuffle. Leafie appears to have escalated her ideological differences with the AFF guys to the point of confrontation. "Fucking dyke!" one of them yells. Real genius level witticism here. But then he grabs her by the ponytail, and Stickie, bless her heart, hits him across the back of the head with a stool. Well, here we go.

The crowd parts expectantly in roughly concentric circles. Initially it is just four AFF guys versus Stickie and Leaf, but then J gets involved, and Kabir and even Tamina, and the trick in a fight is not to get overwhelmed by all the stimuli, stay aware of your surroundings focus on just one person, and there I am with a chair in my hands and Leafie brandishing a milk-crate at those ugly guys. The Indian guy comes at me and could really fuck me up but then Tamina hits him on the back of the head a longneck and I love this about her, love this for us, the way we can be apart but still look out for each other across the room. Then security comes in and they are huge and it becomes obvious both the AFF and us were sort of front-ing, that they were always the arbiters, the boundaries on this particular LARP, as we are marched out of the venue with our arms behind our backs.

Stickie is bruised but satisfied because she got a good hit on the homo-phobe's nose.

"I felt it crunch," she says happily. "I think maybe it broke."

The streets are all quiet now, the al fresco diners all gone home. Kabir is in a good mood, weaving from side to side to aiming a series of kicks at the expensive cars. There is no-one who can take us right now. In our day-to-day lives we are so often alone. But there is no-one on this street who can take us on, not here, tonight.

Stickie and Leaf want to invite everyone back to ours but it's too far. Scott, who is around for some reason, says he has to go home, he has a lot on at work. Why would you do that to yourself on a Saturday? "Great show tonight, let's stay in touch," he says to Brian, who is pretty drunk and still on a high from the performance. It turns out Brian has Scott's phone and after a confusing turn of events, somehow Kabir's address gets passed on by mistake. And then Scott is off to bed so he can be up in time for his responsibilities tomorrow morning, and I envy him for having such an orderly life, where no-one puts lead in their mouth for no particular reason.

"Let's go to the park on the corner," suggests J. "I like drinking there. Feels so free to be outdoors."

"Nah, let's go back to Tamina's house," says Robbie.

"We'll go to mine," says Tamina.

We end up back sitting in Tamina's garden, passing a joint round in a circle. The mood softens and changes. We fall into a companionable rhythm of complaining about other people.

"… Brian is talented, he's charismatic, but he's a cunt. We let him get away with everything."

"How was that gig supposed to be 'Western Sydney power'? We're fifteen minutes away from Central Station."

A breeze arrives, taking some of the tension from the humid evening. Someone offers me a cigarette, and though I've quit I still take it. The little spark, the cocoon of satiation.

"Woah," says Stickie. "Look at this. Apparently Green Revolt just got raided at their place in Tannehill. That's pretty near where we just were. Fuck, it's counter-terror charges." Holding up her phone so I can read the Daily Mail headline: 'EXPOSING the RADICAL group who GLUE their BODIES to the ROAD'. Gotta admire the approach to capitalisation. I take a look at the Green Revolt Insta, where there is a wall of text in classic Green Revolt font. It emphasises the peaceful nature of the protest and the violence of the cop response. It also borrows the Daily Mail's approach to capitalisation: 'WE WERE NOT THE ONES WITH THE GUNS.'

J says quietly, "What if we were?"

Kabir is getting worked up, gesticulating with his enormous hands. "What I'm saying is, I grew up around these people. Normal people, from normal families and communities. They don't care about all this… identity this, identity that. It doesn't fucken matter! We're all the same, ya know? We all just need the same shit to live on this planet. It's not about race! Got more in common with some povo white kid in Western Sydney than you… academic cunts!"

This last bit is obviously directed at Robbie, who shows no visible response. Not gonna lie, Robbie is kind of an asshole but it's good of him to deal with Kabir like this. I guess that solidarity means that you sometimes need to absorb another person's rage, which is broadly justified, although imperfectly targeted. But there has to be a limit. I guess that wisdom means knowing how to tell the difference between these situations.

The Rat looks anxious. I can tell they want to interject, but I also know how much they hate interpersonal conflict. "OK, but look at what you just said. That's also a form of identity politics, but with class. Like how what's-his-name keeps on talking about his mum in the housing commission, but now he's a neoliberal asshole. We are always going to be affected by where we come from, and we are always going to have to find ways to act together across that. I hate talking about idpol, I can't think of one person who hasn't bitched about it at some stage. And I can't think of one person who hasn't reached for it, at another moment, to explain why they think the way they do, what they do or where they are going." The Rat looks sheepishly around. Big smile to defuse any potential tension. "Ah, I'm just shooting my mouth. Go on, tell me to shut the fuck up, like you obviously want to. Only gonna make my politics even worse."

I look around, I am feeling anxious. I look for Tamina and see with a small jolt of the heart that she was looking for me.

Now Kabir has gone into a spiel in his exquisite deep voice, half soliloquy and half monologue: "You know what I'm gonna do? I'm gonna get us a house, somewhere away from this shit. Somewhere with nature, maybe in the bushland, trees and stuff. Fruit trees, an orchard, we can all go and pick fruit. Anybody here, any anarchist, leftist, anyone, you can come stay with me, any time. Heal our minds and our hearts. I wanna do that for you, for all of us."

I am thinking at this moment about loneliness, I don't know why. I think it's something to do with being around other people but still feeling by yourself. Like being hungry and the scent of food when there is no food. There is the promise and the dream that is called up by that promise.

Sometimes I think it would be nice to just fuck off out of here, go and live in the woods like Kabir has imagined. In the Blue Mountains or something. A blue room. Vase of flowers on the table. But the Blue Mountains is a human place just like everywhere else. I know Kabir will never get that house.

Voices continue to unfurl around me:

"… that's what I hate about anarchists…"

"… speak for yourself, *I'm* not an anarchist."

I think of Green Revolt, and my mind swerves away in silence. I think of Green Revolt, and the fear blows through like a cold breeze.

The posse of hot diaspora kids are also here and conferring; they are cuddling and touching each other's torsos. They call each other 'bebe' and 'cuz' and 'my love', it is this lingo born of Internet-speak and diaspora bonding. This is the community I bailed on when I was choosing how to allocate my political commitments. Could have been with them but instead I pitched my lot in with this lot, I mean the climate-imperialism stuff, it seemed important. And of course it is real work but it is not the only work and I don't really know what has gone down with these ones, except that they know things that I do not and it just seems important. And the reason why I chose this and not the other, if I'm being truly honest, is that if I started to think about the genesis of my own self and my choices, like really think about it, who we are and what we do and who we should have been, I would probably just break into a million pieces. Flung up in the sky like stardust, or just ordinary dust, and I don't want to do that yet.

Bombadil and J are gesticulating, not with large movements but with intensity. J is filled with a rage I cannot parse and Bombadil is crying.

"All of us here are just totally fucked," says Tamina, mostly to herself.

There is a pitch of fun you can reach, hanging with this crew, which is impossible to reach almost anywhere else. Some of the people I know are not going to live to be very old. That's why we smoke so much. You have to take your pleasures while you can.

Each day of our lives we are surrounded by people who don't get it. Here we can tell the truth, just speak our pain and be heard for once. And it is not enough. We are not supposed to want one single thing for ourselves and yet we do, we do, we do.

Chapter 27

"Hi," says the rich guy.

"Hi," says the assistant.

"Let's get started," says the rich guy. "Oh, wait a moment. Let me take this call. It's quite awful, and very inconvenient. You would not believe what happened to my car the other day – somebody slashed my tyres."

"Oh no," I say. "How awful."

"I know… the police suspect some of those so-called, 'anti-imperialist' fanatics. It's so frustrating, isn't it? Of course, I support their cause, but vandalism is never the answer."

"OK," I say, once the rich guy's call is done. "I want to discuss the Nilsson sponsorship offer."

"Oh," says the assistant.

"Yes," says the rich guy.

"Yes," I say. "I've decided… I cannot do this. That is, I have chosen not to accept the contract."

"That's a pity."

"That's a shame."

"I wanted to see if we could discuss, some alternative avenues…"

"I see," says the rich guy. "Well, this is disappointing."

"Very much so."

"We had high hopes," says the rich guy.

"All of us did," says the assistant.

"If we can find a way to make this work… perhaps a more minimalist production."

"There's no need to discuss," says the rich guy. "If you're not going to do it, you're not going to do it. That's the main issue. That's all we need to know, from you."

"No need to explore the matter further."

"Well, I…"

"Please," says the rich guy. "On a personal level, I absolutely respect your choice. Personally, myself, I don't agree with mandatory detention."

"It's just terrible."

"Awful."

"Bring them there, that's what I say."

"I've voted Labor my entire life."

"But, well, this is a business," says the rich guy. "And we all have responsibilities. A role to play."

"These are difficult times."

"For everyone."

"Hard times in the creative industries."

"Is there a chance?" I ask.

"No," says the rich guy.

I don't say anything.

"Well, it's been a pleasure to work together," says the assistant.

"I hope we do so again."

"Wait," I say. "About what I said before, about the set. If we could get some technical reinforcement…"

"Well, that's just the thing," says the assistant. "I've had it checked, it should be fine. Absolutely understand your concern. But I've had it checked, by one of the new engineers, a consultancy, yes, they're owned by Nilsson, I know, I know. But just this once, anyway, we were sort of counting on your approval for the next season, nonetheless, they very kindly offered us one of their people, charge by the hour… best as we can, out of our budget… Anyway, as I just said, we had it checked. It was all fine."

"Are you sure?"

"Absolutely."

"Perfect condition."

"Good as new."

"It's a pity," says the rich guy. "Really, I've enjoyed watching the arc with Kit, especially, develop. They have, how shall I say, an unusual charisma. There aren't many roles that would let these abilities in them loose, the way you have. Pity to cut off the story early."

"I'm quite a fan," says the assistant. "It's very sad."

"I suppose," I say, "that I'm going to need to tell Kit what has happened. I suppose I should tell them in person."

The rich guy and the assistant exchange looks.

"Kit wasn't born yesterday, you know."

"Not to say they aren't young."

"Not to say they aren't very young."

"But, they do know which way is up."

"Right, of course," I say. "But I'm sure they'll want to tell me in person, as well, whatever they decide about our partnership. After all, we've been through so much together, as a team."

"Naturally," says the rich guy. "You two are a team, inseparable. In any case, why the long face? Still a few more scenes to shoot, and we'll see both of you at the Gala. Isn't that sponsored by Nilsson too? Oh, don't be purer than the driven. That's right, I forgot – your memoir is coming out! Big day for you, eh? What a culmination. What a capstone on your career, a life's achievement."

Chapter 28

Nothing is obviously changed when I get back to the apartment. And yet even as I step in, the space feels depopulated. The first item tangibly identified as missing is Kit's shoes, which at this time would normally be splayed on the rack in a disorderly shape. Backs of the sneakers compressed because Kit, in their impatience, tends to ram their feet in without undoing the laces first.

A glance into Kit's room confirms it: no more pastel clothes tossed carelessly across the chair. Windowsill bare of small bottles of vape liquid, piles of stickers and stationery, scented candles and small plastic potted plants. Then I see the pink KitchenAid is gone. Kit has taken their small dowry with them.

On Park's official company socials I find a photograph of Kit, tagged and looking beautiful. Wearing more makeup than I am accustomed to seeing – the accompanying post is exceedingly cheerful, singing the praises of the ten-step skincare routine. I download the file and click on 'Properties' to inspect the metadata, and find the photo was taken weeks ago. I call Kit's phone and get sent straight to voicemail.

"So you *were* talking to Park," I say, before hanging up.

Outside Kit's room, and with the exception of the disappearing KitchenAid, all seems to be in order. Vase in the hall, diffuser at the bathroom window. Impossible, really, for such normality to co-exist with this extent of loss. I look at my own face in the mirror, bereft and yet already resigned to the long delayed but still expected event. Later, I will embark on the task of working systematically through my memories in order to delete them one by one, the happy ones first, but not yet. A routine well-rehearsed. *You have loved before and forgotten. You will love and forget, again.*

But first I go into the hallway, where the air-conditioning is turned up to the maximum. There I lean against the wall, staring disconsolately at the rows of lights in the insensible city, just beginning to turn on in the polluted dusk. While the recirculated air dries my tears before they even begin, just as the heat dries the rivers, and as age thins the blood that continues to move, reluctantly and unwilled, through my aging body.

Chapter 29

The Oscars, I learned once, are held in a mall; and so it is with the Gala, which occurs in one of the larger function rooms of the casino. As a locale for heartbreak, it is ideal: people are dressed well but not that well, and for whatever reason their heads all look too large. Within the room, the white tablecloths, chandeliers; underneath, the thousand monkeys at their slot machine typewriters, none of whom are compiling the works of Shakespeare. Perhaps that's what grandeur is, or romance – wilfully choosing to accept someone else's curated version.

On a couple of tables at the side of the hall, are a few stacks of copies of my memoir. They look small compared to the bank of tables used to prop up the lanyards and sponsor packs. Kit stops to pose for a moment, while cameras flash, before walking away as if we don't know each other. We don't know each other.

Seconds later, my phone vibrates. It's Kit.

what the fuck is wrong with you
truly, what the actual, actual fuck

There isn't any point in pretending not to know what this is about. Hovering behind the tables, the piles of retail units with my face on them, I write:

Kit, I am really very sorry. I should have kept you informed. Please, if you can be patient, can we talk about this later? Come home and we can discuss it.

Music plays, with great force and ersatz feeling. There is a human-sized, Oscar-esque gold statuette, next to a temporary wall bearing the names of major sponsors. Nilsson is there, of course. Film feels so meaningless, at this moment – so disappointing to try and turn yourself into an idea.

"Is that you?" says a voice. It's Mandy Lo. She is wearing a dress patterned like a dot painting. "Hey, I got your memoir! Thank you so much for thinking of me, your publisher reached out to my publisher... sorry I didn't have time to give a blurb. My schedule is so hectic... heard on the grapevine you're up for something big tonight!" She blows away. There is a red carpet, but it isn't very good.

My phone vibrates. It's Kit.

there is no 'home'
there is YOUR home
i never lived there
it's fucking over lol

"Can you just take this for us," someone says, and I smilingly oblige as she angles her body. "No... er... thanks, can we just try that again." I try again. A door swings open; a clamour of people is visible in the foyer. The hunger for proximity, pressing into the doorway.

My phone vibrates.

no but let's talk about this
seriously
what did you think was going to happen
you, personally, are going to save the refugees
congratulations saviour

The guests have started to pour in – there is so much noise, and so many people. I am relieved – in the anonymity of sound, my own internal disorder becomes less legible. I write:

Kit, I understand this is very distressing for you to learn, and I admit to my part in not communicating earlier. I'm upset too. In the long term, please believe that this is really the best choice for us, and for our working relationship.

Someone jolts the corner of the table. A few copies of my memoir fall down, and as I bend to retrieve the dog-ears from the floor, an usher comes to guide me to my seat. He does this in an impersonal way, as if interacting with a quantity. Sometimes I like to be manoeuvred like cattle.

My phone vibrates:

oh
oh, I see
'our' show
it's 'ours' now?
ha ha
NO
don't tag me in your mediocre alt-history opera for guilty liberals

Drinks come around. Speeches are made; there is also food, which no-one touches. Kit is supposed to be by my side, but they're not there. And then, horrifyingly, they are – desire turned into fear like a glove inside-out, they have appeared with the assistant, who they brandish before me like a shield. Smiling with technocratic expertise, the assistant withdraws me from my seat and manipulates us both efficiently into place, my arm around Kit's shoulder. Picture. Picture. Picture.

Kit's gone again. I type:

Kit, this isn't you.
I know you're upset, but there's no need to communicate so hatefully.

We have reached the televised portion of the ceremony. Best New Reality Show. Best Background Extra Child. Best Under-25 Supporting Actress In A Documentary Concerning Backyard Renovation. The MC speaks with an intonation that is too large for any of our real feelings. I get up to find Kit, but someone shushes and pushes me back down.

My phone vibrates.

what the fuck lol
'this isn't you'

136

how the fuck would you know anything about that
have you ever, in your life, shown the slightest interest

Human figures moving past. The suits are mediocre, the dresses uglier than usual this year. A young woman moves past carrying a totebag, rigidly and asymmetrically shaped against her body's sleekness – is that the fashion now, some mixed formal and informal trend? There is a feeling of dishonour I associate with weddings and live music. Perhaps this must always happen when one gestures towards what is boundless and infinite – a sad reversion towards what is so inevitably drab and logistical.

My phone vibrates.

let me make this clear
i don't owe you anything
i don't owe you shit

My phone vibrates.

anyway I am done with this
have a good one anyway <3 best of luck with it

My phone vibrates.

you haven't created anything
you haven't made anything interesting in years

There is too much noise in the room, too much stimuli. My emotions unable to converge on a single point. I write:

And you have, O star of TikTok?

If you want to talk about honesty, I wonder if you'd care to share what kinds of conversations you've been having these last few weeks, with Alden Park. While living in my home – living rent free, I might add.

My phone vibrates.

'a lifetime achievement'?
'don't spread it around'?
what is there to embargo?
no-one is waiting
you are a zero
an absence
you were gone before I knew you and you're totally gone now.

My vision blurs with grief. An odd, retrospective emotion – where you are brought, for the first time, into contact with ugliness in a place hitherto known as only beautiful. It isn't lovely, the experience of seeing someone for who they are. Already I miss the sweet, intoxicating rush of romantic belief.

My phone vibrates.

you don't have any talent
i never watched to the end of any of your stupid films
god, you have a fucking ego
you are the easiest person in the world to fool, I swear
i mean whatever, we're done here

My phone vibrates.

your work is shit
take care x

"If you'll follow me, now," says the usher, and we move to the base of the stage, the stairs. As we pass the pile of books with my face on the cover, I notice that my features seem oddly flat – that my face seems flat, more than one would expect even on a two-dimensional representation.

I write:

Kit, I'm glad to hear your feedback! For my part, I have been creating original, well-regarded work – work which doesn't rely on my appearance, I might add – since before you were born. I don't require your services to pursue what avenues of exploration and creation I am capable of, as opposed to venal, mindless climbing of a careerist ladder. Go well.

"Can we have your *full* attention, please," says the usher.
My phone vibrates:

yeah doesn't look like im gonna have any luck getting you to be honest about what u did and what the fuck u are about. i mean what else did I expect from a mediocre maker of just fucking boring, incomprehensible – sorry 'experimental' films. ha ha ha ha. well it's been good working together, yeah it's been some really good times. nice to know u x

How many times, when we were first working together, did I used to beg Kit to tell me what they were thinking. Under the guise of artistic necessity, pawing and prising at the closed box of their essential self. The distinctive look Kit would give me at such moments, compassion and withdrawal. In the face of my unshielded need, filthy as an open wound.

The Nilsson men are gathering on the stage, sponsor-representatives. The future closing in, snapping shut like the lid on an air-tight container. I write:

Kit, that is enough – I have had enough of all this, now. I simply do not have capacity to message you back and forth, ad infinitum – I've already spent enough of my time and capacity on this exchange. Don't think more is going to be productive. I've done my best to shield you but there is really a lot going on, you are not the only stakeholder in this, trying to balance needs, ideas, priorities with different people on both an artistic level and the financial/ interpersonal responsibilities we all have here. Might seem 'trivial' to you but there is a lot going on I think about as well, in the broader environment – trying to facilitate different conversations – be that about technology, climate crisis, flows of refugees, of capital, funding sources more widely, how we can act on that with what small responsibility we have, in our little industry. I've done my best to be patient with you, but my capacity is running out – not sure where any of this is going to go. Have done my best to communicate in a civil manner but my time, my capacity is not infinite, and I'm also rather busy, right now – both in my ongoing role as an artist, and more importantly, broader trends in the world which we both have a responsibility in, and towards – I simply don't have time for this, at the moment.

My phone vibrates:

are you saying you don't have time to be nice to me because of *global warming*

"And the award for Lifetime Achievement goes to…"
And I am there on the stage, I move smilingly towards the podium. We are standing there arrayed, the Nilsson men and I – from this vantage point, I see the girl with the totebag approaching. I sense, rather than directly observe, the look of plastic shock on the MC's face as she steps, uninvited, into the purview of the TV cameras. Breaking into our mis-en-scene. Her hand is in the bag, I can hardly see at all through the scrim of my own misery, I do not understand precisely what is going on –
And then I do, at the exact moment I no longer have the power to prevent it. The girl is peeling back the metal tab. She is opening the can, she is jerking her arm to deliver an arc that curves towards my head. And then it's on my face, on my two hands, it is smeared down my front and over my creased pants. It feels like a judgement, like confession, an unburdening of truth. It feels like tragedy, or farce; it feels like tomato, which it is. It overwhelms my capacity to feel anything at all. It is soup.

Chapter 30

"So, you've changed your mind about accepting the sponsorship from Nilsson," says the rich guy. "Well, then. I see."

"I see," says the assistant.

I don't say anything.

"I can't say I didn't have an inkling something like this decision was coming," says the rich guy. "Unfortunately, the time-window for that particular opportunity has now passed."

"Time stands still for no man."

"Time is like a river."

"That's exactly what it's like," says the assistant.

"Nilsson was very keen on entering into a partnership with us," says the rich guy. "However – just last night, as it happens – I received word that they have signed a deal with an alternative production. *Dumplings with Darren*, a new streaming-only mini-series by Mandy Lo. Follows a group of multicultural young Australians share-housing in bohemian Melbourne suburbia. Exploring their differing, yet authentic connections with their diverse heritage and class positioning. Still at the pilot stage, but it looks like an incredibly promising work. Word on the grapevine is, the *New Yorker* is offering to do a feature."

"Mandy is so talented," says the assistant. "Her work is thought-provoking, confronting and comforting. Love this for her."

"It was quite urgent for them to find a reliable creative to work with. Especially given the recent... er... *unrest*, at the offshore processing centres."

"Awful, isn't it."

"It's very sad."

"All those poor people, it truly makes my heart break, thinking about what is happening to these innocent families, still, rioting is never productive, is it?"

"It is not."

"Do you know, I had a chance to read Mandy's pilot. In the opening scene, there are not one but *two* Asian-Australian characters. Amazing, what she's doing in this space."

"Incredible! our world is changing, so fast and for the better."

"Just *existing* is resisting, Mandy says."

"She was in Forbes' *40 Under 40* as well. Oh, by the way, how is your memoir doing, numbers-wise? Getting some good sales?"

I don't say a word.

As I am heading out the door, the assistant stops me. "Wait," she says. It occurs to me we've never spoken alone before. I don't know how it's possible to so vividly dislike someone you barely know. "I heard about the latest developments, between you and Kit. Have they told you their whole sob story? The abused little child, boo hoo hoo. You know, that director – that man – he assaulted me as well. Followed me into my room, and then, well, who was I going to tell? The grand high vizier of Hollywood? No, I don't expect to be looked after in this industry... that's not my way."

And I wonder if, like Deirdre, I am only able to detect human pain once it is smeared across my shoes.

"No, it's not my way to make a song and dance out of these things. But when people started talking, *I* certainly believed. At the time, somebody certainly reached out to Kit. To request that they not work with – not rehabilitate – that director. 'It's been my lifelong dream.' Did Kit use that line on you, as well?" An abbreviated laugh, like the assistant's smile. "I do admire you, though. Your principles. And you know, we were all very sad to see what happened to you at the Gala. Such pointless, unempathetic, degrading, juvenile, reprehensible behaviour. After you'd turned down the Nilsson contract, too! I suppose *they* weren't to know that ... that is why I am for peace, I reject all forms of violence. There is collateral in every conflict. Always the voice of some innocent, crying from a tower. Of course, *I* support protest, but soup is never the answer."

Chapter 31

Did I mention how Kit is lovely to me? Did I mention their capacity to leave tracks on the deepest landscape of myself. And how the knowledge of falsity makes this feeling even truer. The habit of desire doesn't recede in the face of betrayal, even ugliness.

The thing about shooting for TV is you do not shoot in order. The first scene of the story is not the one which you shoot first and the last is not the last. Thus the final piece of work Kit and I will do together is an incredibly interstitial scene where Kit runs through a corridor, looks out a window and says, "Oh no."

The thing about shooting for TV is that after today I probably won't be doing it anymore, not for a while.

There's an atmosphere on the set – everyone knows that they're going to be out of a job soon, and – though they don't know it for certain – everyone has intuited and engaged in sufficient dot-joining to know that it's probably my fault. There's a kind of deliberate, exaggerated deference in response to my every request, inquiry and remark.

"Of course we can try it a bit faster," says the camera guy drily. "Anything you want." Even the 'you' sounds hostile, and normally he wouldn't say something like 'of course'. He has a chip on his shoulder because he thinks he's not respected enough as a technician. He is right, but that doesn't make it any less passive aggressive.

Kit runs experimentally, a step or two, and tremors move through the soundstage floor. Should have taken the money from Nilsson earlier, perhaps it would have been better constructed. Mostly it's mild reverberations rather than structural unsoundness, but the state I'm in makes it feel like everything is amplified by oscillation, Kit's footfall down through the pine floor then up through the temporary walls. The lighting blinks while the rig bobs its head, the fittings moving up and down.

"Is it supposed to move like that?" asks a technician.

"Ah, fuck," says the camera guy. "They didn't build for winds like this."

And here's the thing: no matter how much you earn or do not earn, what awards you win, how many seasons you last without being cancelled – so long as you work in this industry, you will always be humiliated. Because in the end you are working for your life and other people are only dropping in for the entertainment. No viewer's life is ever changed by a piece of work as much as that work changes the lives of the ones who produced it. I am so tired of needing and wanting other people so much more than the reverse.

Kit bounces up and down on their heels and the whole structure shakes again. I look askance at one of the assistants who shakes her head. "I don't like how this looks," she says. Kit comes over to stand with us, deliberately avoiding my eye. It's strange how we can be here and not looking at each other, and yet I am so aware of what Kit is doing in this moment. Every pore of me is aware of them, how they are standing, how they are feeling, the resentment and the woundedness and yes, still there, still the desire to impress. They are more real when I'm not looking at them than most people who are standing before my eyes. They will be real to me years after we have parted.

"Let's just get this over with," says the camera guy.

Kit flexing their hands, absent and present all at once. Two tracks of mind, the craft and the expression. Control and release, the having and the withholding of feeling. You can't look at a goodbye while it's actually happening, it's like looking at the sun.

I say, "Once more and then we call it."

Kit meets my eye. Things we don't need to speak. Strange, it's like muscle memory – the personal relationship can devolve but the professional remains. Our work outlasts us, it exists without us, it doesn't need us at all. When we are gone, Kit and I, it will walk the earth unencumbered by the desires, the demands of our inconvenient selves.

Kit runs into the fake corridor. And there is a tremor, lights slash suddenly through our vision, beams of light from the fittings that are loose. A noise passes through us before we hear it. A piece of the rig has come apart and fallen. And then walls fall in on walls, and there are pieces on the ground, and Kit is on the ground, and figures are crowding in and pushing away, all anger and confusion. There is no understanding, only reaction. Nothing is resolved.

Chapter 32

"Oh my God," says The Rat, looking at their phone. "Something's happened."

I look. The world washes cold.

"There's been a shooting," says The Rat. As if I can't read it for myself. "Fourteen people dead. Someone's been arrested."

Part Three

TIME PASSES

INTERCISION I

In Philip Pullman's *His Dark Materials* trilogy there is the concept of a daemon, a spiritual projection of self which takes animal form. Usually the animal is lovely and a little elusive: a mink, a lioness, a bird. While you are still young your daemon can shift shape, but as you grow older the form of your daemon becomes fixed. The ultimate expression of intimacy in this world is to lay your hands on another's daemon.

The idea of a self outside the self, a communicative being that is you but also other, recurs in Kim Stanley Robinson's science novel, *2312*. Swan, the gendershifting protagonist, has a qube (quantum computer) implanted into her brain. Swan and her qube, who is named Pauline, engage in banter, backchat and conversation. Pauline is a companion, not just a tool or an enhancement. When Swan's friend declares his love for her, Pauline responds on her behalf.

In real life, Kim Stanley Robinson has said he does not believe quantum computers will ever gain true consciousness.

In *His Dark Materials* there is the threat of intercision, a process used to separate a person from their daemon. This is an act of violence beyond words, a horror that exists beyond the ordinary dimensions of experience.

There you are, all stretched out and without shape. Tubes coming out, a silhouette without body. Lies! It can't be you! It smells like hospital here. Of specificity drained from a human person. Doesn't matter what you did in your past life.

I hate seeing how the ordinary persists, how doctors still get to go home. How can you drink coffee when the world has ended? Stop the clocks syndrome. I could go home I suppose, but home doesn't exist. I'm trapped inside where nobody can help me. I am a stateless person. I suppose the comparison is offensive, I don't care. Let me have my metaphor, it's all there is.

Sleep sucks in this place, it doesn't feel like sleep. Pain is so much, it changes the form of everything, but doesn't have any meaning.

I don't know what I even want, the blinds are drawn down on desire. I want so much, yet this accomplishes nothing. The physical, universal proof of our uselessness. By which I mean to say: love is an emotion through which you may occasionally enjoy yourself. It does not do things.

But where does experience go, because it must go somewhere. It cannot possibly be that we worked together, created beautiful things, and that all that is left of this living relationship is dead art. I am refusing to accept the truth of a physics which allows this to happen. Actually I don't have thoughts right now. I just want this not to happen.

In the *His Dark Materials* universe, it is possible to survive the process of intercision. Loss of, and separation from, one's daemon. But what ensues is a diminished state of being.

Chapter 33

It's been raining again. Near where I used to live they have to call the kids off the ovals at the schools, 'cos of the lead that's seeping up through the soil. I have measured out my life in episodes of peripheral neuropathy.

My parents, who I don't want to talk to, keep on trying to ring me till I give in and answer. They wish to be reassured I have not been in or around the dirty water (my mother read an article on heavy metals leaching through the grass). They don't even want to talk about the killings, which is fair enough.

There is this moment when you walk into a vigil and everyone around is vibrating silently with grief. At the same time, to be honest, you are also a little bored. Because you are still present and there is still the logistical stuff, such as bringing extra water and even sunblock because, after the onslaught of rain, the sun has returned to launch its ozone-poisoned UV attack on us all. Also, honestly, this is not the first time we've been in this situation. Every now and then a fascist murders people. That is not a surprise, that is just how it works. What kind of world did you think you lived in, anyway?

On my way to meet Tamina I bump into J. We hang around awkwardly for a bit, not saying much. Then Robbie and Stickie show up, and bit by bit the rest of the crew.

"Oh no," says Stickie. "I forgot to bring a sign."

There are some Trots hanging round at the pedestrian crossing, trying to sell some papers. Making it more pedestrian by their presence, ha ha ha. Their headline says: HOW THE MYTH OF 'SEX WORK' UPHOLDS CLASS SOCIETY. I have to hold Tamina back from getting stuck into them: "I'm sick of these clout-chasing fake communists. Glomming onto someone else's tragedy, trying to sell their shitty merchandise at a memorial." Robbie has also brought some posters, but he doesn't put them up.

The day is so beautiful. Unbelievably blue skies, a couple of clouds that only serve to amp up the perfect blueness. We are all dazed. That the world can so casually lay out its delights. I do enjoy being present in the world, and I want to stick around for the unfolding narrative. There's so much stuff I don't think that I'll have time to ever know.

"There he is," says Leaf. "All hail the lord high master of the communists, salute."

SwiftBoi, king of the Trots, is getting up there on the steps. Megaphone in his hand, all eyes converging on him as per usual. Bigger than I remembered, also newly beardy, like a discount-rate Che Guevara.

"What a gronk," says the Rat. "Who put him in charge, anyway?"

Tamina shrugs. "I think he just put up a Facebook event quicker than anybody else. By the time it got noticed by people who know he's a dick, too many people had already clicked 'attending' to call it off."

"Ah, that fucking grifter," says Kabir. "Inshallah this speech is short."

It isn't, though. At first it's not that bad. Starts off with boilerplate stuff about capitalism, extraction, exploitation, etcetera. I mean, it all makes sense and the audience (or at least our pals) are primed to agree. So I guess it doesn't matter that much about the exact words. But there's this weird dynamic, where he does these big Marxist quotes to get out the feels ("We have a world to win!"), but then kind of slinks back into the boringest, most futile kind of shit you can think of, namely asking people to join his new groupuscule, the Australian Industrial Workers of the World (A-IWW). Which was formed, I'll tell you now, after SwiftBoi got kicked out of the normal IWW – either because he had shit politics, or he couldn't stop abusing people – hard to tell. I mean, imagine putting the word 'Australian' out the front of your radical formation. That's how you know you've got a real internationalist on your hands.

"We will not be murdered like this. We will not take this lying down. We will not see men and women, little children… murdered in your imperialist wars, wars for lithium. Because it's all the same, all over the world. Ever since the genocidal invasion of this continent… settler-colonialism… the ruling class…"

Goodness, this is heating up. You have to admit, SwiftBoi does know how to psych people up. I hang a lot of shit on the guy, it is easy to do and it functions as an ingroup bonding mechanism to be honest. But when you see him up there on the steps, really getting on the momentum, arms raised in this huge 'V' towards the sky... I have a theory, SwiftBoi's political trajectory has occurred less through deliberate strategizing than some butterfly-wing, sliding doors type activity. It occurs because he has adopted 'world socialism' as his domain of practice, but he could just as easily have been a preacher, a miracle healer, an anti-vaxxer, or a shaman. Even a musician like Brian, if he could actually learn how to sing. Any scene where he can access the romance of the roused-up crowd is like catnip for him. People should see through it but they don't because they want to believe, they want to think that another world is possible and he has convinced him that believing in him and his crew is synonymous with that. As opposed to a pyramid scheme or a sex cult. By the time they realise, they are so burned out and disillusioned, they may never participate in so-called 'radical' activity again. Oh well. Have to learn these things on your own timeline, I guess.

You think of all these things, and at a certain point you know you're just distracting yourself. Because the reason you are here at this memorial, this vigil, is because an eco-fascist has committed a mass murder. The dead are dead because they were immigrants and coloured like you mostly, here for the cash and only that, the kinds of people you would have considered yourself very much better and more politically enlightened than until such time as a white man chose to gun them down. This has happened before, and it will happen again, and no-one will protect you and quite possibly no-one even can. It will happen again and it is happening every day in a thousand different iterations, the sick mutuality of the arms-length dance of the state and the extra-state fash, and the cops and the guards with a thousand different faces, gates and camps and the different co-ordinates of the distributed violence. You hate how shaky you feel and how preachy you sound, and how there is no other way to name it really, the banality and constancy of violence. What is wrong with you? Why must you moralise and analyse? Why can't you look at death? All you can do is be here, showing up for the murdered, who don't exist anymore except in grief and in the past.

We are walking again. The pace is glacial, which somehow makes the sense of loss seem heavier. We are slowed further by the marshals in their bright orange jackets, corralling the disordered sections of the crowd into the middle of the road. Even in my exhaustion I feel irritated – can we not grieve outside the lines? Some of them are wearing T-shirts with the Green Revolt logo.

And then someone bumps into my back, hard; I stagger to the side. A voice yells, "What the fuck!" A car is pushing through the crowd, a white 4WD. The crowd parts raggedly, like cardboard torn along the perforated lines. Shouts of anger and some screaming; a couple of people running alongside the vehicle, banging on its sides before it turns out of view. Someone's been bowled over; but no-one seems seriously hurt. Someone else shouts, "Don't escalate!" A line of cops interpolates itself; the marshals turn to them gratefully. Eyes of the cops dark with sunglasses. We're moving on, we're off the road, we're at a park and a statue and a square, we are out of the path of vehicles, the event goes on.

And now it's time for a speech and it's that fucking Senator, Katherine K. Kelly. "As Australians, we say No! – to violence. As Australians, we say No! – to hatred and division. Why have we failed to invest in countermeasures against this extremism which poisons our harmonious community? That's why, in unity with the Coalition, we've chosen today to pass the National Infrastructure Act. Preventing these terrible acts against our beautiful, diverse Australians, literally building a future for this country…"

"Fuck that bitch," says Stickie in a contemplative tone.

I want to call someone, I don't know who. Just to hear someone tell me I am missed. Is it so wrong to make other people's grief be about you?

SwiftBoi has somehow managed to mount another set of steps. Again he's droning on – this is really obnoxious, I don't get why he thinks we need to hear from him again. Asking us to stay calm, no need to escalate, blah blah blah blah. People from Green Revolt are here as well, holding up their big banner: 'PEOPLE BEFORE PROFIT: NON-VIOLENT ACTION FOR CLIMATE'.

"Such a colonial mentality," says Tamina. "What did any of those people ever do for solidarity with Mob."

The Rat says, *sotto voce*: "What did *we* ever do for solidarity with Mob?"

But then something amazing starts to happen. Kids in the crowd are starting to get less and less deferential. They didn't come here to hear Swift-Boi, they came to show solidarity with the murdered. So they all start to ignore him, milling around turning their backs to him as his monologue goes on and on. Not as a big deliberate gesture, more because he is just not the most relevant thing. SwiftBoi of course cannot bear this and starts to talk louder in this whiny, aggro tone.

But the young people don't care. They are parting and reforming, they are converging round the statue which has become an impromptu point for collective tribute. Laying down their own personal mementos and memorials. There are candles in jars, signs saying REST IN POWER. These signs and offerings change the nature of the space. All of us organically understand that this is now a place of mourning. The crowd's energy becomes focused on this collective grief, not SwiftBoi up there on the steps.

"Oi, look over there – is that the cops going over near Scott and his crew?" asks J. "I'll go check it out."

"Interesting," says The Rat, with J out of sight. "Is Scott OK? Do you think we should go and back them up?"

"No, I don't think so," says Tamina. "It's more important for us to be a part of the memorial."

I don't say anything at all, I don't need to. Eddies of people converge round this central point of our aestheticised grief. I drift away from the others and go to stand near the memorial. Flowers piled up on top of one another, candles in small jars. Small points of light and heat and our unbeaded strings of words. Surrounded now by loss, I take a moment in the company of what is no longer there: hopes for myself and other people; hopes I used to have but don't hold onto anymore. I give a name to my fears: that I won't get what I want, that there are losses which will not be remade. At last, I can allow myself to be afraid.

INTERCISION II

OK but: now they say that you will live. And now, more than ever, I am forced to confront the precise flavour of my own uselessness. Seeing you unpackaged like a broken toy. What's the point in all these words? Comfort for only myself, which is no comfort at all.

And now I'm back and life is more than just a blur. Being present – pain hijacks you in a way that it can't when you're half taken by sleep. All I have now is anger, resenting everything and everyone. I am actively becoming my worst self. Why me? Why now? Just let me go, ffs.

Hospitals suck. That is one thought which I am very willing to get behind. They are the worst places in the world to get better. Actually, they are the worst places in all the world, full stop. Always too much light and chlorine smell and fucking beeping. 'For your own good.' You lose rights over yourself. Hands and feet. No epitaph. No shoes.

Is it so wrong to think of myself at a time like this? The loss of you, not as a tragedy for you or for the world, but for myself. This separation feels like death. Nothing of what I have loved about you is expressed in this particular moment.

It's obscene to think like this, I know. Two nations: of the well and of the sick. And there is no passport to cross one border to the other. Oh yes, I know. Doesn't mean I stop feeling it.

And now, bit by bit, I start to recall. About me, I mean. Sorry, I know you wanted me to say that I thought about my friends, former lovers, my parents, life, whatever. Oh, but I haven't and don't. And probably won't for a while, sorry. Not fighting on anyone else's behalf. Next breath, next breath.

Short list of things I don't care about right now: memories of my childhood; places of my youth; people I have known and have yet to know; sex; the universe; tarot cards; geography; sparkling water; the stream of consciousness; people I might yet grow to love and miss. I don't care about anything, I just don't want to feel like this.

I miss you horribly. I wish I could just care without needing to insert myself, but there it is.

I don't know, man. I'm just really tired.

Is this going to be my sentence? Living on in this unmagical world without you.

I don't know, man. I just don't know.

Chapter 34

After the vigil, we go back to Bombadil's zine place together. Well, why not? It's what you do when you want to keep being together but don't have a reason. We also pick up some drinks, which some might say is disrespectful so soon after a memorial. But, not drinking won't bring back the dead.

Actually, to be honest, drinking is what we do because it's what white people do as their default, therefore everyone follows. And no matter how many or how few of them there are in the group, this is how it goes. I'm getting a bit tired of how we all follow along with their aesthetic, cultural and entertainment preferences. Why is everything about them all the time? Is this identity politics? Maybe I'm just in a shit mood, it's been a long day. The social volume goes up, sometimes I find this charming but today, I can feel another fight is coming on, it's like the Benny Hill soundtrack. Doot doot doot. Another dust-up, more arrests. And then we will all panic and fundraise and go out to support the arrested person for their day in court... and then what happens? Absolutely nothing, or the same thing again. Like we are beautiful lions with nothing to do except rattling our cages.

Someone is playing the news footage of the vigil on their laptop. "How did they get us from that angle?" Stickie asks. "I didn't see any cameras. They can't have gotten pics that clear from the helicopter, surely." I see my own figure, masked and filmed from the side. Weird, my way of walking looks so awkward and familiar. To see yourself through someone else's disembodied gaze. Odd, how close and clear the picture is – I don't recall any cameras. It looks too good to have been shot from a phone.

"Look at the car," says J suddenly. Reality rewound: the vehicle pushing through the people, figures scattering with screams. "Kind of weird, the way it's driving – like, fast enough to scare us, but actually still kind of slowly. And the windows are tinted, so you can't see who's inside. Do you know what... I reckon that's a cop, who's been sent to frighten people. Or

159

just to send a tacit signal, you know, to vigilantes and stuff."

"Oh, for goodness' sake," says Robbie. He seems exasperated, large. "Everything that happens does not have to be a conspiracy. It's probably just some chud who got frustrated in the traffic."

We fall quiet; I am feeling very tired. The footage cuts away from the main rally to a vox-pop with someone from Renewable Jobs Alliance. A guy with a small beard and moustache who somehow still looks clean shaven, explaining how this shows national security needs to be funded better. "The government has dropped the ball on this, they need to step up. Our security agencies are getting politicised, they don't have the tools they need to deal with far-right terror. Tragic incidents like these threaten our multicultural harmony, our diverse Australians…"

"Oh shut the fuck up you fucking greenie imperialist battery fascist," mutters The Rat.

"Oh, come fucking on," says Robbie. All evening I've had a vibe of tension rising between these two. Living together is not working out so well it seems. "This is not the moment for purity politics, mate, you know me. I'll be the first to organise against actual fascists, Western chauvinists – I've been doing the work on the streets for years. Stickers, posters, propaganda, just don't call everything fascism." Robbie's face is turning pink with emotional exertion. I'm not sure if it's more uncomfortable for us to see or for him to experience. "Kind of an insult, actually to people who deal with actual Nazis, like the AFF. Of course, *I'm* ACAB, always will be, but who else is going to deal with a threat like this, if not the cops. That's why I suggested a temporary, tactical alliance, just this once – with our allies in the labour movement, people who build the tech for our security. Who also happen to be people in our communities, who need jobs."

A burst of music from next door, over the fence, apropos of nothing: 'I won't back down', by Tom Petty.

"Mate, I kind of disagree," says The Rat. They are smiling very widely, looking almost nauseous. I've never seen them take someone on like this. "Like, just because it isn't a spectacular event doesn't mean it's not fascism.

Stuff like what's just happened, stochastic terror, obviously it is bad. But the biggest killer is still the State, when people drown, or die of heat, or in prison, or whatever."

Tamina looks at us all levelly and says nothing.

"Look, mate," says Robbie. "I agree with you, I do. But let's be realistic, cops are here to stay. So is the State. *I* want to abolish Australia, of course, but right now I'm just trying to do the best I can, as a white guy. I've read Noel Ignatiev. The framework of the race traitor, yeah, that vibes with me. But speaking here and now, I never promised you a revolution – just doing all that I can, based on our own material conditions."

"Fascinating," says J. "I'm not a theorist, OK. But from the perspective of – what's the word? – being 'material', if you end up homeless 'cos some green energy corp sent its goons to kick you off your land, you still don't have a home. Or if you get killed by a drone – people don't really care if the drone that shot them got made by unionised workers." Downing his drink with a certain flair. I can never tell if he's trying to be dramatic, or if it's just how he moves through the world in a general sense. "Oh, and Robbie – mate – that seems like a pretty big thing to admit, that you're not looking for a revolution."

Bombadil smiles with poorly concealed nerves. I've never noticed it so strongly before, how much he needs other people to like him.

Robbie is amping up. Looming over us, belligerent. "Really? Really? I have one goal here, mate. Getting shit done. And, look, you can talk all the game you like, but right now the State is here to stay. And, I don't mind saying it, social democracy is the best hope that we've got. Do I like it? You bet I don't – always was, always will be a communist. But if this sort of shit is what you're going to call fascism … well, there's a lot of fascists around here." He, too, skols his drink.

The Rat is smiling dissociatively. I want to speak but there is nothing I can say. My words build up inside, black text scrolls through my head against a blank white background.

Krissa says, "Surely we can maintain a distinction between Western democracies which, for all their faults, allow us to exert some real change through the political process. Compared to real fascist regimes like Russia, Iran…"

"Bit xenophobic, much?"

"What is 'real' to you, Krissa? I – " J starts to speak, then cuts himself off, then begins again. "Just because the killing gets externalised to someone you don't care about, doesn't mean that it's not real."

"Very clever," says Krissa. She looks fidgety, uncomfortable – guess J was not supposed to be here. No-one could stop him coming to the memorial, I suppose. "Very, um, stirring, J. But just because you are invested in a particular grudge, doesn't mean everything that is bad in this world has to be retroactively defined as fascism."

"What is fascism to you, J?" asks Stickie. That bright innocent voice of hers. She really wants to know.

J says, "The bullet to the chest. State as a hunter. A unity of government and corporations. The razor fence that is covered in bloody clothes. A screw who shoots you in the back. Break out of a jail and they send you back then somebody makes art from this and sells it to your captors, for their edification. Throw you against the wall and strangle you and say that they're the one in charge. Blood on the wall in the copshop and in other cells, someone spends the whole night screaming. The zone of terror. The predatory state."

"Oh don't be so emotive, please," Krissa says. "It doesn't help your cause."

"Oh shut the fuck up," says J.

There is a silence.

"Don't you dare threaten my wife," says Robbie.

"I wasn't threatening your wife," says J.

"He wasn't threatening her," says Stickie humbly. "He was being an asshole to her, it's different."

"Hey, why don't we all take this down a notch," begins Bombadil.

"Don't you dare threaten my wife," Robbie repeats. "Mate, don't you fucking dare."

The Rat starts to hyperventilate and twitch.

Tamina says: "J, I think you've had enough to drink."

J turns, disbelieving. "Are you serious? All that shit, and *I'm* the one who has to clear out?"

"You were threatening a woman," Robbie interjects.

"You heard me," says Tamina.

Bombadil doesn't look at anyone at all.

J looks around our group for some support. Finding none, he's disbelieving. "Oh, alright then. Fucking fine." He seems both deeply enraged and sort of sullen, like a child. "But y'all should know, what with this kind of bullshit, I'm not always going to hang around this place, you know. Not always going to come back."

"I think we'll risk it," says Tamina drily.

J picks up his jumper and phone and starts to clear out. No-one speaks and the sound of his shoes on the floor and the scrape of his chair is almost comically awkward, against the backdrop of the newsreader's voice continuing to describe the vigil/ rally/ protest. When he gets to the door it's stuck and it takes him a few tries to wrench it open. Once he is out it swings back and almost clicks into position, but not quite. Leafie has to get up and pull it from the inside so it's closed again.

We sit there not saying anything.

"That man is obsessed with identity politics," says Robbie, shaking his head. "These imported American frameworks."

The Rat says, "What are you going to Badiou about it?"

"What?" says Tamina.

The Rat breathes deeply, giggles randomly, and looks around. "This is fucking stupid," they say at last.

"What did you say?" says Tamina.

"This is FUCKING STUPID," says The Rat.

Everyone goes quiet.

"Look at us," says The Rat. "Look at the *state* of fucking us. We don't know who we are, we don't know what we are doing, we just ping round in a circle. Talking to ourselves as if we are the only people in the world. Like, take a word like 'anti-colonial'. We don't work with Aboriginal people, we don't have Aboriginal friends, we don't have SHIT to do with their organising – they are not in our spaces and why would they be? We are all fucking ANNOYING, they don't want to be around us, probably just being around us would make them a worse person. They are on TikTok and stuff, they are making shit that is genuinely FUNNY, while we are circulating reheated memes based on the shittest possible art from the nineteen thirties. Suffocating in cultural forms which were already mouldy decades ago, and then WE WONDER WHY NOBODY NEW EVER COMES TO JOIN US. I mean, yeah, there is 'security culture' but there's also a difference between 'security' and NO-ONE EVEN KNOWING WE EXIST, at least SwiftBoi has friends and knows people who aren't just his friends, like not to co-sign tankies but like, have we ever actually defined the term. Also, do we just pretend that ALL of them are tankies, so we never have to deal with a Black person who hasn't pre-established that they will show fealty to our bullshit? Right? Don't fucking pretend that's not what this is. Fuck my fucking life. No-one has a job – like, what do we have to say to working people – no-one here has responsibilities. Like some of us are 'poor' in that we don't have much money, but no-one is 'poor' 'cos they're supporting other people who actually NEED their support, and that's a big fucking difference. We are not a movement, we are a sub-cultural fucking SCENE. We are a revolutionary cult group, lmao. And here's the thing, we just keep cancelling people for absolutely no reason, or some stupid reason, or we never cancel someone at all even though they are literally the worst person in the world, a useless toxic abuser – it's like a fucking pendulum that swings between 'cancelled' and 'enablement' – everyone white is racist and everyone of colour hates themself, you might as well just ask them at the door, I mean if they liked themselves they wouldn't be running with us, would they? They wouldn't hang around. That's why they're all fucking white people! It is LITER-ALLY A PRECONDITION OF BEING HERE THAT COLOURED

PEOPLE DETERMINE THEMSELVES TO BE UNWORTHY OF LOVE! And there is no ideological UNITY, not discipline but UNITY, when what we truly need is an ideological HEGEMONY of love! 'Cos if you, an individual, come to a conflict with 'love' but everyone else comes with 'destroy' and 'hate', you are going to get FUCKED and this is known as a 'first-mover disadvantage.' Can you see how we are going straight to hell? We just can't keep on DISPOSING of each other, we are not PLASTIC SPOONS, we cannot exist without an IDEOLOGICAL HEGEMONY OF LOVE..."

The Rat breaks off, with a long shuddering moan that subsides into panting, crying, and a loss of bodily control that leaves us all embarrassed.

"Control yourself," says Tamina. For once she looks shaken. "How dare you. I've never heard – I've been doing the work, this work, for years. Where were you, at the Tuggerah detention centre breakout of 2005?"

The Rat laughs dementedly. "I was born in 1994," they say. "So, at the time of the Tuggerah Detention Centre Breakout, I was eleven. That's where I was. *Being eleven.*"

There is a pause.

"Get the fuck out," says Tamina.

The Rat begins to weep, and I put out an arm to comfort them. "Leave them," says Tamina.

"No," I say. Everyone is staring.

"But Tamina," I say. My voice is trembling a bit. "The Rat is really upset, let me just take them home." No-one else will say anything, they won't even look at my face.

"Bro, this is not a game," Kabir says to no-one in particular.

I don't know where the words come from, I just know a decision is affirmed for me. A line, from a movie perhaps, beats round my head: *this far and no further.* "Tamina," I say. "I am going to take The Rat home with me. We are going to go – I am going to call an Uber so that we can go home together. That is what I am going to do."

Tamina's whole bearing has become very still. "You've been warned," she says.

I put my hands around The Rat and start manoeuvring them out the door. As I pass Tamina, she gives me the smallest of nods; Kabir also gives an apologetic little shrug. I am surprised by the delicacy of the gesture. After a moment, Leafie and Stickie also come, so it is the four of us on the roadside. The night feels enormous, uncharted. The empty street spilled out before us.

"Come on," I say to The Rat. "You can come home with me."

Chapter 35

The Uber driver doesn't say anything but just plays some loud, high energy but not-too-bad pop, which is a relief. When we get home Stickie and Leaf just sort of smile at us awkwardly in the kitchen, then go into their room. In the presence of their gentleness I feel new, disassembled and raw.

The Rat and I are left together in the lounge. "Do you want some tea?" I ask. Trailing dissociatively, they follow me into the kitchen while I end up rummaging through the leftover boxes from former housemates, some of whom haven't lived in this place for years. I look to charge my phone, then see I must have left the charger at Bombadil's zine factory. Always something left behind in the grand departure.

While the kettle is heating, The Rat starts to cry and I let them do that for a while. "Sorry I'm so fucking useless, it's just, Tamina, she is like, you don't understand, it's been like this for years. She's your best friend and then she turns on you and then the others turn on you as well. Everyone's so fucking scared, it's doesn't run on trust, it runs on fear. Fuck me I just can't fucking go home, I hate that place, I hate my housemates, fucking Robbie doesn't even close the pack of chips once he's finished eating it. Can't even leave my room, I'm so sick of this shit. I can't remember when I last… oh, those are nice, those are really nice." Looking through the tears at one of the old posters: DIVERSITY OF TACTICS, DIVERSITY OF TARGETS. "I remember that one, I think I helped to paint – God, that must have been years ago."

At this point DojaCat!!! comes thumping into the house. "Oh, hi," she says before crashing into her room. Sometimes it drives me mad how she can't do one single thing without making a bunch of noise. Then I remember she just got out from the psych ward. There is so much human need. There is just so much need, and we never have the time to properly consider it at all.

The Rat is still talking, full speed ahead. "I keep saying… I just… it's hard, I don't know where... don't even wanna hang shit on Robbie, like don't get me wrong he is a total cunt but he is also a good person, like, he has copped some shit from the State, I don't even blame him for liberalising, really. Tamina fucking hates me, so does Robbie now as well, just because I won't just hate people who they hate as if it's really political when it's not, it's just a fucking excuse. 'Security culture', don't make me laugh. Even with SwiftBoi, yeah, he's a cunt but it's fucked up how they all laughed when he got arrested. You shouldn't celebrate that shit, it is fucked up. Circle jerking forever. They say that SwiftBoi is a snitch but I don't really believe it, I haven't seen the fucking evidence, it could just be some shit that people say. I mean 'we' are all supposed to be part of the collective but what is collective about it, who the fuck is 'we'? Security blah blah blah blah blah. Have you noticed if you challenge their authority, suddenly everything is all about 'security'..."

I let The Rat talk it out. The light is still on in Leaf and Stickie's room. Something about the moment, the unformed tidal wave of feeling, brings me to the edge of panic. It's like I don't really know where I end and other people begin. It does not feel safe, but we are never safe. We have to look after each other, even when everything else is not all right. The sky is full of smoke – there are fires again. The future keeps on coming for us, despite our best intentions.

I let The Rat talk it out, make up a bed for them and then walk out into the acrid evening.

Chapter 36

The zine-palace looks empty by the time I get there but the front door is unlocked. I creep inside using the torch on my phone as a guide; somehow it would feel like a small violation to turn on the main light. I see my cable plugged in where I left it, in the corner. While going in to pick it up I am startled by a sound – someone else is in the building. A yellow tendril of light is creeping out from the closed door leading to the back room. I bend over for the forgotten charger, then freeze.

The door swings open, and the light widens into a bright wedge. It's J, carrying a cardboard box of empty bottles. Our eyes meet for a moment; his expression is closed. Feeling caught out, I scamper off.

When I get back to my house The Rat is curled up on the couch, cradling one of the cushions. They look a lot more relaxed than when I left them behind, less manic, "Hey, guess what," I say. "When I went back to the zine palace, no-one was there except for J. I think that he stayed for a while after everyone left. Cleaning the place up."

"Hmm," says The Rat. "Why is that weird?"

"Well, I don't know. It's just, he said that he was leaving ..."

"Words words words words words," says The Rat, yawning in my face.

Tired now, I go into my room to sleep. Before I turn off the light, I pull the box of zines out from under the bed. Such beautiful titles. Words words words words.

I touch the box lightly with my fingers, then push it back under the bed and the next morning The Rat is gone without a message or a note.

'To Hate The Ones Closest To Me'

I came across a story about an Italian soccer player which
I found deeply affecting, in a complicated fashion. He was
a Black man and all the things you think would happen
to him as part of a soccer club had happened – audience
members, teammates chanting the n word, giving him
bananas as a 'joke', etc. He couldn't really let himself think
about it. Even looking back in hindsight he could barely
speak. He said that he tried not to think too hard because
the game and team were his true passion, it had been
that way since he was a small child. Thinking too hard
would put him in a place where he would be isolated from
those he loved, with whom he knew there could be no
reconciliation: 'to hate the ones closest to me'.
An intimate, unsolvable betrayal.

Lorenzo Ervin, author of *Anarchism And The Black
Revolution*, writes: 'The radical socialist and Anarchist
movements have the same kinds of figures of colour, who
perform the same role. They are slaves on the white radical
plantation, have no voice and tolerate all kinds of abuse,
just to be part of the movement… It is an unhealthy,
oppressive relationship'. It is both funny and tragic the
extent to which this drives him mad because Ervin is not
an armchair radical. He was a Panther before he was an
anarchist. He spent 15 years in jail, nine years in solitary,
was drugged before his trial, hijacked a plane to Cuba to
avoid the KKK. They extradited him to Germany where
he was tortured for a week. He has been targeted by
fascists, state and extra-state, and has delivered his share
of violence against fascists as well. Yet judging by this piece

of Ervin's writing what really keeps him up at night, what drives him truly up the wall, is the behaviour of white leftists. Genuinely, he has devoted more words to how racist they are, how annoying their music, than being subjected to actual torture while he was in prison. 'The progressive plantation' – it is an amazing, spot-on rant. You should read it.

Fanon writes that colonised people have 'muscular dreams': 'I dream I am jumping, swimming, running, and climbing... I burst out laughing, I am leaping across a river and chased by a pack of cars that never catches up.' It probably isn't right to call myself only, or primarily, a colonised person; I am a coloniser too. But I too have dreams where I am flying, where I exceed these bonds... you have to understand, it's been my life. It's been my whole life. You can't just unlive your whole life. Can't just go.

INTERCISION III

So what happens now. Pain beginning to release its iron hands. Time exists again – a future that feels like a threat. So, then. What next.

And now I inch back to the land of the awake, world in colour again – growing technicolour palette of available feeling. Humiliation, that's the one. Hate to see you see me in this condition. Used to be cute as hell, don't you remember? The way I could move, writing out a whole poem using my little body. Now look what I've become, a broken puppet. A tool which outlived its usefulness. Probably still think of me the way I was before. Oh, please don't look at me. Don't visit.

And now you're back, and here I am a little sheepish. Extreme feeling, or feeling in the presence of extremity, is always like this I think: clarifying but embarrassing after the fact. Note how I said *always*, a subtle slippage to imply that I have been in this place before. I am very experienced and very clever, nothing is new to me, I have always the capacity to name and to catalogue an experience. Need to remind myself that though you are everything to me, I still have my history. Still have other options. Even if the main 'other option' right now is sinking back into an endless treading and recycling of said history.

OK but: I really don't want to see another sunset. Sometimes the blinds go down on desire. I really don't want to meet new people, reconnect with beloved friends. They say that everything is beautiful if you really look, but I don't want to look. I don't want love and I don't care about politics. From here the sound of water or of cars on the highway is impossible to tell apart.

That is fair. To be clear, I'm not actually grieving for you, at this moment. But rather for me and for an idea of us. Nostalgia for things which haven't even happened yet. I say yet as if there was ever a thing to call a future. As if there was ever an us. Where does experience go? Grieving all out of order since I only started once it became clear that you were going to live.

What is the point of pre-emptive mourning. Each love story a preview of mortality.

What a sickening thought – that I care more about keeping you, or retaining the vision of me and you, than for you living, existing. Image over the reality, concept over the person. Doesn't stop me from feeling it, though.

No-one knows anyone as anything other than a concept or an image, this is known.

Fuck, that sounds bad.

It is, man. Just admit it.

Well, if you must.

Sometimes I hate you, I admit. Hate you with the jealousy the sick are entitled to feel towards the well. Yeah I know that it's gross. Parading my powerlessness so you just have to suck it up because I'm hurt. But so fucking what. This really sucks. If I can't have love, pity will do.

I wonder: did I ever tell you about the different places that I've been. Harbours and bakeries, boardwalks and ruins. Believe it or not I used to be young, back when that was even possible. As a result of this extended backstory, my dearest Kit, you are not the only one who I have existed in relation towards, at one moment or another. A lot of different people have been special for me over the years; and I have also, on the occasional occasion, rendered myself special unto them.

This is what happens to you, when you are with someone a very long time: you build up a shared lexicon, a joint narrative of experience. It is memory outside of memory, a repository of self outside the self. Then when it ends that repository goes, and your entire reality changes. Language itself is taken from you, any old narrative can be true. It is through these experiences I have learned that experience is real, and that it evaporates in the time it takes to check the weather. Tears in rain, etc.

Yes but: you still have your words. You have your tools. My tool was my body, and now that's fucking gone. People wanted the dance but now who the hell wants the fucked up dancer. I mean I'm pretty but I was only ever that on someone else's behalf. What even is my job. What am I to you, a ventriloquised sex doll?

A container for dreams. Channelling other people's truths. It's art.

Or else, a trashcan for their trauma. Acting and re-enacting other people's pain, their processed and re-visited ordeals. So cathartic for everyone else and so sad for me.

When you put it like that, it sounds kind of exploitative.

Hey, don't worry about it. It's you who gets caught up on the whole morality trip, not me.

So what do we do now?

I don't know. I guess we will have to find a different way to be around each other.

And how to be in general?

Yes, that as well.

Chapter 37

I've been trying to get started writing for a while. Tell you a bit about my day. Because, you see, I am so fucking tired. And to be honest, I do wonder whether it has all been worth it on some level. I mean whatever happens, life goes on in mostly the same shape. But underneath the surface, everything is different. Or not. You can tell that I get existential when I'm nervous.

It's around this point, when I am really starting to spin out, that my mother calls. "Hello ___, don't you remember you are coming home for dinner?" Feels so weird to hear my government name. "Your father is not here, he will be away on a site visit. But Vishaal will be there with Darshna, also your cousin Ishan – you remember Ishan. Please dress properly, none of this gender stuff. Remember we are family, that is my only wish. I may not have much longer on this earth, but I am still your mother."

Not gonna lie, I kind of loathe my older brother Vishaal. But maybe it will help to be somewhere else, just to change the texture of my day. Sometimes it feels there has been so much experience I do not know where I can possibly keep it, and sometimes it feels like not much has ever happened to me, at all.

Riding on the train, I observe a gradual increase in the concentration of Brown people – waiting on the platform, getting on and off the carriage. The fact that they are travelling with each other, too, as opposed to at the edges of larger groups of mostly whites. Listening to their own music. Going to and from their jobs, talking on the phone. Not like the suburb where I live, or Bombadil's zine-palace. Where for all our differences, we are all really the same kind of people: unemployed or with an NGO job or something menial, but also having government support, or access to it and the support of their friends. We aren't really responsible for other people. Well, that's me, I guess. I don't really know how to fit this into my sense of things in general.

"Hello darling," my mother says, when I arrive. Kissing me on the cheek. "Your face looks so dark. Have you been wearing sunscreen? SPF 50 and up? Please, please, cover your face when you go into the sun. Do it for my sake, as your mother. I will not live forever. That is my wish, for after I am gone."

Being back at my parents' house is a trip, to be very honest. Disorienting to land in a reality which feels so real and so normal and yet has not been normal in my life for over ten years now. The TV in the living room on as usual; on the table there is Bhuja mix, and a can of wasabi peas, and my mother offers us a selection of Coke Zero, Fanta Zero, Low Sugar cordial and No Sugar Sprite. Far, far too many gadgets – apparently my dad has installed a Smart Energy system for no discernible reason, except that now the doorbell and fridge can co-ordinate. Cool, I guess. There is a carrom board leaning in the corner, which I haven't played in years; also a big tub of idli-dosa mix which I haven't bought in ages since I don't live with people who would eat idlis or dosas in such quantities as to necessitate such a purchase. And an Instant Pot, obviously. Each of these details functions like a rope looped round my feet so that I am yanked forward, utterly face-planting, into the past.

"Oh, hey there," says Vishaal, who is older than me. Looking at my face like he is going to smirk right through it. He only wears black, grey and white; this is modelled off Steve Jobs. Asshole. I hate him so much.

"Hello ___, nice to see you again," says Darshna, Vishaal's wife of four years. She is very pretty. She is also very pale; of course my parents both approve of this without overt comment. Darshna is a practising psychologist. Though she only moved to Australia as an adult, she has acculturated fast and now wears a lot of Gorman.

"How is your practice going, Vishaal?" my mother asks.

Vishaal spreads himself out, like Toad from the first X-Men movie. "Well, it's been hard work. Done a few 80-hour weeks, which is kind of ironic – I thought the point of radiology was that you could see patients in your own time, not theirs. But, since I've branched out into my own practice, I understand that it's part of the deal, you have to work like a dog, at least for the early years. Although, we're almost at the point where we'll be looking to hire a new specialist. That will bring its own difficulties, of course – having to deal with more people."

"Terrible," agrees my mother. "Dealing with people is the most stressful, the most tiring, the most inconvenient. The worst."

Vishaal nods and gives an expansive sigh. "Absolutely. Absolutely. But I'm confident that with the kind of base we're building, both in terms of clients and our staff, we will pull through… and you, Ishan. How are your studies progressing?"

My mother is wearing this expression of sick worship, like she wants to kiss Vishaal's ring, or lick his face – I know that this sounds gross and mean but I don't care. The thing is, she has never really forgiven me for not being Vishaal. And I have not forgiven her for not forgiving me. What tangled webs, etcetera. Ishan straightens up, nervously. "Oh, yeah, it's going well. I got a credit average last semester. Also been doing some extracurriculars – I got elected as co-president of the bumper bowling society, it's cool."

To be honest, Ishan is a pretty good guy – he is very photogenic and twenty-one years old. Always wearing the same uniform of white shirt, jeans and gold chain because, why not? Last time we talked he was developing a scam to steal food from UberEats; trying to make sure that it wouldn't screw over either the restaurant or the driver, which I thought was quite touching. While we are talking, his phone rings – as he swipes left on the call, I see that the background is a scene from *Avatar*. Ishan loves that movie. "Anyway, next year I wanna go on exchange to Amsterdam. Although one of my friends, she went and did one of those aid work trips to Bangladesh. She went there, like, a normal person, and came back wearing this massive bindi… I think it's a feminist thing," he adds contemplatively. "Got nothing against it, totally I'm all about the social justice, stay woke."

"Social justice, hey," says Vishaal superciliously. Whenever Vishaal speaks I straight away have the impulse to disagree, no matter what he says. "I mean totally, yeah, I support all that stuff. Old man like me, some of the kids these days, I can't keep up. They get offended at everything – I just wanna tell them, I'm not a bad person, you know? What do you think, Darshna?"

Darshna gives a little laugh, shaking her bangles, but doesn't choose to venture an opinion. "Oh, Darshna, did you remember? The sweets you brought, in the refrigerator." At this point we take a conversational break for Darshna's home-made gulab jamun, which are frustratingly excellent. I think of The Rat as I drink the syrup in one gulp, like it's a shot.

While we are still recovering from the sugar, Darshna turns in my direction. "And what about you? How are things going at... erm... the toy shop?"

Vishaal's wife confuses me. By rights you'd think I would hate her; I both don't and kind of do, for reasons that are not really her fault. To start off with, she is beautiful, well-educated, smart. She's also really nice and is probably a good person. But whatever the reasons Vishaal stays with her now, I think I know why he wanted to be with her at first and when I see how she is FAIR and everyone keeps remarking how she is FAIR and my mother looks at me and wonders, even just with her eyes, why I am no longer FAIR, it really shits me to be honest.

I say, "Um, work's going well, yeah, it's fine I guess, it's going fine."

"Your own private practice, wonderful!" says my mother. Expertly diverting attention from my failure to achieve. "And Darshna, how are you doing with your Masters? You study so hard, at the same time as work and looking after the house. I could never have managed. Life is so much more stressful for your generation."

"Darshna is so focused, isn't she?" says Vishaal. "Inspires me to get all my mess together – take my word Ishan, you should find yourself a girl like her, when you finally move out of home... hey, do you have a girlfriend?" Ishan goes red and laughs embarrassedly. I'm pissed off at Vishaal, even if I know he wasn't actively trying to be a cunt at this particular moment. He just goes round being a dick and lets the chips fall where they may, which is usually in a pattern not conducive to happiness for me.

"It's not easy living away from your parents," my mother interjects. "Every day there is so much stress. Cooking and cleaning, a big headache all the time. Ishan, you are lucky, you must be very thankful to your mother and father. If not for them, what will you eat? Cheese sandwiches. Apple. Muesli bar. Cereal."

Ishan looks existentially disturbed as he contemplates the hypothetical. At this moment his phone goes off again: it's the song from the *Avatar* sequel.

While Ishan is silencing his phone, Darshna says, "It's very hard! School and work and taking care of the house all at the same time. But in one semester, I will be finished with my Masters… it will be a big relief. Vishaal and I are thinking we can take a holiday once the business is set up with the staff. First we must train them properly. But then, we will go somewhere wonderful together… I've heard that Indonesia can be cheap for the snorkelling, very nice." I don't like the little public-private looks Vishaal and his wife are swapping across the table. Grosses me out, physically speaking. At the same time, I don't like the extent to which I am put off, which probably says something about the essential pettiness of my emotional response. There are so many questions and they all make me nauseous. Who we want and are wanted by. Who we want to be wanted by, and how.

"And what have you been up to, ___?" repeats Darshna. Busting me out of my reverie. Oh God, she is not going to let this drop. "Have you thought any more about taking an internship with Vishaal? If nothing else, I would enjoy the chance to see more of you. We always have such interesting discussions."

My mother, who perversely gets off on denouncing my failures in public, interjects. "If only ___ would accept this! But ___ is so extreme in personality. No moderation, no discipline, that's why you don't get anywhere," she goes on, addressing me directly at last. "Even when you were a child, I always used to say, you have so much potential. But you squander it. You have to be the change you wish to see in the world. Not just arguing and fights."

"___ thinks she's so smart," interjects Vishaal. Wow, thank you for the commentary, dearest older brother. "Too much social justice lingo, not enough job. Nothing ever gets tested. Thinks she's better than us sheeple who have to go to work every day, ha ha."

"I *am* better than you, dickhead," I say, *sotto voce*.

"It's *they*, not she," says Darshna. Shooting Vishaal a censorious look. Oh Darshna, I do believe you will see heaven.

"Language, please!" says my mother. "Dear God, why have I been punished with such children. It is my dying wish, to see my children to get along – my dying wish, and yet you both deny me."

"Where's Pa?" I ask.

"He's away on a site visit," says Vishaal. "Don't you remember? Or is it because you don't have a job, you think nobody does? Do you care about anyone besides yourself?"

"Every day your father is shortening his life," my mother says. "Working so hard 24 hours per day, seven days per week. I have looked on the internet, there is severe metal leakage in this area, lead contamination. I have dreams he will get cancer and then die."

Ishan looks longingly at the carrom board and says, "Have you seen any good movies lately?"

"Don't be upset, ___," says Darshna, putting a hand on my arm. "Your mother only says this because she loves you. And really, what is the point of all this activism? What's the purpose of saving the world, if your own mother cannot tell you when she is hurt? Recently I read a novel, it was very deep. It said the reason we survive as a species is because we care more about our families and our friends than anybody else – it is enlightened selfishness. And the author is a communist! I have started to read much more – sometimes it is good to have, not just entertainment, but a deeper theme or thought. Not just Ishan's blue person movie." Ishan once again goes red. Well, fuck you, Darshna. I thought you were the nice one. Don't be superior about *Avatar* – yes it's super problematic but isn't everything, the whale rips off the arm of the coloniser guy and it flies across the screen. No, let me rephrase – the whale rips off the arm of the WHITE AUSTRALIAN coloniser guy and it flies across the screen IN 3D. Say what you like about James Cameron but the man puts his money where his mouth is, he is a sailor truly in love with the sea. He went to the bottom of the Mariana trench in his own submersible. Did you?

"See, this is why you should marry a humanities major," says Vishaal. "Darshna understands it all, a simple doctor like me doesn't get it. Books, movies, music, arty stuff – to help us escape, but also to help us understand reality, to live within the world."

I say, "We know that operating within reality does not mean that we accept it; we're operating within it so that the reality can be changed. For what we did as revolutionaries is abstract, but the people are always real."

There is a pause. "What change would you like to see in society?" Darshna asks kindly.

"I want to see dead imperialists."

The silence which ensues is pretty funny if you think about it. "There she goes again, talking like an extremist," Vishaal says at last. Addressed to the company at large. "Of course, I sympathise with this desire for escapism. If you think that I enjoy working seven days a week... capitalism isn't fun for me either! But when you say things like that, you only give more fuel to those who write you off as being silly extremists. The police, government, companies, professional people. Sensible people – none of us believe in violence."

"Yeah?" I can feel my blood pressure rising. "Well, it believes in you."

Vishaal's eyebrows go up. That habitual supercilious little twitch. God, do they inject you with the smugness, is it part of the graduation ceremony? "What do you mean by that?"

"I mean, Vishaal, fuck your 'belief'. Violence exists whether you believe in it or not. People die when there's no water, people drop dead of heat in the fucking street. Is that a question of 'belief'?"

My mother's voice like a damp rag over the conversation. "Please, ___, don't swear. Why am I cursed with such children, you are shortening my lifespan. You don't understand these things, you have been here since you were a child... over in those places, life is cheap. Even my own friends, in my own hometown – of course I am sad, but you must see, some of these people have so many children. Four, five, six, not two or three. What can we do, there will be too many of them like that. You want to play the hero, one person cannot change the whole world. But, you know, we can be there for each other as a family, you are always welcome here with us, your mother and father, you know that we are here, eating much better food, you will save so much money on the rent."

I don't know why it is this exact moment which sends me over the edge. It's not the exact words which do it – you see, nobody wants me. Not as I am, not even in my so-called home. They would prefer I was a totally different person. Well, I can give them that, I guess. I walk away from the table.

I walk away and I go into the back garden and it's there that I start to cry. It's only meant to be a moment but then I keep going, really getting in there, all the accreted adulthood washed right off. I am crying for the wave of death that is already here and there is no-one here to stop it, it's so much, we don't even think about it anymore. I am crying with the impossibility of telling the people I love the whole truth about myself or about anything at all, things most important are things that can't be shared and I don't know how to fit all these experiences into a whole that would mean something other than bullshit, it is too incongruous, the variegated stories of my life. I am crying because in another world Vishaal's wife and I might have been friends but in this world I really fucking hate her and it's not even her fault, it's just the way things are set up. That she is stupid. That she will always be stupid, for reasons out of her control, and that I will show no kindness nor forgiveness for this involuntary stupidity, the consequences of which are so grotesquely and unevenly distributed. I am crying for the dream or the sick trap of revolutionary love, so many people have written of this, Malcolm X and Joy James and Frantz Fanon, and what would it take, what would it take to make conditions which would make such a connection really possible in the world, between two structurally different people. And why do others not write of this, is it because they don't care or they just haven't even noticed. How so much of our praxis consists of begging for love from those who will never ever give it to us. How pathetic this is. How we still want it. I am crying because this world is just violence for some people and ever contracting circles of normality for others, but what the nice people call 'violence' isn't really that, it's just the inversion of authority, and when authority does violence their little eyes glaze over and all that is left is a blurry view of their own self-regard. They are so insatiable, these people. It's not enough for them to be useless, they actually expect to be praised for it. They need infinite and constant applause, to be told each and every day that their narcissism is not only forgivable, it makes them better than other people. Will you remember each other's birthdays in the fucking plantation. Will you be nice to your friends on top of a pile of fucking skulls. I hope the wretched of the earth show up on our doorstep, like, next week. I hope that they take what is theirs by force.

I am crying because you do these things, you take these risks and make these decisions because you wanted to fight white imperialism and yet you remain a little bitch to your friends, basically. Always subservient to their priorities except that now you've become a soldier in their redemption narrative, not only the dirty work of doing the work but you took on their white guilt for them as well. In their fucked-up way my family has been there for me and I have not been there for them. Do you understand why I have to believe my friends and I are better than other people? Is it possible to punch imperialists and be a fucking coward? Here I'm not Brown, I'm just skin-coloured, how did I get to this point, describing myself in the same terms as a swatch of paint. I bailed out on the diaspora kids because I am better than them, I mean that is what Tamina says, I have to tell myself they're liberals and not the real radicals because if they are just as good as us then why did I give all that up and who the hell am I? I am crying because 'we' are supposed to be the special ones, the collective narcissism of The Resistance (TM) who I have determined to be My People (TM) and I sometimes have an inkling they, by which I mean we, are not very good people at all. I am crying because I want my family to stay the same forever, I want to be completely different and still have them to go back to, you can't step twice in the same river but I'm the one who has changed and therefore it's my fault, I am the one who fucked up this particular river. Social movements got the best of me and the ones who loved me best got what was left over and now there is so little of me left to give to anybody, going forward.

I am crying because I have worked so hard to construct this thing that is called 'myself', this shitty work of art which is the outcome of the process of self-creation all those of us who are 'radicalised' must go through. No-one is born to this politics so we have to construct ourselves as if we were artists but we are not actually artists and that is why the selves we have constructed are such an ugly fucking mess. Sometimes things that didn't happen live with you as much as things that did, but then the waters just close over as if nothing ever happened, but it did, it really did and I'm not sure how we are supposed to just go on and live with the unreality of that. I am crying because my friends are so fucked up but paradoxically, given our relationship with violence, these are the only people in my life who I do not regard as being natural born killers. There should have been a place for us to go. We deserved so much more than we ever got and we will never ever see it.

Darshna comes out to find me, puts a hand onto my arm. Of course this sets me off again. She's actually quite kind, is Darshna. Soft, in the way people can be when they've never had to fight for their place in the world or gone against what other people told them they could do; but still, soft she is. So it's an untested softness, but it's still genuine and right now to be honest, it makes things worse, like someone threw me a rope as a lifeline and I just fumbled the rope. I don't care about this stuff, I just want dead imperialists. I want the people I love to see me whole and I know that this is never going to happen.

When I go back inside, Vishaal is somehow still talking. "Please ma," he is saying, "don't listen to ___, don't take the things they say to heart. Darshna and I are so inspired by your story. You are a *perfect* mother. Making a life here for your family, starting your own business – you know, Ma, I think you should write a book. No, really! Darshna can help you with the drafting, there will be a market for it, I swear that I'm not joking. There's a lot of people out there who would want to hear your story."

Chapter 38

I can't sleep and I don't want to. The concept of sleep feels unrealistic for these times. I lie in bed for X hours every night and all that exists in my head is white noise. I am unmoored, drifting from the ordinary co-ordinates of reality.

The day scrolls by and there is nothing to do. Already afternoon and I'm still lying on my mattress, exhausted from not crying. I see a video on Facebook live. Fucking prison guards rallying for better gear. Someone is giving a speech – he has a face like a ham and a self-righteous look. "Coming together across industries," he is saying. "Technology for the front line… the public service… Aussie workers, going step by step towards a greener future." The voice sounds familiar. I look at the captions. It's Mark Miller, the manufacturing guy. The one who did the interview with Scott. Images blink through my brain. I look again.

I look again on my phone and I turn on my laptop. Some adventures on the internet, cross-checking various points of fact. So much I have learned from the Rat and Robbie. It doesn't matter if the latter turned out to be trash – I remember reading once about missionary schools, you might not believe what they believe. But once you've learned to read the Bible, you can read anything. I pick up the phone to message Tamina. Look what I found! Surely she'll forgive me if I drop this in her lap, my abject gift. My resolve flexes away from me like a fish. I put down the phone. I pick it up again, thinking to message J. In the end I message no-one.

Before I head out, I remove the red cord braided through my hair.

When I arrive at the familiar Tannehill street, lined with brick warehouses and silence, the sky is so dark that the black looks like blue. It's really cold tonight, windier than you would expect. My hands are shaking: why am I so frightened? Because this time I made the choice. I'm responsible.

The building is surprisingly unsecured, or maybe not so surprisingly. I guess it's better for them to make it look like there is nothing special, here. I climb the fence and make my way up the fire escape, no, don't look down if you're scared of heights. I'm scared of heights, I'm scared of everything. The night unfurling like a printed scroll.

From the top the view is wondrous, the sky criss-crossed with electric lines. Oh god I love the panorama. The slant of the saw-tooth roofs, and banks and banks of air-conditioners. Yes, that's how you know there's a server – you don't need to cool a normal factory so much. I think about The Rat's old laptop, whirring and slowing in the heat. Is this how I get Legionnaires disease, lmao.

It's so easy once you're up there, you would be surprised. Swing crash and swing. Oh to always be in motion.

And then it's over and I'm shimmying back over the edge, making my own escape into the unlimited evening. Later, it occurs that I should have looked more at the stars. I should have taken the time – these days I hardly see them 'cos of the pollution, though the sunsets are so beautiful. This, too, because of pollution – I want to have them both, the clean air and the sunset. I want to have it all and always be alright. Wish there'd been someone to come with me, but I accept that this is how it might be, from now on. Turns out that when you want to do something honest, it always ends up being something you have to do alone.

INTERCISION IV

OK, let's have it out: what do you actually want from this?

From me, or from life?

Well, both, really.

Oh, I don't know. I know what I don't want, though – I just hate this sensible apportionment of feeling. Morality-based endeavours. I want someone to want me even more than morality, you know?

Coming down from the emotional onslaught(er).

What does that mean?

I don't know, but it feels true.

Feel like I've been living my whole life wearing a T-shirt which says COME HERE GO AWAY.

Yeah, something like that.

Want you to see me, but not to look too forensically.

Look at what?

At my dumb face.

Two of my friends committed suicide and both of them were clowns.

Hmm, fair enough.

Want to be wanted, but not so much I get obliterated.

I will never get over how comfortably normative people slip into telling you how you should be. Like a warm jumper, fits like a glove.

What does that even mean?

I just know whatever I've been doing, it's all wrong. Living someone else's borrowed life.

I haven't even read *His Dark Materials*.

Nor will I. It's OK, I don't mind. You don't have to read everything to steal a metaphor off Wikipedia.

Imagine that you dream my dreams and see things through my eyes.

I don't get the feeling that you've actually asked me the thing you really wanted to ask.

Perhaps I haven't. Which of these describes what you want: love as an affect state, or love as a verb?

The affect state, of course! Actually, I have some specifications. Memorialise me and make me beautiful – isn't that the thing you know how to do? Frame me here and not there.

How would you like me to frame you?

Oh, you know, the usual. Interesting, pretty, mercurial, pretty, lightning in a bottle, turn on a dime. Heartbreaking work of staggering genius, in human form.

I'll do what I can.

I still want more reassurance.

I see. As I suspected. Well in that case, does this help? There is no lie I would not tell, no morality I would not transgress, no sense of self I would not perjure, if that was what it took. I don't wish to exaggerate. I'm not going to pretend I couldn't live without you, clearly I could. But I also know the whole universe would be fundamentally less alive without you in it. Not better or worse, mind you. Just less.

OK... these layers of irony unfurling to reveal a shocking sincerity. What?

The city, any city, is beautiful in the rain.

I still don't really know what you're trying to say, but thanks for saying it.

I thought you said you wanted the truth.

Yes, but not *that* much truth.

How much is the appropriate amount?

Less than one hundred percent, more than zero.

I need to have a dream to hang my sense of future around.

What kind of dream?

Oh, I don't know. It doesn't have to be likely, just lightly plausible.

All right, then. Here's a question. Enduring love in which we both tell the truth and no-one is diminished. Is this possible?

Well, I don't know! I'm just a puppet. You tell me.

Part Four

EVERYTHING THAT
YOU CAN GIVE

Chapter 39

"Brian's been arrested," messages Tamina. "It was a dawn raid, counter-terror squad. I don't know all the details. It's under the Kelly amendments. They don't even have to say what he's been charged with. I spoke to his lawyer – same person who Robbie used last time, she's really good. Even she doesn't know what the hell is going on."

"Oh my God," says Leaf. "Is this the Infrastructure Act? Fucking hell, he could go away for years."

"His brother's been detained," messages Tamina. "Cops were waiting for him – four cars. Picked him up from their dad's place while he was coming back from work."

The silence is the worst part. Well, that and everything else. Terror: just an enormous blank for your mind to fill. Where are our friends? Nobody knows.

"What does his brother have to do with anything?" asks Stickie. "Was it just wrong place at the wrong time? Where are they being held? Maybe we can send him something."

"I don't know where they are," messages Tamina. "Even the lawyer doesn't know. Cops are on a roll, won't tell us anything. They don't have to. They know that with these laws, they can do anything they like."

Chapter 40

"It was messed up and really fucking scary," Leafie says. "I had no idea what was going on. These four guys just came in the front door and started smashing our stuff. The common areas first, and then the bedrooms. Then they went out to the garden and destroyed the raised beds. Even came into the living room and tore down all our posters as well."

"It wasn't cops, was it?" asks Bombadil. "Did you recognise anyone? Did they seem like professionals, or just randoms? Does this mean you've been doxxed? Do you think it was the AFF?"

Leafie and Stickie on the old mouldy couch, holding hands. I want to protect them – I'm ashamed, because there's no reason for me to protect them. Just because they are femmes. I'm also ashamed because I can't protect them. I can't protect anyone, not even myself.

"I have no idea who it was," says Leafie. "I don't think they were professionals, though. They murdered my tomato vines and also my strawberry plants, and kale."

Stickie says nothing but quietly holds her girlfriend's hand. How, even now, can I be jealous of their shared affection?

"Maybe the cops passed on our details," says Leafie. "We'll never know."

Confusion everywhere, we don't know where to turn. Are we safe or are we not? What does safe even mean? Where to turn is so apt, I'm looking left and right, I can't focus on things. I can't sleep, my short-term memory is fucked. My hands have stopped working, I put things down and I forget where I put them. I had a handful of beans in my hand I was going to cook and I lost the beans. I dropped a plate and it took like an hour to sweep up the fragments.

"Just letting you know, they have picked up Kabir," messages J. "The counter-terror squad – believe he's being held in solitary right now."

"Fuck fuck fuck fuck," says Tamina.

"I heard again from Brian's dad," messages J. "He's been held in solitary as well. They've let him out now, still in jail but in the normal part. Screws said it was because the rest of the jail was flooded. Makes you think, lmao. He got beaten up – I don't know how, if it was the screws or another prisoner. It was quite serious – head injuries, apparently. Apparently his dad thinks he should be under suicide watch."

Catastrophe and normality, catastrophe and change. I can't feel my feet, even while I am walking. I keep on losing things – sunglasses, water bottle, hat. I don't have object permanence right now. Can't find things in my room.

"We're gonna get kicked out of here, aren't we," says DojaCat!!!. Finally dropping the pretence she doesn't live with us. "I don't know where else I can go." Without malice or rancour, just stating a fact.

Chapter 41

"It must have been The Rat who snitched," says Tamina. "That's the only explanation. No-one ever vouched for them – no-one *I* trust, anyway. Robbie, I'm so glad they're not there anymore with you and Krissa. The way they disappeared straight after their little brain explosion! Even their old housemate says that they are a liar and unstable."

Current of fear, currents of exhaustion. The creeping unreality of time. Again there are bushfires and you see nothing but smoke on the horizon, air you cannot breathe. And yet the shops are still open. It all goes on as normal, workers from the offices going to the offices to work.

"I heard from Brian's dad," says J. "It was a concussion, pretty fucking severe – took a couple of days for the screws to call a doctor. Hope this doesn't leave him messed up in the head for life."

"I heard from Kabir's lawyer," says Tamina. "Best not to talk about this stuff. Apparently he is not going to be let out of custody for a while."

Catastrophe and normality, catastrophe and sense. Why is my body like this? My heartrate accelerates at weird times, my swallow-reflex doesn't work. Why can't I sleep properly? When I go to bed, all I can feel is white noise.

"Brian tried to hang himself," says J. "Luckily the cord broke, he is still alive. Physically he is OK, according to his dad, just a bit messed up."

Catastrophe and normalcy, catastrophe upended. I don't know what is happening, which way is up and which is down. A life goes into fragments, a self into retreat. The stock market fluctuates. A brick goes through a window and life goes on regardless. Don't know how many times I can reconstruct.

"It must have been The Rat," says Tamina. "Why have they gone? Where have they fled to? Who spoke to them last? No-one else could have dogged us like that. I never trusted them, the little shit."

"I haven't spoken to The Rat," says Stickie humbly. "But, Tamina…"

"I agree with you Tamina, it was The Rat," says Robbie. "They were always fucking weird to be around. Emotionally incontinent. And it happened just after the night that they melt down – when they went home with you." I pull back in surprise – things must be bad, Robbie never addresses me directly. "That must be how The Rat got hold of your address."

I say, "They always knew where I lived…"

"It was definitely The Rat," says Tamina.

Catastrophe and normalcy, catastrophe and change. I guess it's time to pack my bags and go looking. Queer-friendly household, no pets. Queer-friendly household, must love cats. Queer-friendly household, vegans only. Queer-friendly household, all groceries shared. Queer-friendly household, must do chores. These sad simulacrums of a family. What is a commune? Does it even exist? That's how it is with state violence – always something to wait for, but nothing to react to.

"Stickie wants you to know that she was sexually assaulted," says Leaf. In a small voice. "When they came and wrecked the house. She wants you to know 'cos it explains some of the trauma but doesn't want to have to tell you directly. So, now you know."

Catastrophe and normalcy, blood in my eye. Blood on the walls. What was it like in prison, Kabir? Will you ever get out to tell me? God, all my art is so bad, I don't know why I even framed this. Take the removable hooks down from the bedroom wall. I hope they haven't left a mark – the agent will be, like, 'that's your whole bond now.'

"Has anyone managed to check in with Brian's dad as of late?" asks Bombadil. "I haven't been able to reach… also, have you been in touch with DojaCat!!!? Haven't seen her round the zine-stop these last few days."

Catastrophe and normalcy, catastrophe and loss. The point of change; a fulcrum on which the future turns. Do you know how it is with state violence? Can't even think – go to the edge with a rope tied round my ankle. Pull me back if I fall in. What day is it today? So shocked to go outside and see the sky is blue. How far I've been removed from my normal reality.

"I told you not to speak to The Rat," says Tamina. "You disobeyed my instructions. They were always unstable and just fucking weird. You should never have trusted them."

"You disobeyed me," says Tamina. "That night after the memorial. I told you not to talk to them. You should not have let that little, scab, traitor piece of shit inside your house."

"Hang on," says Bombadil. "We don't know…"

"No, you listen to me," says Tamina. "Who else could it have been? That little bitch, I told you not to talk, I told you not to have anything to do with them. Go off. Just get out of my sight."

And that was it. I never saw or spoke to Tamina again.

Chapter 42

Silence falling on you piece by piece, like blinds being drawn throughout the house.

Stickie and Leafie aren't the kind to turn things into a big conflict. And to be honest, they didn't even tell me what Tamina had said to them – I wish they did. You could just tell from how they looked at me, those two can't lie with their faces. Awkward while we were still living together. After we got kicked out, they just went dark – changed their handles online, didn't even tell me their new address.

Robbie, surprisingly, seemed a bit torn, but then he blocked me on Telegram, Signal, Instagram and Facebook and some others did as well. That was how I came to understand I had been expelled from the formation.

Shortly after we all moved, Brian was finally let out on bail. He didn't answer my messages asking if there was something that he needed, any way that I could help. I don't blame him. There is nothing you can say into a silence.

Kabir got denied bail a few times, the trial's been delayed again, I don't know how it's going at the moment. There's not much else to say or do about it, at this stage.

I don't really remember what happened, to be honest. I mean I know but I don't know. It's so hard to explain how cognition becomes when you are not in control of what will happen next. You are there but not there. You can turn away and the thing you were looking at becomes unreal. It becomes undone. It has no permanence.

Tamina put out a post saying The Rat was a snitch and a collaborator, that anyone who kept in touch or worked with them or even knew them was a collaborator as well, and that they and their associates should be removed from all collective spaces. Robbie shared the post and so did Krissa and Scott, so that was that. Mission un-accomplished.

The Rat blocked everyone, including me, and fell out of touch. I was hurt by this but maybe they were just retaliating, who knows. Some people took this as evidence of their guilt, that they had to flee the scene, socially speaking. Someone told me they had seen a screenshot of a post where they said that Tamina was a 'groomer'. That she would use you and discard you; that they, The Rat, were not the first to be used or discarded in this fashion. But I never saw the post or the screenshot, so I can't vouch for it.

Do you know how it is with state violence? They don't actually have to do it, you just have to know that they can do anything. We are not the primary victims of state violence. They held me for a bit; there was blood on the walls but it wasn't mine. I don't want to tell you now what went down because that is not really the point; in the end nothing happened, it was fine. It all turned out fine and I walked out on my two feet and don't you know it. Someone else was screaming the whole night and I don't know if she left the cells or not. They bring the guns and the dogs and the copters and don't even have to use them; knowing what they could have done to you is enough. What they are saying is, if you take us on head-on then we will crush you. Yes I know, and I know. We are not the primary victims of state violence.

One day, just to hurt myself, I went on Robbie's Insta. I saw the latest post – 'SEMINARS FOR SEDITION – NEW RAD READING GROUP'. The accompanying picture showed the seminar leaders – four people posing in a line, their features blurred. What do you have to blur your faces for? It's a reading group.

Even without faces, I knew who it was as I would know them even in a dream: Tamina, Robbie, Bombadil, J. Et tu, J? There was a crowd-funder, too, and a recent donation – a figure with a number of zeroes in it. The donor was the Renewable Jobs Alliance. The title of the seminar was, 'Breaking the Jobs-Climate Standoff'. No, it can't be so simple. You can't unmake the story of my life in a manner so banal.

Here, I bestow freedom on YOU and YOU and YOU and YOU and YOU…

For a while I was sure the cops were going to come back, that it was going to be just fear for me from now on. I waited and I waited, for that moment which divides a before from an after but the cops did not come. Maybe they were biding their time, maybe they lost interest. Or they couldn't find shit on me and gave up. Maybe it really was The Rat who snitched, who knows; maybe they took pity on me, didn't pass so much on, 'cos I stood up for them in front of the others. I'll never know, I guess.

As griefs pile up they become invisible.

I sent so many messages to Tamina – it was just grovelling, really. Wanting for her to understand. Or just to explain why she was so very sure it was my fault. But I never heard back from her and I didn't think I would.

Political relationships are like romances really. They are the bearers of so much desire. And when they end it feels like death.

Tell me, you fucking genius, what would you have done? Should we have been more open with our activities or less? Tried for a mass movement or gone completely underground? Organised the workplace? Insurrected the streets? Oh, you've got all the answers – and yet we're all still here, and we are losing. What was the most frightening part, that you were not in control of what would happen to the movement? That you were never in control of what would happen to yourself?

Chapter 43

In which The Rat, in their absence from our narrative, takes an unexpected foray into free-form poetry

well I seem to be going a little bit mad over here
how did that happen

well you tell me we can't win
i say lie to me, baby—

what if
for every death in custody
they had to pick
a random prison administrator
and hang them in a cell
see you in hell

what if
every time they tear gassed an uprising
we pulled out a random guard
and just beat them to death
still wearing their red hat
imagine that

(lie to me baby...)

well they say violence begets violence
but what if it's a good begetting
like they say about the planet
like they say about sex

spinning between different realities
thinking about violence on the edge of mania
in a room with no floor and no walls
and no door either
well you say that we can't win
i say lie to me baby, tell me it's alright—

Chapter 44

Towards the bottom of my bottomless spiral I drop by Bombadil's place to see the new zines he's been putting together. Piles of pamphlets, photocopy and collage. Orderings of words and image which maybe two or three people will read and digest properly, tops. A once-living culture ossified into a museum of resistance. I feel a deep cringe that penetrates right to my very bones. I can't believe I reshaped my whole life around this shit.

"Oi, don't condescend to my zine-ism," says Bombadil, seeing my expression. "You were here too, not so long ago. Now you've had your glow-up you wanna break out, make something bigger than a sub-culture. Revolution something something – very well, you're probably right. But don't forget where you started, you weren't born knowing all that you know now. And at least, you know, I have my own form of *positive* politics, as opposed to just kicking the shit out of people, even if they are imperialists. Oi, did you ever talk to Bridget? She's had some pretty interesting experiences around this."

I say, "I'm not sure about Bridget. There was some problem, Tamina used to say that she was homophobic…"

"Are you serious?" Bombadil looks at me incredulously. "Bridget, anti-queer? That's not the reason. It's because she used to date Tamina's ex."

And I stand there wondering if literally anything I've been told has come even close to the actual truth.

"Oi, don't worry about it! I'm sure you'll have lots of little moments of minor delayed realisation, over the coming weeks. Yeah, I heard about what happened, you got excommunicated from your little groupuscule. Well, it's very sad. I'm sure you're going to miss your periodic Live Action Role Play expeditions…"

I like Bombadil, but sometimes he can push things way too far. "Bro, give it a rest, OK? I know you have your detached joker persona, but this is some real shit that's going on. Brian got the shit kicked out of him in pre-trial detention. He got a concussion that's, like, brain damage maybe. While you're giving your talks, your fucking crowdfunder, your reading group. And Kabir – "

"Yeah, yeah, whatever." A quick flit of grief across Bombadil's face, followed by a reassertion of joviality. "Going to jail doesn't mean you're not LARP-ing. Come to that, being *dead* doesn't mean you weren't on a great big LARP. Wanna hear a secret? This is the true meaning of the LARP: it is what it is, but it's also a stand-in for something else. What did you think you were really accomplishing, your little band of friends and ex-friends? Knocking the shit out of a few fossil executives? Putting the fear of God in them, or whatever?"

"Um, yes? That is literally what I thought I I were doing..."

"Exactly! Face it, you guys kicked a few goals. But you were not going to undo this whole rancid reality, which is what we really need. Well, let's be real, *I'm* not gonna undo capitalism, imperialism, eco-fascism, the settler state. We know no singular act by our own hand can accomplish this, but we live as if it will. That's what I mean by the LARP."

"But... "

"Oh, I'm not saying it's useless, doing what we do! I should say, doing what *you* do – honestly, beating someone up is a lot more real than whatever some wordy dickhead like me is ever going to accomplish. Just remember that we are all just pixels, and we do what we can, and that is all. This is the price of our dreaming. We are living in relation, not just with cunts that we know, but with the cunts of the whole world, past and future. Each victory attained is but a shadow of the victory we seek, and each violence we experience is but a microcosm of a greater violence. Even and most especially when we are winning, we will always feel helpless because we are. Helplessness is the difference between one's desires and the plausible reality, so we who want everything for everyone will always feel entirely inconsequential. And yeah, I see that you're just starting to ask questions, and you have a right to hate me. Probably one day, when you've thought it over a little bit more, you will. I know that I am not what I had promised you to be. Just remember that I did what I could, and if some of it is messed up, well, here we are. And you know I'm just a guy, and I have my friends, and you have yours, and I've taught you what I know, and maybe you don't need to come around here anymore."

"OK, yeah, but Bombadil?"

"Yeah?"

"Was it worth it?"

Bombadil sighs. Turning over his massive stapler, pretending to fix something. What is it with this guy? Never in a million years will he allow you to perceive a true emotion, but it's all there. "You can't compare, it's not the same units. Anything that we won, it was all incremental. Tiny fractions out of the lives of millions. But what we lost came in pieces from our lives. Of course it wasn't worth it. It never was." Straightening up, handing me a small card with a square of words: *To Sanction All Revolts, All Desperate Actions*. "Oi, you should take this. Just had it printed, thought it might appeal to you, personally. Keep it somewhere safe, OK? Oh, and FYI? Take a look at this footage."

I look at Bombadil's phone, where a video is playing. 'Disturbance at Mount Helliar Correctional Complex'. A blur of smoke, jagged shouts on the audio. Young people in the prison yard with dirt flaring at their feet. Some of them on the roof, bracketed by barbed wire. Shirts off, an act of display. *We are alive and we are here.*

"How terrible," I say dutifully. "Solidarity with all uprisings."

"No, no," says Bombadil impatiently. "Well, yes, but also, *look*."

"I don't see anything."

"*Exactly*," says Bombadil. "Where are the drones? Normally you'd have those evil little shits buzzing around, shooting pepper-balls and stuff. Pretty weird, isn't it? Almost as if someone's been messing with them. There's a lot of technical stuff that goes on to get those fuckers working. Something which may render them increasingly vulnerable, ever since they moved the data centres to Australia…"

"How interesting," I say. "Probably coincidence. An unrelated fault.

We'll never know…"

"Indeed, we will not!" Bombadil shakes his beard and laughs. "Oh yeah, and did I mention? There's a snap action happening tomorrow. It's in Redfern, I think. Some annual dinner or fundraiser featuring the board of directors of Nilsson Security, your old mates. I can't make it – too old actually, my knees – but would you consider putting in an appearance? Oh well, and hello, look what the cat dragged in."

I see the figure and I freeze. "Oh hey," I say.

"Hey," says The Rat. "Yes, it's me. You can trust me or you can not. I can give you words and facts and whatever other bullshit but in the end that is what it comes down to. I don't know what Tamina said and I won't ask. And in the end, we do not understand what has happened to us. Things happen to us, and we do not know what they are. That is the essential issue. But I trust you. Do you trust me?"

"Yes," I say.

At this moment DojaCat!!! comes wandering in. She just got on the disability pension; this has changed her life and by extension mine. We are planning to move into a new place together; we are going to install a lead-filter for the pipes. DojaCat!!! is wearing a sparkly gold crop-top, a fake-feather bolero and a pair of gold booty shorts. Behind her she is dragging a baseball bat, brand new with the Kmart label still on. Her expression is doleful in the extreme.

"The Revolution will be a shitpost or it will be nothing," she says, dragging herself into the back room and closing the door behind her.

Chapter 45

A Distributed Dream With No Particular Narrator, Since It Happens To Be
Shared By Many People

You are walking in a labyrinth, Alice in Wonderland style. Hedges are high, you can't see through. You've been in there for hours, all you can hear is the silence. And the inhuman song of birds. You keep walking, time is empty, phone not charged, you could be walking here forever. Perhaps at some point the sun will move.

At last you can hear something different, the sound of cars. You push forward, you are running now in spite of your exhaustion, there are brambles and vines, your face is scratched. You are exhausted, exhilarated, so tired and so close to the space of freedom.

You reach the edge of the maze. And there you see another hedge, which is tall but sparse. You push through; beyond this hedge is a wire fence, at least twelve foot tall and made of wire. Razor wire on the top. But you can see through.

Through the wire fence you see that you are standing on the edge of a bridge, overlooking the highway. You see different lanes, and cars. There are lights, there is traffic and a service station. You are so very tired, it is so close. But you can't get across.

Out there are people going home to ordinary lives. But there's no way to get through.

Either you wait here forever or go back into the maze.

To turn back into the maze is not to say that you know the solution. No-one can tell you in advance whether you will be able to find a way out. Rather it is to commit yourself to the idea that 'out' is possible, that it is possible at least to tell the truth.

Love is a normative statement about the kinds of desire that are found to be desirable. Whatever, man. I say 'man' a lot, it conveys a kind of stoner-egalitarianism I find personally appealing because it lets me say *I love you* without being exposed as a person who would feel/do that. I love you, man. Whatever.

Part Five

IN LOVE AND AGITPROP

Chapter 46

Director: And now Kit and I pass into a new era, days of quiet fulfilment and of satiated yearning. I watch the sky out of windows, work through sentences in notebooks, and am warmed by the certainty of Kit's daily presence. A new pleasure of returning – counting the seconds in the lobby, place of white curtains and blue walls, that moment in the lift where I am left alone with my desires. Sometimes during the day there will be a message, and I will see my phone, see Kit's name, I feel a comfort that is public and private all at once. The machine is so private. It is under your bed. It is the cord running to the wall. Kit progresses through rehab, pain but of a kind which has its own significance and trajectory, quietly accumulating towards a new form of wholeness. Am I adored, or am I the last in a series of next-last-resort supplies of adoration, a commodity as necessary to Kit as bed linen or breathing? We don't talk about the future.

One day, the culmination of many calls, questionnaires and no small amount of money changing hands, a new wheelchair arrives. It is electric, battery-powered and much heavier than expected. The flat becomes alive with unpredictable motion, happy minor chaos as a wheel catches a bookshelf, a stray pair of shoes, an extension cord. Kit's so very pre-occupied with their own sphere of motion, the machine as extension of their own body, playful as a toy. Quietly, without communicating, we count the days – when and whether Kit will walk again, how much motion they'll regain, whether they'll stay. This mutual, ongoing dance of calculation.

"Holy shit," says Kit one afternoon. "Oh my God," says Kit. Over the sound of the orbiting KitchenAid paddle, which they are using to make mooncakes filled with cheesecake filled with mochi. "You would not believe what is going down right now in Asian Baking Obsessions. So, there are rules in terms of what you're allowed to post. Didn't used to be, but there was that incident with the air-fryer pork... it's a long story. Anyway, the rule is that either it has to be traditional, like gulab jamun, or it has to incorporate Asian flavours, such as black sesame. Totally sensible compromises. There was some back and forth – someone actually tried to stop people from posting those jelly cakes – it was a kind of personal vendetta, I think they were upset the pork got banned. Thank goodness, that was overruled. But THEN – well, will you look at this. Will you look at the *state* of what is happening. Someone has made a cake… made out of jelly… which looks EXACTLY LIKE A PIECE OF AIR-FRYER PORK! It is photorealistic, it's an incredible replica. Have they no shame? No touch of bashfulness? There are already forty-seven comments, and I hope to see more."

"Hey," says Kit. "Look what I saw on Facebook." Hesitant, standoffish – as though they are looking for my approval. Why do they want it? "Apparently there is this, like, rally, some people are holding, to protest Nilsson Security. Is that like… I mean… is it the kind of thing you would be interested in? If so, do you think it would be good if I could come?"

*

"Water, bandaids, mask, spare mask, ear plugs and snacks," says The Rat. "Such talismanic ordering of objects. I got some extra ear plugs as well, just in case. You never know. How does the saying go? 'Be water'. And failing that, at least remember to *bring* water. Not sure what's going to go down – but, I have a certain vibrational feeling in my bones, tonight."

*

Director: Approaching from the middle-distance, we see veins of human traffic flowing in the same direction. I am reminded of how eyelines in a classical painting converge towards a single point. The venue for the annual company dinner of Nilsson Security directors and their associates, including politicians from both parties, is in a converted railyard and industrial precinct. Some of the old equipment has been retained for conservation purposes, metal tracks embedded in the ground. I am reminded of violence, the kind of force which it takes to drive steel pylons into concrete. And how it lasts.

The crowd has a distinct and yet unformed, emergent character. Some older, clean-looking people, holding signs with slogans like, 'NOT IN OUR NAME'. I recognise a couple from the meeting with StandUp. Students, looking clean and excited; some rainbow flags, trans flags and Pride symbols, and some people selling newspapers, who most of the others politely ignore. A few people wearing T-shirts with the Aboriginal flag; not all of them appear Aboriginal. There are some young people with banners saying 'Green Revolt', looking skinny and somehow more disreputable than I have previously associated them as being. There is the Communist Party and the Party of Australian Communists. I think of the Monty Python skit, the People's Front of Judea and the Judean People's front. I think of darkness and the taser, armoured figures and vans.

There are portable loudspeakers, clashing strains of music. One man with a friendly, ham-like face is playing the tuba. He pauses briefly to nudge me on the shoulder. "Not a great call that they would hold an event like that in a suburb like this, eh, is it? Most of the people here didn't even need to catch the bus."

There are young-ish looking people roaming round the outskirts of the gathering, wearing fluorescent orange jackets. They move their arms in a half-informative, vaguely chastising direction, motioning for us to stay within the lines of the defined protest area. There are also white women whose jackets are also fluorescent but pink, marked with the words 'Legal Observer'. They have a lawyerly look and are holding up phones. And then there are a few strange people, looking disorderly and cross-eyed. Seen on their own each appears unremarkable, but when two or three are gathered together it becomes apparent there is something in their way of being that's distinctly odd. Like a pie which rose on one side of the oven but not on the other.

And, standing silent in dark glasses so we cannot see their eyes are the police. The bulk of armour on their bodies, of tasers and guns at their holstered sides. Mostly they are positioned near, or next to, the protest marshals.

Cruising round the perimeter, face masked in black bandanna and hair covered by a hoodie, is a dark-skinned teenager on a skateboard. While we cannot see their face, their external affect is serene and yet indisputably wired for action. In their hands they hold a cardboard sign which reads, 'FUCK THE POLICE.'

"Well," says Kit. "This certainly is a mood."

*

Kit: The many-pronged potential of the thing you haven't done before.
That inimitable feeling, just before you go on stage.
Going out to meet an unknown sea of bodies on an electric night.

*

"Oh my God," says The Rat. "I can't believe she had the cheek to show her face. Is that Katherine K. Kelly?"

It is indeed. Ascending a stack of pallets that have been brought out so she can tower above us, declaiming her righteousness at large. She has that weird zone around her, that twilight vibe of nothing-is-real that surrounds politicians. God knows who invited her to speak.

"I stand before you today, filled with deep shame. The deepest shame, at what our country has become. These innocent children, families, held in detention under the LNP. It is a stain on our character, as citizens, as mothers, as Australians."

"She looks like IKEA furniture turned into a person," says The Rat.

Katherine K. Kelly is still speaking. "I hold in my hand – I show you now a bracelet that was given to me as a gift. Gifted to me by one of the most beautiful little girls in the world, her name is Preetha. Imprisoned by this terrible LNP government, for two years. I sat with little Preetha in their small church, where the family has continued to pray for the whole term of their imprisonment."

A voice screams, "FUCK YOU, KATHERINE!" There is a murmuring from the crowd; one of the orange-marshals raises his hands in a placatory way, and we fall silent.

Kelly goes on. "I prayed side by side with little Preetha. And we have had many conversations. Such a bright, precocious little girl. Her mother said to me, 'I still believe in Australians'. And my heart began to break, because I thought of how this little girl has put her trust in us, in our capacity for justice, for kindness, for the fair go. So let us raise our voices. Telling the truth to this government, standing up to this extremist, right-wing government, bearing witness to our shame"

"FUCK YOU KATHERINE, YOU MADE THIS HAPPEN!"

A different anonymous voice, this time. I look over and see that the speaker is unidentifiable, masked. There is a rumbling from the crowd, an upsurge of energy in a shape that is disordered, unpredictable, in how it crests and peaks. Again the orange-jacketed one puts out his placatory palms; he is joined by several of the more lawyerly-looking attendees of the protest. Two competing forms of energy, colliding like waves out of phase whose amplitude cancels each other out. And then one wave overwhelms the other; it overwhelms the ordering hands of the orange-jacket marshal. There is an upsurge, a seething of people, of hate; there are people climbing on the pallets. Her security are pushing but they are now swarming Katherine K. Kelly. She is separated from her guard; she is stumbling, she's lost a shoe. Someone grabs her jacket, bright blue; she falls, she is jerked back, the jacket rips. And we see, as if we didn't know before, that she is not made of IKEA furniture. She is a person who is breakable. The cops on the edges of the crowd try to push past but are unable to move due to the density of people. We look at her security, and at her, and we smell fear.

"I do believe," says The Rat, "that when people say 'it's going down' this may, indeed, be what they are referring to."

*

Kit: People and people and people; the seething of bodies. Stuck on the ground because of this fucking chair. What's going on? I want to see!

*

Director: Senator Kelly is speaking from a raised platform into a microphone, and I think: no matter how far you go, in time or space, there are always more speeches. The words sound distorted and Kit can't see from their chair, and I can't see either above the many heads, the roiling mass of the unruly crowd. And it seems unreal, as if the speech is not reflective of the full reality of the event. It is not the focal point, so much as one event that is occurring among many.

And then there is some sort of kerfuffle and Senator Kelly is no longer visible from where I am standing. What is left is just a centre of intense inferred activity, ripples moving out through waves and flows. By the time these ripples reach us they are hardly discernible as evidence of human conflict, just an unseen disturbance in a moving sea of people.

Kit and I are moving too, we are being pushed out towards the periphery and what we can see are the glass walls of the function centre, which I recognise as a place where I have given talks on film before. Where good art goes to behead itself and good thinking comes to die. And where, on this fine evening, the Nilsson Board of Directors and their esteemed associates have come to consort over dinner.

They are coming out in pairs, men with pink faces and blue suits accompanied by their awful wives. And one or two women in bright suits, flanked by their appalling husbands. There are no official lines but the crowd makes its own, pressing in but not quite getting to the point where the movement of the executives is blocked. The movement of the executives, the music of the spheres. They are walking as if nothing is happening – at least, that's what they're aiming for – gazes fixed on the ground, or into the middle distance, these men who are used to seeing everything through the gaze of ownership. The police dotted unevenly through the crowd flex around us, like fish: an impromptu corridor forms, allowing the executives to pass. From either side of the space, scattered insults and shouts. But as yet no-one steps into that corridor.

"Fuck off Nilsson!"

"Dogs, racist gronks!"

"Fucking imperialist cunts!"

There are more officers behind us, I think; but they can't get to us through the moving throngs of people.

One of the pink-faced executives looks rattled. Younger than the others, blue-suited and in pointy shoes, he breaks ranks and grabs one of the protestors. Shakes him hard by the collar, screaming in his face. "Bloody hippies! Go take a bath! Go get a job!" Many hands pushing around, and he lets go.

Another protestor, who looks like a student, runs suddenly into the makeshift corridor. A policeman steps swiftly in and, with a practiced movement, throws him to the ground, pressing a knee into his back. Then just as quickly lets go. The young man gets up, shaking and dazed. Many hands draw him back into the crowd, reaching out to help. But no-one raises a hand to the police. There are more of them here now, they wear wraparound sunglasses. You cannot track the movement of their eyes.

That is when it occurs to me. We can scream as much as we like at the Nilsson executives, individually and en masse. The Nilsson men can scream at us. But that is not really the stage we are on, and we are not the only players. The police are the unspoken parameters of this interaction.

*

Kit: Still can't see a thing. Scared people are going to fall on me, I keep running into people's toes by accident. I want to break free, I want to break free, I want to get out.

*

"Hey, we're moving," says The Rat. And so we are. The little dribble of Nilsson execs and associates coming out from the building seems to be finished, disgusting as it was – I can see only the backs of them, standing on my toes to look over the variegated heads of my comrades-in-crowd. And in front and behind, the blue shapes of cops, their block-like bodies bulked with armour. Weapons at their hips – we see them and don't see them. A couple of the orange-ones on the periphery, gesturing here and there. They seem a bit lost, not really a match for the crowd's energy and volume.

And now we're all walking with shared, distributed purpose. Though we don't really know what that purpose is, moving up the tree-lined street with the quiet houses, terraces framed by pretty leaves and no suggestion of the violence it took to obtain them. No cars, such silence on the periphery of the evening. The Rat and I look at each other, elated. The crowd is spreading out and we jog ahead as the texture of the suburb changes, we're approaching the station, we're in real Redfern now. Past the brick walls with the murals, railway turnstiles you can see from the road. It's a real road, artery to the city. Not a place where you're protected from the sounds and smells of trucks.

We're on the footpath, the pedestrian crossing. The little green man is meaningless because either way, the crowd is moving on. Walking in loosely concentric waves to the middle of the street, people begin to sit. One row and then the next. The lights change but we're not moving, there are cars sounding their horns but we're not going anywhere, not yet. The Rat and I crouch on our haunches, but don't sit down. Cars are on the highway with their lights on, backing up.

*

Director: I sit on the road and Kit locks the wheels of their powerchair, warmth of the unfinished day radiating up through the asphalt. The sky draws its blinds, the orange trace of colour darkening into evening blue. Cars now on our level, headlights staring like animal eyes. The thought occurs to us both and our eyes meet – how very helpless we are. It only takes one driver. But then we look at each other, and we know we are not leaving.

"Check it out, look up," says Kit.

On one side of the intersection is a park, and on the other a block of apartments. Either dark and unoccupied, or occupied and lit into golden squares. In one of those flats we can see a young man working out for the evening, topless, with a magnificent torso, rotating his chest and extending his arms. In the illuminated square in the midst of a blue evening, he could be a young god. People in the crowd see each other noticing and notice too, they start to crouch and point. A ripple of suppressed laughter moves through the group;.

The young man pauses in his exercise, confused. You can tell that he can sense he is being watched but doesn't know where from. Recommences his rotations. Someone giggles loudly. He stops again, a very legible look of confusion flitting across his handsome face. Comes to the window and he sees us – oh God, his expression – snaps down the blinds. And our little bit of crowd goes off in spurts of laughter. No unkindness, just delight.

*

"Oi, look over there!" says The Rat.

At first I can't see much. They're refurbishing the apartment blocks, so what. A temporary steel fence, and those white and orange blocks that they use to keep you out of construction sites. And then I notice. "Oh yeah, I see."

There is a pallet of bricks. No, two pallets, three. And without a word The Rat and I are in motion, scrambling over the orange and white. We are unwrapping the bricks, a few others have joined us, vaguely familiar faces – out of the corner of my eye I see SwiftBoi – OK fine, he annoys me, but right now he's doing good.

An impromptu production line forms, ferrying the bricks back onto the road, assembling little arches. Mini Stonehenge. More people join us, converging into a shared, purposeful wave of movement. Several are wearing badges with the Green Revolt symbol. And then my heart jumps because I recognise, it is Stickie and Leafie. All masked up, but I would know their silhouettes anywhere in the world.

"Hey," I say to Leafie when we are close enough to speak. "Why are you wearing brown pants?" It just slips out, it's the first time I've seen her dressed in something which doesn't look like she is on her way to a steampunk riot.

"Oh," says Leafie. "I wanted to look like I was going to the shops."

And I know it is all right. The way our bodies move in sync while we are ferrying the bricks. The shared experience of weight, bend and release.

On either side of us the cops are massing with their horses. Even when you're not looking, you know that they are there. Horses huge and very beautiful. And so very still, apart from the flicker of their noses. To bring them here, into this evil act, is the most evil thing on Earth.

Cars are still backed up; we can hear distant horns, the extent of the disruption on the highway is impossible to tell from here. Headlights so intense in the blue evening. One of them revs threateningly at us; we keep on making Stonehenges. The Rat still by my side; I watch them bend and straighten up, with their strong skinny arms and their dextrous hands. It's a long time since I felt such elation on a falling night.

*

Director: Lines of horses on either side of us, as evil as minotaurs

This is the stage, but we are only waiting here. Who are the players?

The police are now directing the cars to go back, doing U-turns on the highway. Men in fluorescent jackets, not protest marshals this time, more official; vehicles peeling off into the cross streets. Still kneeling in the middle of the intersection, next to Kit who has unlocked their chair. It is now well dark.

More and more police, massing around like silent fish. They are so close. They are close enough to look you well in the eye, those who are not still wearing sunglasses underneath the fluorescent streetlamps.

One of the police, a large, bearded man, looks me right in the face. He is wearing a name patch and a number. Deliberately, he removes both, making sure to keep eye-contact all the while. Someone links their arm around mine; the warmth is stabilising. Chaining to each other's bodies, one by one. We are all being unmade under these blue lights.

Kit: I miss the freedom of a world that was made for me, physically speaking; I want to go where I like. But it's a while since I've been in a story where the ending wasn't pre-determined.

*

"Doing good here, comrades!" yells SwiftBoi. In his dumb, bloviating voice. "C'mon, everyone get down, link arms, link arms!" And my heart sinks. None of this is real to him, even though it is happening before our eyes. It is so real I can't even speak.

The Green Revolt people keep on going at their work without talking about it. Their energy, their ability to act in unison, is exemplary. One of them, wearing a surgical mask, looks at me and smiles with their forehead and their eyes; I smile too, although they can't see through my masked face. We're all moving in sync, sharing the momentum. We're feeling good.

There is a different calibre of cop showing up now. Black-clad and blockish, armoured, with shields over their eyes. Cop vans, also huge, back blackly up onto the pavement. Bring out the firepower, bitches.

"Attention! Attention. Immediately vacate the road. I repeat, leave the road immediately. You are in violation of the law. We are directing you to leave."

Cop on a loudspeaker, the opposite of music of the spheres. Uncertainty that ripples through the gathering. Some get up obediently to go as if shocked from a dream. "Don't move!" barks SwiftBoi. The Generalissimo. "Lock arms, stay in place!" A few of his people kind of freeze in a mid-level posture, half-out and half-in. A couple leave with a small shrug at SwiftBoi; I respect that, as well.

People are still sitting, they are locking arms on the asphalt. Some of them look very young, they are so brave. But why lock arms? Be water, not a fucking lump.

Rows and rows of us, a densifying core surrounded by police. Nowhere to go from here. I touch the ground with my fingers. The asphalt radiates warmth, but the feel of the bricks is rough and cold against my hands.

*

Director: Screaming and crying and choking and wailing and scream-ing. I'm too close to the ground, can't see. And then my eyes sting, a harsh, serrated feeling. Awkward shapes of arms around me, the distorted chain; someone has tipped over and I'm dragged forward with them, sharp commotion of impact. Elbow bone striking someone else. The night is violently yellow now, not blue.

"Fuck!" screams Kit.

"Fuck!" screams someone else.

"Don't touch your face!"

*

Kit: It hurts me too but I didn't get the worst of it.

Pepper-spray – other people's panic.

Other people's pain.

With other people's pain all around, I never felt so alive.

Before the guns are even touched, they change the shape of the
  interaction.

*

Director: One of the teenagers from the crowd is lying on the road, he is moaning. His friends drag him backwards by the arms. Friction on the asphalt, an exposed square of flesh on his belly as his shirt is hiked right up. Indignity.

Cops without number; in motion it seems like there are dozens, though in our vicinity there are only five or six. Someone is on the ground, surrounded by three or four officers; motions of violence, a knee in the back. Young person prone on their front with their arms splayed out; and then, with practiced movements, the elbow to the head. One, two and three. A small space parts around the centre of violence; several people have their phones out, filming. Someone holds the phone right in the officer's face and then his colleague sprays her, right in the eyes. Now she is on her knees, weeping and screaming in their faces. "How dare you, how dare you, shame on you, for shame."

Two or three others are still filming, an ouroboros of spectacle. Transitive shame, to voyeuristically partake in someone else's humiliation. No-one goes to help; I don't consider it, either. I am ashamed to say that my response in this moment is primarily aesthetic. Total dissociation of feeling. My primary sensation here is exhaustion; I came to get away from the unreal, not to embed further within it. The pathology of pain that seeks an audience. We could fight them, I suppose, but so what? *We were not the ones with the guns.*

Over my career I have created so much media for so many audiences. It isn't clear who the audience for this piece of media is. It feels almost disloyal to articulate the question: *Who is this theatre for?* And how can we ask it, in the proximate shadow of immediate violence.

*

Kit: God help me, I know I should care, but I don't care at all.

How much can you hurt yourself before you know that you are real?

*

Oh my God, it's Kabir's ex-girlfriend, the one with the dreadlocks and the shitting dog. Another day out with the pepper-spray – and to be honest, I don't give a shit. I would like to feel righteous rage at this moment but I just don't, just kind of bored and pissed off. I'm ashamed of this response but that doesn't mean I don't feel it. The moment when you start to pre-create your own feelings in response to things you see around you, that is one dangerous moment. That's when you know you have been taken by the role play, a participant in theatre, the LARP.

The Rat brandishes their squeezy water bottle, tilting somebody's head to flush their eyes. On the grassy square beside the station, water runs diagonally down their face. Their hair is wet – I am so fucking tired. Down to my very marrow. What will it take to obtain escape velocity from this performance? I see the face of the cop, smug, brutal and uninteresting, I see them pacing in their sick, predatory way. Spraycans looking so ridiculous. Crazy how something so quotidian can hurt so much.

And then someone else in the crowd, someone I don't recognise with their face all covered, hair covered, grey pants, sneakers and hoodie – from their bag they are pulling out one of those novelty, super-compact, foldable umbrellas. One of the ones from the shop which Stickie got done for writing stuff on, before.

"Well, go on then," says The Rat.

I take the umbrella and push through, people mill densely around but it's amazing how you can work your way into the crevices if you really need to. A skill I learned as the shortest person at various gigs. I make my way to the front and I am opening the umbrella, Grey-Bloc person is opening theirs. And now the ridiculous has met the sublime, umbrellas versus pepper-spray, my umbrella has a little green frog picture on it for some reason and so it should. Is this an innovation from the Dragon Diaspora kids, lmao.

Others are joining us, you can't really call it a crew, it's just people who have seen and understood the logic of the act, there is a row of us out front blocking the rest of the crowd and from underneath I see the cop with the round stupid face who sprayed Kabir's ex-girlfriend right in the eyes. He looks juvenile and sullen, now that his weapon of bullying first resort has been revealed as somewhat stupid and resistible, all being told.

*

Director: Behind the wall of umbrellas, there is a feeling of privacy. In spite of the noise, a sense of peace and silence. It reminds me of hiding in a blanket fort when I was a small child. Shelter is an idea. You can dream it up, magic it into being.

From behind our umbrella wall, someone lobs a projectile, something like a can of Coke. It follows a high, lovely arc over the top of the umbrellas; somewhere in the middle distance we hear a thump. A policeman yells, "Ow!" And we all start to giggle. The slapstick moment passes through the crowd, sense of release.

"Leave the area now. You are in violation of public order. Leave the area. You are in violation. Leave."

The voice, robotic and vibrational, doesn't sound like a real person. Passed through amplification to the extent it isn't human anymore, this person doesn't exist. The sound lacks the fuzz, that unclarity round the edges, which I associate with a loudspeaker. This sound is precise, it is aimed at us like a beam of light.

The noise comes on with no warning; shrill. It oscillates. Like a car alarm, but a thousand times worse. It seems to shake your organs from the inside. People are reeling, doubling up. I bend over and retch.

The noise cuts out. Moment of relief. "Clear the area now. You are in violation of public order. Clear the area…"

And then it's on again. I unfold myself just long enough to see a black hexagonal disk mounted on top of a van. Lights red and blue – time there was I would have correlated the image with safety. And then I'm doubled up with pain, we're falling back. Kit's wheelchair fizzing and jerking as they mash at the controls. In a confusion of movement with the others. We are staggering, crashing into each other; we move backwards but the sound doesn't get less intense.

Someone is gesturing from the sidelines, one of the people in masks. They are wearing guards over their ears. Motioning with their hands – *move to the side, move to the side*. And we do. The sound grows less, it is almost miraculous. Like moving your head out of a jet of scalding water.

Move further, keep moving. We're on the grass, someone is handing out earplugs and we are putting them on. The whole world is muffled, as though we are living underwater. Why does everything seem so unreal when the sound is off.

The horses tall and beautiful. This evil thing that is happening is not their fault. But the thing they are part of is so evil. Mounted by police, they are like minotaurs.

*

Kit: One of the horses is going totally fucking beserk. It's in the path of the noise, reeling back and forth and then the horse is on someone and there is screaming. Can't see above the heads of the crowd but I can see it.

*

Director: Mouths stretching open, grotesque shapes. I can hardly see through the scrim of my own anger. I have never felt such hatred in my life.

*

Kit: Someone falls across me, on my chair; an elbow in my nose, somebody pulls them off. People clear space for me but it's getting closer, centre of gravity unstable, that last guy almost tipped me over. God, I never learned to drive – the suspension on this chair is pretty good, but every jolt in the pavement, you know I'm really feeling it. For fucksake please don't tip me on the ground.

*

Someone is getting crushed underneath the horse, and they are screaming. The Rat drops their pack and runs over; I would go as well but there are too many people, staggering, reeling, I'm being moved on by the crush and there's no point. The last thing I see before I'm pushed all the way up the road is people rocking the van with the mounted LRAD, the hexagonal disk, people are rocking the van and the cops are pushing back but the swell, the sheer quantity of people, it's rocking harder and harder, it is going to flip. But before I see this I'm pushed forward by the trampling momentum of the crowd. The Rat has found me again, I see they're speaking, I pull down my earmuffs.

"Hey," says The Rat. "I'm not certain, but… do you think over there is the crew from BLKPWR?"

"Oh, wow," I say. And then, another jolt of recognition. "Hey, look over there! It's that movie director, what's their name, the one who wrote the memoir. I think I saw it in the discount bin at Target. And hey, look over there in the powerchair! Is that the actor, you know, the cute enby one, Kit Phuong?"

*

Kit: Yeah, you assholes – what are you going to do, are you going to shoot us?

Go on, you fucking cowards.

*

We were not the ones with the guns. But what if we were?

*

Kit: One thing I understand is the threat which is the image of the threat.

The trick is that the ending is pre-determined, though you pretend that it's not.

Theatre and violence, move and countermove.

One thing I understand is theatre.

*

Director: The momentum of the crowd has not ceased, it is pushing us en masse up the still human-blockaded street. Train station on our left – amazing to see it, the timetable boards and the turnstiles where the commuters come out. Kit has regained their elan, they throw their head back and laugh, and I know what they are thinking. Ridiculous to think of people validating Opal cards. Getting to work on time due to their daily commute. We have entered a world where such experiences, so determinative of our everyday lives, have become utterly beside the point.

On the other side of the road there is the Redfern police station. With a kind of distributed force of decision-making, a current of the crowd is converging towards it. We are all moving at our own pace, separating off into these small, emergent groups: people drawn ineluctably towards these strange found affinities of the crowd.

There is a whole group with powerchairs; they are forming a row before the station, locking down their brakes. Kit and I make eye contact for a moment and then they are off, taking their place in the growing line without looking back. There is a pack on the ground someone has dropped; I pick it up. I'm being pushed away by a new current of people, I am back on the grass. Someone is crying, touching their clothes and whimpering; someone else barks, "Don't touch your face!" Instinctively I look at the bag in my hands and there it is, a plastic squeezable bottle with a tip. Then I am washing out the person's eyes just as I observed done previously, and I think: *Oh, this is easy, I can do this.* This is nothing so special, I am not a super soldier or a hero but I am here, I know that I am real and this is utterly possible. New sensation of apprehended competence.

For some reason I think now of my mother and father; people who came from somewhere else. And now I, too, am going to another place. In a strange way I feel closer to them than ever while they were still living. There is a time to stay and a time to leave, and I now know what that means. I look back once into the unknown masses of the crowd and say a quiet goodbye; because this is not, at long last, the world of theatre, of the performance. Not the world of the circulated image; what has occurred and what will continue to happen has not yet been pre-determined. Don't know how this is going to end, and I don't need to.

*

Kit: There's only one way this can end but you can't not feel it.

*

They're coming hard for us now but they're blocked off by the row of powerchairs, they can't get through. And the cops can't get past, the chairs are heavy and they're locked in place and in any case they are thwarted and swarmed by the sheer force of numbers, we are huge in ourselves, grown enormous in togetherness and in our shared, amplified rage.

We're close enough to see into the copshop, walls and glass. A brick curves through the air, hits the wall and bounces. Another one is thrown and strikes a window, the brick falls to the ground but cracks are snaking through the glass, like when you drop your phone on tiles. And then another brick, with even greater force; this time it meets its target. In caves the glass, laughter and screaming.

And then, as though from nowhere, one of the marshals pops out from the crowd. Still in his orange shirt, flapping his little hands. Facing the crowd with his back turned to the cops. "Please – don't escalate, don't give them an excuse! We aren't anarchists! This is a peaceful protest… please, let's bring an end to this, no violence!"

"Who the fuck are you calling not an anarchist?" someone screams.

There is a hiss, a smell of methylated spirits. And then like a bright fish, the thought swims up in my consciousness: *what happened on that dam on the Murray-Darling?* And then a confusion and an energy of movement, bottles being passed along the line. And there is one in my hand and I am hurling it, wildly but with intent, desire meeting the reality in perfect synchronisation as the bottle curves through the air. It goes into the open glass maw of the window, the building now undefended; orange flicker inside. We're already on fire. The smell is so unbearable, it's perfect, it is so very silent, you can't hear a thing. You will be amazed at how quiet it can be when flame and smoke drown out the night. And you know there is a whole load of fucking bullshit but if you just turn around it has no hold on you, no power over you whatsoever. I am not an anarchist, there's been too many betrayals, but I'm not *not* an anarchist, either. And it is possible to love a person, a place, an era without wishing to remain there, as incensed with the clarity of real stakes I turn my face towards the heat.

And then there is a *whoosh* and the whole building is on fire, scrim of smoke and orange tongues jumping through the roof. We fall back, heat trapped between our teeth; we fall back, we can't see each other; the wind blows and we look, amazed, upon the work of our own hands. Yes this is the magic hour. You see it really is possible for us to do things. It doesn't mean that we'll be right for all time or that we'll be together for all time, either. But it is real and it means something. A streak of self. A moment of intensity. A choice. Looking now at the flames leaping from the burning copshop, now all engulfed in smoke, it occurs to me quite suddenly that maybe I do deserve love after all.

To Sanction All Revolts, All Desperate Actions

We are not pragmatists, since none of this is sensible. We are not dreamers, since the catastrophe is real and at the door. Our historic mission: to sanction all revolts, all desperate actions. And we will get free regardless. Maybe I'll see you there.

Epilogue

Here's what I know: I can't promise that we'll win this. I believe we can fight. The 'we' I raise here is an offer, a proposal, not ventriloquising, a coin tossed in a fountain. Take it up if you like, or don't. I believe this is a fight rather than a puzzle; a lot of people don't want you to puzzle that one through, but I believe that you can. Go on then, amaze me. Yes we have taken some losses but one day we will know who we are to ourselves and to each other, not to 'them'. What I'm trying to say is, don't underestimate this act of *preferring not to* – this withholding is an act, it is more than a zero, dreaming of the good apocalypse as we go into a crack between a *no* and a *maybe*. And I do not know if I, personally, will get to see what I am talking about; nonetheless I will gesture towards it in fragments, silly dreams, in these meandering conversations. Oh, I'm not real until I'm seen by you, till I am consecrated by your touch. And yes, we are still losing – but when something so terrible happens, walls between the fictional and the real start to break down – change coming through like a slit of unfathomable light. I believe in the kindness of strangers. I believe in Kit. I believe in love.

Acknowledgments

This novel was written on the lands of the Gadigal people in 'Sydney' and the Kulin nations in 'Melbourne'. I acknowledge that these lands were seized by violence and are held by violence, and commit myself to their return by all necessary means.

My deep appreciation to Rach Crawford, my agent, for her competent, respectful stewarding of this manuscript. Rach does a lot of work for very little; the only explanation I can come up with is that she believes in it. Thank you.

And to Ed Wright, publisher and editor. Thanks for taking this strangely shaped book on.

For this novel to exist, I also had to exist for an extended length of time. This was more complicated than it seemed. My thanks to the following people:

Abdallah for constancy, wisdom and a couch

Nate for being 'good' above nice, not running away

Anh for holding on to me as I've changed

Alana for friendship, scholarship and introducing me to many generative readings and relationships

Zowie for strength, sincerity, memes

Lucy for healing, gentleness, artistic honesty

April and Austin, the warmest weebs

Ashwin for some of the best lines

to Nic and Ben, who took me in when I needed it. Nic, you were so enigmatic and loyal. The world was more whole when you were in it.

to 爸爸

And to the others. 'Stories most important to me aren't/ Stories I can share' – Wendy Trevino. But here is one.

The excerpt that begins 'But first the state sets the scene for such violence, you see...' on page 40 and 'We know that operating within reality does not mean that we accept it' on page 181 are quotes from Dr Huey P. Newton, co-founder of the Black Panther Party. The first excerpt is drawn from Newton's eulogy for George Jackson, in which he quotes Jackson quoting Marx: 'the unjust would be criticised by the weapon'. In the same speech, Newton also extensively paraphrases Mao, who likewise counterposed the meanings of a revolutionary and a reactionary death: 'All men must die, but death can vary in its significance. The ancient Chinese writer Szuma Chien said, "Though death befalls all men alike, it may be weightier than Mount Tai or lighter than a feather."' The inclusion of these passages is intended as a tribute to this lineage of radical thought and action.